# BEASTS OF ANTARES

by

Dray Prescot



*Illust*
RICHARD HESCOX

DAW BOOKS, INC.
DONALD A. WOLLHEIM, PUBLISHER
1633 Broadway, New York, N.Y. 10019

Cover art by Richard Hescox.

FIRST PRINTING, AUGUST 1980

1 2 3 4 5 6 7 8 9

DAW TRADEMARK REGISTERED
U.S. PAT. OFF. MARCA
REGISTRADA. HECHO EN U.S.A.

PRINTED IN U.S.A.

# THE SPIKATUR CYCLE

Beasts of Antares is the first volume of the Spikatur Cycle chronicling the history of Dray Prescot on the marvelous and horrific world of Kregen four hundred light-years away under the red and green fires of the Suns of Scorpio. Reared in the inhumanly harsh conditions of Nelson's Navy, he has been transported to Kregen through the agencies of the Savanti and the Star Lords. Dray Prescot is a man above middle height, with brown hair and level brown eyes, brooding and dominating, with enormously broad shoulders and superbly powerful physique. There is about him an abrasive honesty and an indomitable courage. He moves like a savage hunting cat, quiet and deadly. The portrait he presents of himself is enigmatic and attractive.

The people of the island empire of Vallia, cruelly oppressed by invaders, call on Prescot to shoulder the burden of leading them to liberty. This he has vowed to do to the best of his ability, and then thankfully relinquish the imperium, for there are other tasks set to his hands on the unforgiving and rewarding world of Kregan.

The Spikatur Cycle brings Prescot closer to the realization of many of his dreams and each book is arranged to be read as complete in itself. He is determined to do what he feels is laid upon him; but he finds it is not so easy, particularly when the Empress Delia and his comrades are determined to keep him out of trouble. But—he is Dray Prescot, Lord of Strombor and Krozair of Zy, and that canny old leem hunter will not be prevented from buckling up the brave old scarlet breechclout and with a sword in his fist hurtling off beneath the Moons of Kregen into fresh headlong adventure.

"They sought to attack us from below."

# Table of Contents


1 At the Sign of the Headless Zorcaman 7
2 Of the Disobedience of Nath Karidge 22
3 In Which Nath Nazabhan, Kapt of the Phalanx, Is at Last Named 29
4 Concerning the Power of Phu-Si-Yantong 37
5 On the Day of Opaz the Deliverer 45
6 Swords for Delia 59
7 Sacrifice 66
8 Zenobya 77
9 "You'll be just that, Dray Prescot! Arena fodder!" 91
10 Unmok the Nets 103
11 A Shot at a Swordship 115
12 Beasts for Huringa 124
13 Of an Encounter in a Skyship 129
14 I Amuse my Friends 137
15 Of Questions and Reminders 144
16 An Armorer Raises an Echo 152
17 Of the Eye of a Vollerman 160
18 In the Recalcitrants House 167
19 Mazdo the Splandu 177
20 Combat, Blood and Death 187

# List of Illustrations


"They sought to attack us from below." II

"A sedan-chair borne by eight womoxes swayed up the steps." 50

"My fist wrapped around the throat of the speaker." 179

"He leaped up, his sword flashing out at me." 198

# CHAPTER ONE

## At the Sign of the Headless Zorcaman

Naghan Raerdu was a most entertaining character. He had a remarkable penchant for laughing so much the tears squeezed out of his closed eyes and no one took much notice of what else he was doing. His face expressed habitual surprise that people never took him seriously, and his body, short, stout, robust, supported on thick waddling legs, conveyed an impression of undirected manic energy. He was apim, a member of Homo sapiens, with brown Vallian hair and eyes and a blobby chunk of gristle for a nose. He'd been a soldier in the Phalanx, rising from brumbyte to Relianchun. With his bright popping eyes, his highly colored cheeks, his glistening mouth from which a glass was seldom absent, he looked quite unlike what he was.

Naghan Raerdu had turned into a first-class spy.

His jolly red-faced exterior concealed the mentality more often associated with the gray, inconspicuous secret agent. And he liked to laugh.

He finished laughing now as he said, "This fellow Chuktar Mevek—leastways, that's what he calls himself—means what he says. In a matter this important he will deal only with the emperor."

"It's a trap." Turko spoke in a dismissive way, perhaps a little warm at having to state the obvious. He stretched his arms in which the sinuous muscles spoke eloquently of the enormous man-crushing power of him. He had the wrestler's trick of emphasizing statements by physical movements. Since his elevation to the nobility he had flowered wonderfully and yet he remained a good comrade. Naghan Raerdu's spying mission had been into Falinur, near the center of Vallia, Kov Turko's new province.

"I think not, kov." Raerdu spoke up stoutly. He was often called Naghan the Barrel for obvious reasons. "I took soundings." He laid a chubby finger alongside that blob of gristle that passed for a nose.

"A trap," repeated Turko. He half turned away, and his profile showed, keen as an eagle's. "That unhanged villain Layco Jhansi wants to lure the emperor into his clutches by this story, and then—chop."

"With respect, kov, this Mevek has suffered and has no love for Layco Jhansi."

"He told you this?" Nath Karidge, that tearaway cavalry commander spoke up. He happened to be here because a new task was to be set to his capable hands. Now his reckless face was thoughtful in the shadows under the trees. "Or—you saw for yourself?"

"Both, and yet it was the way Mevek spoke that impressed me. I have seen men's faces when they talk like that. I was Relianchun in the First Phalanx at the Battle of Sicce's Gates, and, after we were beat. . . . That was a bad time for Vallia." Naghan the Barrel did not laugh. "It is my view that Mevek speaks honestly and can do what he promises."

The problem was a knotty one. Around the heap of tumbled ruins that had once been a pretty village, up here in the north of the province of Vindelka, the trees grew vigorously, thrusting their roots into crevices and completing the work of destruction. The streaming mingled radiance of the Suns of Scorpio fell in a muted, wavering undersea vision of green and russet gold. A short way off the animals snorted and stamped their hooves, tossing their manes. The cavalry escort waited beyond the line of trees. By the slanting rays from the twin suns the day was waning. Night would soon be here. A decision had to be made before the twin suns, Zim and Genodras, sank beneath the horizon and the first moon of Kregen, the Maiden with the Many Smiles, swam roseate and shining into the night sky.

Naghan the Barrel cocked his red face up and squinted at the position of the suns.

"Chuktar Mevek will wait for you, majister, at the Sign of the Headless Zorcaman until the hour of midnight."

His golden beard glinting in that dappled light, his four arms and tail hand relaxed, Korero the Shield coughed one of his dry little coughs. A magnificent golden Kildoi, a marvel with his shields, an adept of Disciplines, Korero was, like Turko, a valued comrade.

"Mevek may speak the truth," said Korero, "but the risk is not worth taking."

"I agree," said Turko. "You'd be running your head into a noose."

With a flick of his pelisse, furred and smothered in gold lace, Nath Karidge added, "Majister, the danger is too great."

In that uncertain light they all stared at me. The scent of evening hung sweetly on the air, and insects buzzed. The zorcas snorted and stamped their hooves. Overhead the trees bowered us in shadow.

I stared back at them.

"Three of you," I said. "Three right-roaring rapscallion hellions. Since when has a little danger, a few risks, bothered you?"

They each found it necessary to make immediate and finicky adjustments to their clothes or harness or weapons. I did not add, as in justice I ought, that if anyone trembled at risks taken and dangers dared, it was me. Korero the Shield, with four arms and a tail hand and an enormous competence in the midst of battle, with a dry humor and practical outlook; Turko the Shield who was now Kov Turko of Falinur, a Khamorro, a feared man who could break the strongest opponent, a man with a gently sarcastic manner; these two were good comrades, trusted friends, and right tearaways. And Chuktar Nath Karidge, the beau sabreur, a cavalryman—no, a *light* cavalryman—who swore on Lasal the Vakka and had no great expectations of living beyond the next charge, he was here because I wanted him to put his talents to good use. And, all three, all three reckless daredevils, all cautioned me gravely, with long faces, direfully warning me of risks and dangers.

By Vox! It was enough to make a fellow laugh.

"With your permission, majister, I will have to take back an answer soon. Mevek is somewhat touchy in these matters." Naghan the Barrel laughed his wheezing, tear-splattering laugh. "I fancy it is how he has kept his head on his shoulders for so long fighting his guerrilla actions against Layco Jhansi's mercenaries."

"Risks," said Korero. He pulled his golden beard. "I do not hold with them."

"Nor me," said Turko.

They spoke seriously. I considered. Yes, it was true that

both Korero and Turko were among the more sober headed of my boon companions. They were not as foolhardy as most, not as ready to jump in without a thought. Both had carried shields at my back in battle. Perhaps that was why they were less reckless, or perhaps their function as shield bearers to the Emperor of Vallia had made them more cautious. All the same, the humor of the situation remained.

"You say this Chuktar Mevek will deal only with me directly?"

"Yes, majister. And, in addition, he was firm on the point. We can take no more than three companions to the Sign of the Headless Zorcaman."

"Five of us," said Turko. "And I daresay he'll have a little army waiting."

"As much as any man may," said Naghan the Barrel, and he spoke more strongly. "Chuktar Mevek has my trust."

Nath Karidge put his fist onto the hilt of his sword. He carried a curved sword of a pattern of his own design, specially made for him. He looked at me. "If we go, majister, at least let me bring on my two half-squadrons in support."

"Would that not be breaking faith?"

He stirred the dust with his cavalryman's boot.

"Aye. But, by Lasal the Vakka, when you treat with rogues you must watch your back."

The others nodded. There was no need for them to amplify. This view was one commonly held among my comrades concerning certain eventualities and certain people. What Karidge had said merely cloaked a deeper meaning.

There was no need to amplify, yet Turko said, "Honor is a precious commodity. Yet honor cannot stand in the way of our proper duty."

I refused to allow myself to think about this at the moment. Later on I pondered the implications deeply, as you shall hear; but, right now, the decision must be taken.

And, really—and as they knew only too well—there was only one conclusion I could come to.

I said, "We go. We go now. Rather—with Naghan *I* go."

At once, speaking all over each other, they were baying out their outrage. I calmed them.

"If you wish to accompany, you will be most welcome. But, if you think the risks too great, why, then—"

In mercy I couldn't go on. Their faces expressed the utmost consternation and chagrin and downright fury.

They knew—I trusted they knew—that I merely baited them.

In the language spoken over most of Paz, the Kregish language which had, I surmised, been imposed on the people, there are many fine terms of abuse and contempt, many resounding oaths, many expressions of love and fidelity. Some have a reasonably exact counterpart in the languages of Earth; some are purely Kregan. To call a fellow a fambly is to express your opinion of him in gentle, friendly terms, and yet you also let him know you are giving him a little stick. When, half under my breath and turning toward the zorcas, I said, "Famblys!" these men of mine knew exactly what I meant. Mind you, the oafish of two worlds might misunderstand, that seems obvious. To call a man a fambly is not the same as calling him an onker, or a hulu, or any other of the colorful names available in the Kregish tongue.

"I shall station my two half-squadrons—" began Karidge.

"No. I judge Chuktar Mevek will scout the approaches. Anything like a follow-up cavalry force—and he'll be off."

"Quidang, majister!"

Yet, as he spoke, Karidge indicated that he might bellow out "Quidang!"—a standard acknowledgment of an order—but he didn't like the idea at all. He was a cavalryman. It was hard for him to grasp any idea that anything at all valuable could be accomplished without the exciting jingle of harness and the onrushing stamp of hooves.

We mounted up and Karidge gave orders to the cavalry to await our return, and we set off as the suns declined. Up ahead lay a rich and fruitful land between the generous arms of a loop in the Great River, She of the Fecundity. This part of Vallia was blessed with richness; the land sent forth its goodness in thickly growing crops, in trees heavy with fruit, in grasslands where cattle grazed and grew fat. Westward on the outskirts of the semi-desert Ochre Limits the land yielded many rich minerals. This land was called Vinnur's Garden. It lay between Falinur to the north and Vindelka to the south. It was coveted by and laid claim to by both provinces.

Just who was the rightful claimant no one now could say. I had partially solved the squabble by an arbitrary parallel dividing Vinnur's garden in half. The locals didn't much like the solution, but had to acknowledge there was not much else to do. Falinur had been the kovnate province of Seg Segutorio until he had relinquished it and I had appointed Turko. Vindelka was the kovnate province of Vomanus, half-brother to Delia. Both were blade comrades. Neither would press his claim against the other.

Some of the annoyance felt by the southern Falinurese against Seg for not actively advancing their claims had led, coupled with his attempts to put down slavery, to the people throwing in their lot with Layco Jhansi. Jhansi had been the old emperor's chief minister, and he had betrayed him. The plot to kill the emperor had misfired, Jhansi had fled to the safety of his own province, Vennar, to the west of Falinur, and in the Time of Troubles he had waxed strong. He had troubles on his northern borders, but just lately he had attempted to invade southward into the imperial province of Orvendel, having subjugated Vindelka. We had bested his army at the Battle of Ovalia and had subsequently campaigned successfully northward to liberate Vindelka. My projected trip to Hyrklana had perforce been postponed yet again. . . .

So, now my spy Naghan the Barrel brought word that the people of Falinur were grown tired of Layco Jhansi.

The time was ripe to strike the blow that would free the province. All the island empire of Vallia had been in turmoil, invaded by mercenaries and reiving barbarians and by the iron legions of our rival empire, Hamal. We had won back most of the south and the midlands, and the northeast stood for us. But there was still much to do. If Turko could take over in Falinur that would be another good step forward to the final liberation of all Vallia.

The twin suns sank as we trotted past fields rich with crops. Very few lights showed from farmhouses or villages; these people had grown to live with waves of invasion. The miracle was the land was in such good heart. We moved on, silently.

Just what we were trotting so silently into did not bear thinking of. I looked ahead at the dark squat figure of Naghan, who clamped his short legs around his zorca and hunched down with your typical infantryman's handling of a mount. After the disastrous Battle at Sicce's Gates, where the Phalanx had been upset by the clansmen, Naghan had been cut off. He had lived off the country, saved his life, kept his spirits and had kept out of the way of our enemies. In the fullness of time he had reported back. His story had interested me, and on meeting him I realized that here was a man of parts, resourceful, hardy, and like a chameleon able to survive in places where no one would expect him to last a couple of heartbeats.

He had proved ready to take employment with me, as a spy, a secret agent—the name did not matter overmuch. The interesting aspect of this was that Naghan Vanki, the emperor's chief spymaster, did not know of Naghan the Barrel or the other agents recruited in similar ways. A small corps of intelligence men was being built up, quite distinct from the large-scale organization controlled by Vanki and which served Vallia to the best of its ability in dark times and in good.

We halted on the brow of a hill where the road, dim and barely visible before the rise of the Maiden with the Many Smiles, trended down toward the shadowy and misshapen lumps of darkness that indicated a village. Not a light showed.

"Chuktar Mevek risks much in coming this far south to meet you, majister." Naghan the Barrel wiped his face with his neckerchief, a gaudy article of red and lilac and green with brown spots. That kind of neckerchief the Kregans call a flamanch, and very useful it is, too. Usually it is fastened at the front by a brooch or a pin or a nolp, and now, having wiped his face, Naghan slid his nolp up and down as he spoke. "We are in good time. And his men have us under observation already."

Not one of us showed the least surprise or consternation. We were old campaigners. If Mevek had not scouted the approaches and kept a lookout we would have been far more concerned.

"All the same," said Turko, following on that line of thought. "It means we may have some difficulty if we have to pull out quickly."

Although we had only Naghan's assertions to guide us in this enterprise, we felt we were not going in entirely blind.

I, for one, felt confidence in Naghan Raerdu the Barrel, and his opinion was that this Chuktar Mevek would hold to his word, even if we did not reach agreement. If Naghan was wrong, why then it could easily be a quick scramble to get free. . . .

I nudged my zorca.

"No sense in hanging about."

We rode slowly down the path which glimmered into smokey grayness as the first moon lifted. The Maiden with the Many Smiles shone bleakly, it seemed to me, cutting a pallid sickle in the sky. Soon she would take on her usual pinkish hue and the shadows would warm to a russet fuzz. We rode on.

This little village was called Infinon of the Crossroads, and the inn with the sign of the Headless Zorcaman squatted in one angle of the cross. The other houses were fast shuttered. The stillness and the ghostly moonlight were broken as men rode out with a clatter, casting bars of shadow across the road, to surround us. A few quick words between their leader and Naghan and we went on, riding up to the inn and dismounting.

A warm fug of ale fumes and cooking and sweat met us as we entered. The place presented the appearance one would expect from a small village in a prosperous countryside, and the ale would be good.

The floor was swept clean. That floor was made from sawn planks, not beaten earth. Pots glittered. The enormous fireplace gaped black and empty, save for a brass jar filled with dried flowers. The men who escorted us and the others who awaited our coming wore ragged clothing of a raffish, free-flowing kind. They were much burdened with weapons. Almost all were apims. They sat about on the settles and benches, and I surmised they would keep quiet as their chief spoke. If there was trouble—I gave them a glance that appeared casual and which totted them up and assessed them.

Twenty. Twenty ruffians, guerrilleros, as ready to slit your throat as to greet you with a pleasant Lahal.

One of them, a fellow who wore a gaudy sash of a color I took to be plum, so dirty and festooned with gold lace was it, walked forward. His face looked like an old boot. His hair was lank. But he smiled.

"Llahal, koters," he said, giving us the name of gentlemen of Vallia. "The Chuktar will be here in but five murs."

Karidge would have started hotly demanding to know why the emperor should be kept waiting, but I silenced him. I looked about, saw a long lanky lout with his feet on a bench. Walking over, I pushed his legs off, so that his heavy Vallian boots crashed to the floor, and sat on the bench. I took off my wide-brimmed hat, placed it on the table, and said, "I will wait five murs."

As a mur is shorter than a terrestrial minute, the ball was, as they say, in Mevek's court.

The long lanky lout glowered, but he said nothing and straightened himself up. The eyes of the others in the taproom—by Krun! You could feel them, like a pack of drills.

My companions remained standing. The fellow with the unmentionable sash and the face like an old boot swallowed.

"I am Vanderini the Dagger. I will fetch the Chuktar—"

He went out through a rear door in something of a hurry.

Karidge chuckled nastily. A chuckle can express many profound emotions.

Turko and Korero looked as though offensive smells were obfuscating the pleasures of life. Naghan the Barrel let one of his wheezing laughs shake him up, the tears pouring from his eyes. He clapped his belly.

"I am parched. Will no one fetch a stoup, for the sweet sake of Mother Dikkana, who brought forth the saint who gave us ale?"

Someone laughed—that was easy to do with Naghan the Barrel—and tankards were forthcoming. I sipped.

Four and a half murs, all that took. On the fifth, as the calibrated clepsydra on its shelf above the mantlepiece showed, Chuktar Mevek walked into the taproom.

To sum him up in a single glance would be easy, and probably completely wrong.

This Mevek, who called himself a Chuktar, the equivalent of a brigadier general, was quite clearly hard as nails, hard-bitten, hard as old leather. He was strongly built, with a flat, impassive face in which his brown Vallian eyes were deeply set. He looked like his men, save that he wore more ornamentation. Yet I judged that to have accomplished what he had, in raising so many people willing to stand against Layco Jhansi and his mercenaries, he had a spark, a charisma, a touch of that genius Kregans call the yrium. He looked at me carefully. He reminded me by that stare, by his impassivity, of a wild animal in the moments before it leaps.

Then: "Llahal, majister. I will not give you the full incline as all emperors are due. I hear you have banished such flummery."

"You are right. Llahal."

"They say the kov who ran off is a friend of yours."

"You are right and wrong."

He merely lifted one dark eyebrow.

"Kov Seg Segutorio is a friend of mine. He did not run off."

"He was not here when—"

"I have heard this before. It is unworthy of you if you wish to prove your friendship. Kov Seg Segutorio was about business for the empire—for the old emperor—and those to whom he confided the care of Falinur failed him. He did not fail them."

"You fight for your friends—"

I broke in. "This wastes time. The past is dead." Well, that is not strictly true. . . . "What do you wish to tell me?"

Now he did not exactly lose that coolness, but he reached out and fingered one of the many loops of precious gems encircling his neck and depending on his harness. His eyebrows drew down.

"Perhaps it is you, majister, who has somewhat to tell me."

I stood up.

"Shilly-shallying, Mevek, is for those who have all the time in the world. I do not. There are mercenaries, reiving rasts, cramphs from Hamal, abroad in Vallia. The people called me to be their emperor and free them from tyranny. That I will do, although I did not seek the task. If you can help me win back Falinur, all well and good. If you are powerless, then we have nothing to say to each other."

He digested that. Then, as I had suspected he would, he picked out the item that touched him most nearly.

"Powerless? Me? Oh, no, majister, I am not powerless."

"Do not think these men here can stop me from leaving." And here I put on a little of the bravado I detest and which, sometimes, serves well. Sometimes it is a disaster. "I do not think you could stop me if you had twice as many men."

He wiggled those eyebrows of his again, and I came to the conclusion that, impassive as his flat face was, those eyebrows were weather indicators to his state of mind.

"I have been told you are Jak the Drang."

"Yes."

"Then I believe you."

I nodded. "Then we understand each other." I pulled my riding cloak off and tossed it on the table. I sat down. "I do not think you are powerless. Now, let us Rank our Deldars and see what we can agree."

At that familiar opening challenge from the famous game of Jikaida, Mevek, nodding in his turn, visibly relaxed. We had sparred. His amour propre had been maintained. Now we could get down to cases.

His story followed the lines I expected. When Jhansi's mercenary troops deteriorated in quality with the hiring of more and more of them from dubious sources, the countryfolk began to suffer. That was a normal risk run by any commander who hired mercenaries. The defeats in the south were almost matched by unhappy encounters with the Racters in the north.

The Racters, once the most powerful political party in Vallia, were now penned in the far northwest where a concentration of their estates gave them a base. Jhansi fought them and the battle did not go well.

"What you are saying is now that Jhansi's fortunes are at a low ebb, you wish to change sides."

His eyebrows flared.

"No, majister, not so. Many of us have opposed the Kov of Vennar from the moment he crossed our borders."

"As I am the emperor, you may understand that Layco Jhansi is no longer the Kov of Vennar. His province lies under an interdict. His head is forfeit to the empire. He is a traitor."

"Just so. But he still runs his kovnate, whether he is kov or not, and he still sends his damned mercenaries to keep us down."

I said, "You have intelligence of the battles we have won? You know our armies have cleared Vindelka?"

"Aye."

"Then you must realize that the time will soon come when we will march north, through this very spot, and go on into Falinur and west into Vennar, and Layco Jhansi will swing very high indeed."

In a low tone, almost surly, he said, "You will need my help."

"I welcome your help, Mevek. As to needing it—that may be a different matter."

Vanderini the Dabber, he with the sash and the face like an old boot, stepped up. That face wore a scowl.

"By Vox! But this new emperor has a stiff neck! If I did not hate Jhansi so much, why—"

"There will be a place for you, Vanderini," I told him, without a smile. "In the new Falinur after we have liberated the province. At least—" And here I judged the time had come to apprise these desperadoes of their new lord. "At least, if the new kov I have appointed listens and approves of you."

They swung to glare at me on this.

"New kov?" growled out Mevek. "What new kov?"

"Kov Seg Segutorio is about vital business for the empire. He has relinquished Falinur. Your new lord is appointed. He is Kov Turko, whom you will obey in all things."

Now, as you know, the rights and the law on Kregen regarding titles and property and inheritance are not quite the same as on this Earth. Necessarily, they must differ.

Mevek hoisted his eyebrows. I began to suspect that he was well aware of his eyebrows, and used them on purpose, to fool credulous folk into thinking they could read his mind.

"If this Kov Turko proves himself—"

"He will."

"Then we will give him the welcome that is his due. But I recall the old kov, Naghan Furtway, and his nephew Jenbar. They had little love for the emperor. Their seed still grows here."

Perhaps this was the root cause of the disaffection in Falinur. The past is not dead, its tendrils twine and choke the new bright growths. . . .

"You know Naghan Furtway proved a traitor and fled overseas. He is allied with the Empress Thyllis of Hamal, and that mad woman seeks only evil for Vallia. You know."

"I know."

"So that Kov Turko will bring a new light and spirit to Falinur. You will see."

Now, all this time Turko had been standing there silently. I could see him. His face, that handsome Khamorro face, remained impassive. But the muscles in his arms roped and jumped. He would wait just so long for me to fiddle around like this and then, why, then Turko the Shield would start to show these hardy, near-bandit guerrillas that he was their new kov and they'd better get to like it. . . .

Korero the Shield stroked his beard with his upper left hand in a most judicious way. He had kept his two lower arms well inside his cloak, and his tail with its powerful grasping hand was tucked up out of the way, so that he did not look like a diff but could pass as an apim like us. Now he smiled.

"It seems to me we are all agreed, but we cannot reconcile ourselves." His voice carried that tinge of mockery he knows so well how to intimate; goads to infuriate his listeners.

Mevek almost bit.

"Agree! Of course we agree that Jhansi must be put down, but as for this new kov—" And then he caught himself, and that dull, impassive look settled again on his features.

"Good," I said brightly. "When do you think the Kov of Falinur should show himself to the people? I do not think he is a man to wait until after the victory."

"Indeed, no," put in Korero.

Turko said nothing.

Mevek said, "If he is the kov for us he will lead us in battle. I have Freedom Fighters, in hiding. We lack weapons of quality, but we fight. Send for this new Kov Turko and bid him join us—if he dares!"

Turko opened his mouth. I lifted my hand.

"We will send weapons. Our armies will march north. They will be commanded by Kov Turko of Falinur. You will send word to your people. They will rise. Together, we will sweep Jhansi and his mercenaries back to Vennar. Then. . . ."

I had overlooked a point. Not all the Falinurese felt the same fierce detestation of Jhansi shared by the men in that room.

As Turko looked at me, his head up, his handsome face verging on a scowl—for I sensed he was not completely sure of what I was about—I went on in a heavy voice, for what I had to say did not please me.

"When we beat Jhansi's men at Ovalia, they were led by a damned Hamalese, a Kapt Hangrol, and by Jhansi's toady, Malervo Norgoth."

"Hangrol has gone back to Hamal—"

"Poor devil," I said, whereat they looked at me strangely. They did not know the kind of punishment the Empress Thyllis handed out to people who failed her.

"And Tarek Malervo Norgoth skulks somewhere in Vennar. He is out of favor, serve the rast up stewed black."

"We were attacked by hordes of screaming savages—yet they were once ordinary citizens of Vallia. This is sorcery." I did not miss the flicker of fear in many faces. "This displeases me. Can you contain this? Can you handle these misguided fanatics? Will you succumb to the sorcery of Rovard the Murvish?"

This did not go down at all well.

Many were the protestations, many the oaths, many the knotty fists thumped on tables. But these men had felt the breath of fear. Rovard the Murvish, an initiate in the Brotherhood of the Sorcerers of Murcroinim, an adept of real powers, had almost trapped me in a web of sorcery. Jhansi had a trenchant tool in this sorcerer.

At last Mevek said over the hubbub, "We have seen the misguided men this wizard has spelled. Yes, they fight like crazy animals. But, they may be killed."

This, then, was the nub of my displeasure.

We talked for a space, with Turko growing more and more tense and showing every symptom of blowing up, quite unlike his usual distant mockery of me. I inquired about various people whose welfare in Falinur obsessed me, including Lol Polisto and his wife Thelda and their child, and learned he was known in this part by reputation; but his guerrilla deeds took place dwaburs away across the hills. The problem of the men under the thrall of thaumaturgy, fighting like maniacs for Jhansi, would have to be faced. When we fought and met them in battle, they would, as Mevek had so crudely said, be slain if we were to free the country.

"At the least," I said, "you can always smell Rovard the Murvish a bowshot off."

They ventured hesitant laughs at this. Sorcerers, to the ordinary man, are no joking matter.

A man wearing a fur cap poked his head in the doorway and said, "Nath says there are men skulking about to the north of the village."

My first thought was that I'd misjudged it badly when I'd tallied Mevek's band at twenty. He still had outposts.

Mevek jumped up at once.

"That will be that damned rast Macsadu and his foul masichieri." Masichieri are very low-class mercenaries, barely better than bandits. "He has been scouring the countryside for us. Well, we owe him, and tonight he'll bite off more than he can chew."

Vanderini walked quickly to the door, drawing his sword. The others followed, their weapons making a fine show.

Mevek eyed me. "It is best, majister, if you remain here where you will be safe. Macsadu does not know I have more men than usual, more than he expects."

"No," I said in a mild voice. "I do not skulk—"

"You are the emperor!" Now Mevek looked astonished, and his eyebrows formed a black bar. "Emperors do not—"

"Jak the Drang does," I said.

He nodded, convinced at once. He jerked his head at Turko. "The stylor had best hide when the fighting begins."

Because Turko bore no weapons, Mevek had judged him to be a stylor, outside the scope of fighting men, a stylor being a man who can read and write and as a scribe carries pen and ink and paper instead of sword and spear.

Now Turko's mouth opened in earnest.

I said, "This Macsadu. I hear he is a by-blow of Jhansi's."

"Aye. A vicious man-hunter. He slew his own mother when Jhansi tired of her. Now he extorts taxes and tortures for pleasure. We have a score to settle."

Turko got out, "I'll be at your side in the fight, Mevek, and judge how you conduct yourself."

The guerrilla chief gave Turko a puzzled look, started to say something, changed his mind, said, "Please yourself, stylor. If you are chopped, do not blame me."

Nath Karidge drew that curved sword of his. "It appears to me, Mevek, that you have been lax in your scouting and have sucked us into a trap. You had no business arranging this meeting if you were being followed."

Very quickly I stopped the argument. Outside the inn the sudden sounds of combat flowered in the night. Perhaps Mevek had made a mistake; we were in for a fight and that was that.

Somewhat surlily, Mevek said, "I have enough men to thrash that cramph Macsadu, do not fear—"

Vanderlnl catapulted through the doorway. His old boot of a face bore a huge bloody gash. He was yelling. He twisted and slammed the door, shoving the bar across.

"Scores and scores of the bastards! They've tricked us!"

The noise outside faded and then increased. The door bulged. The bar broke. In a smashing welter of splinters fierce armed men thrust through. Their weapons glimmered darkly with blood.

"You stupid onker!" yelled Karidge.

He fairly hurled himself forward, shouting, "Into them before they deploy!"

Korero threw back his enveloping cloak. His four arms raked up and his tail hand curved. Steel glittered.

With a whooping rush the mercenaries charged.

In the next instant a confused and murderous struggle began across the cleanly swept floor of the taproom in the Sign of the Headless Zorcaman.

## CHAPTER TWO

# Of the Disobedience of Nath Karidge

The windows exploded in fountains of splintered wood and patterned glass and struggling men collapsed inward to sprawl, still fighting, over the tables and settles. The guerrillas and the mercenaries hunting them fought madly across the floor.

Korero's glittering figure swirled like a lightning bolt of destruction.

Nath Karidge, characteristically the first to get in among his foemen, swung his curved sword with precision and gusto.

Naghan the Barrel whipped a stout clanxer, a straight cut and thruster of Vallia, into his adversary and then stiff-armed it about in a horizontal slash that dislodged the Adam's apple of the next.

Vanderini, swearing horribly and the blood running down his face, cut back into the pressing mass.

Chuktar Mevek, a sword and a dagger swirling, fought madly, as though working out a private grudge eating away his soul.

And I, Dray Prescot, I fought too, seeing that these miserable masichieri sought to kill me and I didn't have the time to die, not right now, with all I had still to do waiting to be done.

A screaming wretch flew over the battling throng. He turned a complete cartwheel as he whistled though the air. He departed from the taproom through the only window so far unbroken. Wearing the windowpanes like a collar, he vanished.

So I knew Turko the Khamorro was in action.

The fight, for all its shortness, was exceedingly ferocious.

One of the problems with low-class mercenaries is their rapid loss of interest if the day goes against them.

Not for me to judge any man in what he does, unless that happens to be against the well-being of Vallia and he is hauled up before me in my capacity as emperor. I did not condemn, nor even cavil, as the mercenaries, seeing that we were not to be easily plucked, lost interest. By ones and twos, and then a half dozen at a time, they ran out of the shattered doorway. A few hardy souls left were either cut down or persuaded to depart. I noticed that Mevek far preferred to cut them down than let them escape. He had his reasons, I did not doubt.

Some of these dubious fighting men were not apims, not Homo sapiens, being diffs of various races. A Rapa with his wattled neck and vulture head and waving tufts of feathers pressed me and I cut him a little, so that he shrieked and, turning, ran off. A Fristle, his cat face a bristle, spat at Korero, whose arm—one of his arms, the speed made it difficult to see exactly which one of the assemblage—raked out and biffed the Fristle through the gaping window. Korero used the hilt of his sword.

A Brokelsh, coarsely furred and coarse of manner, sought to drive his spear through Mevek's guts. Mevek was, at the time, hotly engaged with a fellow who tried to bring a cleaver down from the crown of Mevek's head to the junction of his collarbone.

Mevek dealt with the cleaver fellow just in time, and swung about. He saw what happened.

Turko hove up, twitched the Brokelsh's spear away, upended him, twirled him as a maid twirls a feather duster in all the old plays and heaved him over the heads of the rest of us out the window. Then, without pausing, Turko slid a long thrust of a sword in the grip of the next mercenary who had delusions of grandeur. The Khamorro grip fastened on the screaming wight and he was twitched up, up and away.

Turko, perfectly balanced, breathing easily, not in the slightest discommoded, looked about for the next one.

Mevek stared at Turko.

The fight was dying. A few more quick flurries, the shriek of a fool who hadn't the sense to duck, and the masichieri departed.

But the battle was not over yet, and we had not escaped

scot free. A number of Mevek's men sprawled on the floor in their own blood, wounded, dead and dying.

"It seems," said Mevek, breathing hard and his eyebrows twitching uneasily, "that I owe you my life. And I do not know your name."

Turko smiled.

A commotion outside drew our attention to the open doorway, and once again we grasped our swords ready to beat off a fresh attack. Introductions could wait. Crossing to the door, I peered out cautiously.

The Maiden with the Many Smiles illuminated the crossroads. The shuttered houses remained dark and mysterious. The folk of this village of Infinon of the Crossroads wanted nothing to do with the night's nefarious doings.

The stink of spilled blood and the tang of dust obliterated the smell of the flowers of the white shansili trailed on its trellis over the door.

A group of riders astride totrixes were bringing their clumsy six-footed steeds up in a rush, and the moon glinted from their lance tips and harness. These were the fellows come to finish the job the masichieri had failed to do. I did not doubt that Jhansi's illegitimate son, Macsadu the Kroks, rode at their head.

"They mean to finish us off once and for all," growled Mevek at my shoulder.

"Aye," panted Vanderini, shoving up with his sword crusted with blood. "But we'll—"

"Yes, you old wart," said Mevek, by which I judged there was a comradeship between them.

"We can but fight," I said. "We would never reach our zorcas in time."

"And if we could," said Karidge, stepping out and, surprising me, looking in the opposite direction, "I do not think, majister, you would gallop off."

"I would, Nath, and thankful to be able."

His reckless face looked shocked as he swung back.

"But, majister—"

"I have work to do for Vallia, Nath, work such that it would ill betide me to get killed before it is done."

"Ye-es," he said. The doubt was alive in him. "I see."

"No, Nath, you do not see now. But, I think, you will see one day. And, if we get out of this scrape in one piece, soon."

"Where is this marvel who makes men fly?" bellowed Mevek. "By Vox! I would have him stand at my side in the fight."

"I am here, Chuktar Mevek," said Turko, in his silky tones.

"How you manage it, and without naked steel in your fists, passes me. But, by all the names, you are a marvel."

"Men have said that before, Mevek," I said. "I am glad to see you share their opinion."

The totrix riders were now almost on us. They rode knee to knee, in a jingling, ominous trot, and it behooved us to duck back into the inn before they speared us where we stood.

Again Nath Karidge looked away at the crossroads. The intensity of his stance, the piercing stare, gave me to think. So, when the first shafts arched and the steel birds struck in among the totrix riders, I was not surprised.

Zorcamen rode swiftly from the shifting shadows. They bore on in a close, disciplined mass. Archers in front, loosing with the fluent rapidity of experts, lancers following on, they galloped along the road.

The archers fanned out, still shooting, using their nimble zorcas with superb skill. As the zorcabows opened out so the lancers bored on through in a solid bone-crushing charge. The lance heads with their red and white pennons all came down. The steel heads glimmered cruelly in that wavering light.

When the half-squadron hit, they plunged in like a fist into a tub of butter. In a twinkling the individual combats broke out as the melee swirled along between the shuttered houses. Caught utterly by surprise, thrown into confusion, the totrix men gave no thought to fighting—only to flight.

A trumpet pealed the recall. As one, the lancers disengaged. The archers shot until their targets flitted into the shadows and were lost.

Karidge yelled in his strong voice: "No pursuit, Jiktar Tromo! Form up, emperor's guard!"

With drilled precision the two half-squadrons swung back and formed at the door of the Sign of the Headless Zorcaman.

"Well—by all the names!" declared Mevek.

His men huddled, gaping at the red and yellow uniforms, the feathers, the furred pelisses. Yes, zorcamen, archers and lancers, make a fine show, by Krun!

Nath Karidge was staring at me in great uncertainty.

Mevek, however, voiced the mutual thoughts first.

"So you brought a bodyguard, emperor, after all."

"It was necessary," said Karidge, very firmly, brooking no argument, no recrimination. "The emperor did not order the bodyguard. I did so on my own responsibility." He looked down, and then up, defiantly. "I disobeyed your orders, majister, and now I accept that I will be sent as a simple trooper, to pay for my crime."

"You assume I would send you to a cavalry regiment?"

He suddenly looked aghast.

"But—majister—"

Karidge was a zorcamen first, last and all the time.

"I am minded to send you to the Phalanx, to be a brumbyte." I said brumbyte deliberately, and not soldier, for I wished Karidge to understand the situation.

"Majister. . . ." He spoke in a weak, strangled voice.

"I shall speak to you, Chuktar Karidge, about this later. For now, I thank you for your two half-squadrons. They judged it nicely. Jiktar Tromo? Send him to me later on."

"Quidang, majister!"

Then it was a matter of clearing up and finalizing what was understood between the guerrillas and myself. I heard Karidge saying to Korero, "In the Phalanx—I admire them, of course—but to trail a pike as a brumbyte! One of your muscled fellows with a vosk-skull helmet and a damned great pike and the view of the fellow in front's backside! By Vox! I couldn't bear it!"

"Cheer up, Nath," Korero advised him. "The emperor has a funny way with him at times."

"Aye!"

Keeping a straight face, I walked over to Turko and Mevek who were arguing about payment for the damage to the inn.

"These folk have been badly treated," Mevek was saying, his flat face now filled with passion. "I shall pay for the damage. And then—" and he laughed—"I shall find a damned convoy of Jhansi's and take from it what he owes."

"I feel I have a better claim," said Turko.

"You are then a rich man, you who save my life and refuse to tell me the name of the man to whom I owe it?"

"No, I suppose, if all goes well, I could be rich one day. But wealth does not interest me for itself. It is what may be done with riches—like paying for this damage."

I said, "Let Mevek pay and take the gold from Jhansi. I like the sound of that."

"There, you see!" burst out Mevek. His impassivity had quite deserted him. "The emperor speaks sense."

"I shall return to Vondium now, Mevek. You call yourself a Chuktar?"

The note of interrogation prompted him to a long, circumstantial story about once having served in a mercenary army raised somewhere in Pandahem, and he was a Chuktar by that right as well as being the leader of his guerrilla band.

"Then Chuktar it is, Mevek. An ord Chuktar, I would say." Ord—Kregish for eight—meant he had only two more steps to go before becoming a Kapt.

"Thank you, majister—"

"And now you serve the new Kov of Falinur, Kov Turko?"

He squinted up at me.

"What has passed cannot alter my decision—"

Turning to Turko the Shield, I said, "Kov, I would like to introduce to you Ord-Chuktar Mevek, a fine fellow and one whom you must watch. Mevek, you have the honor of being presented to Kov Turko of Falinur."

Well. . . .

I suppose to a tired old cynic this was all childish stuff. I am tired, right enough, even though I recognize tiredness as a mortal sin, and I am cynical enough betimes; yet I viewed this confrontation with a quiet relish. The sight of Mevek's eyebrows was reward enough.

Turko maintained a marvelous composure, and yet I knew well enough that superior Khamorro was thoroughly enjoying himself. And, with all this fun and games, we had made a significant breakthrough in relations with some of the people of Falinur. Oh, there were many of them who would side with Jhansi, and detest their new kov. But we had to be patient, and do the right things—the right things in our eyes, of course—and eventually demonstrate that we were not bloodsuckers, not slavers, and were seeking the good of all the folk of Falinur.

That was just about impossible, given the tenacious clinging to slavery of many of the masters of Falinur. But I felt strongly that Turko would succeed. He was going to bring a different technique to Falinur from the mild methods of Seg. I might deplore this. But, as the surgeons say, you cannot amputate without losing a little blood.

We left Chuktar Mevek with promises that we would soon return with the army of liberation. At least, Kov Turko would lead that army; I planned to travel to Hyrklana. With the cavalry escort fore and aft, we rode back south as She of the Veils, the fourth moon of Kregen, rose to follow the Maiden with the Many Smiles between the stars.

## CHAPTER THREE

# In Which Nath Nazabhan, Kapt of the Phalanx, Is at Last Named

"A sorcerer was reported sniffing around one of the university buildings."

"Ortyg Voinderam has absconded with the Lady Fransha, and her father, the Lord of Mavindeul, having recovered from a fit occasioned by his paroxysm of rage, vows vengeance, and his agents have been seen in Drak's City."

"Filemon, the shoe contractor, has defaulted on payment for a thousand hides."

"An outbreak of horn rot is reported in the zorcas of Thoth Valaha."

"It is reported that an idol of Mev-ira-Halviren opened its eyes and spoke, since when a multitude of the credulous flock to the temple of this outmoded religion, and the priests wax fat."

"A Hamalese spy has been apprehended in Delphond and is being brought to Vondium in chains."

"It is reliably reported that. . . ." "The latest situation appreciations show that. . . ." "What are your orders concerning. . . ."

And so on and so on. . . .

The motives of anyone who takes on the job of putting a country back together again after seasons of unrest and destruction surely need very close scrutiny.

While the process of reconstruction is going on there is little time if any for introspection. It is all work, work and more work, from long before the twin Suns of Scorpio rise to long after they set. All the same, despite the constant crushing work load, doubts must creep in. Self-analysis is probably engendered by the pressures and fatigue. And then, as they say in Balintol, you'll forget which hand to use and stand there, motionless, like a cartwheel.

Enevon Ob-Eye, my chief stylor, had recruited a large and growing bureau to handle the paperwork.

Every death warrant was seen by me, personally, and in many cases with discussions with the magistrates concerned to delve deeper into the matter, the sentences were commuted to lesser punishments. This damned Hamalese spy, for instance. . . .

"Hang him," said Nath Nazabhan, the fierceness of his words matched by the anger he felt against the enemies of his country. "Hang him from the highest branch in all Vondium."

I sipped the wine, for it was evening and the lights had been brought in and the curtains closed. My small workroom with the books and charts, the arms rack, enclosed us. The wine was superb—Vela's Tears from Valka—and I swallowed down, keeping Nath waiting before replying.

Then: "Nath. It is high time this vexed question of your name was settled."

"You will not hang this Hamalese spy?"

"Probably not. If you ask him which he prefers, to be hanged by us or sent back to the Empress Thyllis, what do you think he will reply?"

Nath's face creased. "So we hang him?" He could see the funny side of that. "Because it is more tender?"

"He might be won over. At least, we must make the attempt. Naghan Vanki will earn his keep as the chief spymaster in this."

"I am privileged to command the Phalanx. We are the most powerful fighting force Vallia possesses. I leave spies and darkness of that kind to Vanki's faceless minions."

"And, Nath, that is the problem. Your father's rank of Nazab gives you the right to call yourself Nazabhan. We have talked on this. You are the Kapt of the Phalanx. I have warned you often enough that the Phalanx is vulnerable—"

"And have we not overturned all who came against us?"

"Yes, yes. We have done well together. And you keep shying away from this business of your name."

Enevon Ob-Eye rustled papers at the side of my desk where he had brought in the latest reports. A small folding stool allowed him to sit down to the job. His own offices were large and crammed with people and files and papers.

"If I may speak for Nath, majis? He wishes to remain in the Imperial service, with your blessing, as a justicar governing a province or city. He has no ambitions to be ennobled in the main ranks of the peerage—at least—" and here Enevon squinted his one eye up—"that is how I read the situation."

"That is so, Enevon." Nath spoke crisply.

I said, "You know that at any time you wish you may be appointed justicar to govern the city or province of your choice. The imperial provinces around Vondium are in our hands once more, and arrangements can be made that will not unduly upset the incumbents." Nath Nazabhan was a good comrade, a fine man, who led the Phalanx and who was devoted to that immense cutting instrument of war, as the brumbytes within the ranks were devoted to him. So, I added, "You'd have to leave the Phalanx, of course."

"That, I am not prepared to do."

Enevon closed his eye. I leaned back and sipped the wine.

"So, as you are set in your ways, Nath, and it is necessary that you be rewarded—"

"It is not necessary, majister!"

"Oh, but, Nath, it is."

Nath, as a superb example of the splendid young fighting men who had fought shoulder to shoulder to liberate Vallia and stave off the attacks of the predators feasting on the prostrate empire, a blade comrade, a man of unquestioned loyalty, Nath must be seen to shine in that galaxy of gallants who had stepped forth to save Vallia in her Time of Troubles.

"You remember the Battle of Kochwold, Nath?"

"Who can ever forget it?"

"We had three Phalanxes there. It was a famous victory."

"Aye."

"It appears to me that Nath na Kochwold has a ring."*

"Majister?"

Enevon rustled more papers and pulled out a large sheet much embellished with fine writing and scrollwork. He placed this down before me and then fussed in his meticulous way with the sealing equipment. I looked steadily at Nath.

"Kyr Nath! No more shilly-shallying. Your rank will be formally announced when the lists are promulgated. You are

* na. The word "na" in Kregish for "of" carries connotations of higher rank than the other common word for "of"—"ti"—and is used more of provinces and cities rather than towns or estates. —A.B.A.

Nath na Kochwold." Then, and I hoped in no testy way, I added, "There are so many Naths on Kregen you have to accept the needle in this." And I signed and sealed the patent.

Nath opened his mouth, shut it, opened it again and his lower jaw moved sideways before he spoke.

"And I keep the Phalanx?"

I nodded.

"Then, majister, I thank you. By Vox! I shall have no difficulty in remembering my name!"

The feeling of relief I experienced in having pushed that problem to a solution lasted for some time as we worked on. But, inevitably, more problems came crowding in and the proverbial light at the end of the tunnel remained obscured. Mind you, to call rewarding Nath—or anyone of the people who labored so hard for Vallia—a problem is to be foolish. It was just Nath's insistence on remaining with the Phalanx that prevented my using him in a wider capacity for which he was perfectly suited.

Plans for Turko to march northward to Falinur pushed ahead. An army had to be collected. It had to be equipped and fed. And, at the same time, the rest of the territories regained in the island had to be protected.

Two new plants for processing the bumper crop of mergem we had been blessed with this season had just reached completion. Mergem, a leguminous plant, when dried may be stored for long periods and then reconstituted. It is rich in protein, vitamins and minerals, with trace elements—although at the time I knew nothing of them, by Vox!—and has seen many a beleaguered city safely through a siege. With little persuasion from me, the Presidio, to whom I was delegating more and more responsibility, had ordered the planting of vast areas of mergem. These two new processing facilities would give an even larger return than the traditional methods of grinding and drying in the suns light. Now we could use not only the pods, but the stalks as well.

And, as all good Kregans know, you can flavor your reconstituted mergem with all manner of tasty fruit juices.

Delia burst into my room as I shoved the mergem file away. She looked marvelous, rosy of face, brilliant of eye, quivering with passion.

"Dray! You sit here! What are you about? Why haven't you done something?"

I stood up. I think—I am not sure—Enevon killed a smile. I searched for meaning, and for words.

"Come on, Dray! We can't just do nothing! We must hurry!"

"Yes," I said. And I tried to put a snap, a ring of decision into my voice. "We must act!"

"At once!"

"Of course. . . ."

Now my Delia is the most wonderful person in two worlds. That goes without saying, although I have said it, will say it and continue to say it. But, all the same—what in the frozen wastes of the Ice Floes of Sicce was she talking about now? By Zim-Zair! It was enough to make a plain old fellow like me jump up and down on his hat.

And here came Jilian, recovered of her wounds, roaring into my little study, shouting that we must hurry. Jilian with her black leathers and her pale face with those dark brilliant eyes brought a heady wash of action wherever she went. Jilian, with her whip and her claw.

"Don't just stand there, Jak!" she called.

Delia said, "Oh, you have to take a two-handed sword to stir him up when he gets like this. Come *on*, Dray!"

I swallowed. Venturing all, I said in a voice that was little more than a husky croak, "Where to?"

Both women—both gorgeously beautiful women—stared at me as though I was bereft of my senses.

"Well, *I* don't know!" said Jilian.

"I've no idea," said Delia. "But we must hurry!"

Now I shut my mouth most firmly. I put both hands flat on the desk. I closed my eyes.

Enevon coughed. "I think, majis, this matter touches the business of Ortyg Voinderam—"

"An imbecile I'll sink my claw into if—" began Jilian.

Now I grasped what was going on—well, some of it. Ortyg Voinderam had eloped with the Lady Fransha, and Delia as Empress of Vallia no doubt knew far more about the affair than anyone could guess. From this knowledge I judged that young Idiot Voinderam had not obtained an opinion from the empress. Delia would not interfere in matters of the heart. But, as she was the empress, these were matters that were of concern to her.

After all, in the mating of noble houses coalitions formed and business was transacted and heads could be parted from shoulders.

I ventured again, attempting to sound as though I was fully apprised of the situation. "So no one knows where Ortyg has gone?"

"Where he has taken poor Fransha!"

"Now, Jilian," I said in my reasonable voice. "Perhaps she went willingly. Perhaps they are in love—"

"Of course they're in love! That's why she went! And that's why we have to get her back!"

I shook my head. I reached for the glass of Vela's Tears. I sipped the strong red wine that comes from Southern Valka. I was all at sea again. These women . . . !

A kind of brain wave occurred to me then, and I spoke up with a firmer voice. "Call all the members of both households. Call all our chamberlains. Contact Naghan Vanki. Order a fast voller. Saddle a dozen zorcas and two dozen totrixes. Have the Emperor's Sword Watch stand to arms—No." I felt I'd gone far enough. I didn't want the Emperor's Sword Watch given unnecessary burdens, turned out of barracks at all hours, their training program interrupted. "No, cancel that last order."

Delia saw through all that nonsense on the instant.

"You may think it all very funny, Dray. But it is serious. Ortyg and Fransha are passionately in love and the match is generally regarded with great favor—"

"Well, why—?"

"Because if they run off like this the families will never agree, old Larghos of Mavindeul, Fransha's father, will turn against Ortyg Voinderam and make his daughter wed that Fridil Goss. *Then* you know what will happen."

I did. My old antagonist, Natyzha Famphreon, with the wizened face and lush body would rub her hands with glee when she heard the news. She was a leading member of the Racter party, once the most powerful political force in Vallia, able to dictate to the emperors, and now sadly fallen away and confined to their locus of discontent in the northwest. After Turko had regained Falinur we had to deal with Layco Jhansi who fought the damned Racters to the north of him. Many men expressed the pious hope that they'd kill each other off before we had to march against them.

I looked down at the cluttered desk. A paper protruded from a file—a thin file, just opened—and on the paper two names were written out fairly. Weg Wegashtorio. Nath Karidge. The next file concerned the state of our airboats. We could buy none from Hamal, seeing Hamal was at this time our mortal enemy. We could not manufacture airboats ourselves, only our flying sailing ships. Embassies had gone down south into the Dawn Lands in the hope of buying fliers. I had to go to Hyrklana not just to find our friends; making deals to buy fliers was also on the agenda there. I sighed.

All these pressing problems of empire, and I was being entwined in the passions of lovers. A world might shiver and shake and empires totter and fall, but two foolish young people in love must take precedence.

Well, there is a justice in that, I suppose. . . .

The other three people in my study were well aware of the network of agents—spies—I had set up distinct from the empire's chief spymaster, Naghan Vanki, and his organization. Enevon had been an active participant in our plans.

So now Delia could burst out hotly, "We have worked hard up there in Mavindeul. The stromnate is ready to declare for us if they are guaranteed support. And old Larghos has no love for Natyzha, despite he holds his stromnate at her hands."

A strom, the equivalent of an Earthly count, has certain powers. We had promised to make Larghos, Strom of Mavindeul, a strom in his own right with his own province if he threw in with us. The marriage of his daughter Fransha was a part of this, for young Ortyg Voinderam was the son of the Vad of Khovala, and Khovala's southwestern border marched with that of Mavindeul. If everyone agreed, Mavindeul would rise, Khovala would march and we would send troops across the Great River to join in the attack from the imperial province of Thermin, whose governor just happened to be the father of Nath of Kochwold. It all fit perfectly.

And now passions could not wait, and the couple had eloped.

Enevon coughed. "If the Lady Fransha is married off to Fridil Goss, a puppet of Natyzha Famphreon's, Mavindeul will not dare declare for us, for they will get no support from Khovala."

"I suppose," I said in a vague way, "Khovala will not support, anyway, seeing their vad's son has the girl he wants?"

"It will not rest with them. Mavindeul holds the key."

A vad is the rank of nobility below a kov, which roughly equates with a duke, and a vad is very high on the tree of rank and power and prestige. Old Antar Voinderam wasn't going to stick his neck out for nothing, and nothing would be all he would get if he tried to march against Natyzha Famphreon without the support of Mavinduel. Rather—he would get something—a great many dead soldiers in his forces.

The situation was perfectly simple. It was not at all complicated. After all, this was just the kind of problem your real emperor would tackle and solve twice a day before breakfast.

But—I wasn't a real emperor—at least, not in my own eyes. I was just plain Dray Prescot, tackling a colossal task with all the wits and cunning I may be blessed with. The sooner I could wrap up this business of liberating the Empire of Vallia and hand the lot over to my son Drak in working order, the better.

By Zair, yes!

And together with that, there was no denying the fascination of handling these problems. How did you perform the balancing act necessary to gain your ends? How did you please everybody? Well, that can't be done, of course. There is a pull, a dark tide in men, that urges them to meddle with the lives and destinies of other people. We felt that we were acting for the right reasons in attempting to free Vallia from the hordes of mercenaries and slavers who had descended on the islands in the Time of Troubles. We believed that, these people gathered together under the new flag of Vallia. The moment I suspected the tiniest suggestion of corrupting power—I'd be off, by Vox, off and away and out of it.

It is not necessarily true that absolute power corrupts; it does do so, lamentably, but it is not a rule that it must.

Anyway—how many men in history have possessed real, true, genuine absolute power? Perhaps it is having only the illusion of absolute power that corrupts. I did know that the passions of young lovers were, if not more important than, at least certainly as important as, the devious political maneuvers we were forced to in our struggle to clean up the mess in Vallia.

Rather heavily, I said, "Send everyone suitable to try to trace Ortyg and Fransha. We can hope they have left a trail. I'll go and see Antar Voinderam if he is still at his villa here. And I shall try to catch Fransha's father, Larghos, before he departs."

I closed the next file on the desk. It concerned the Opaz-forsaken zorca horn rot, a frightful business.

"I don't like the idea of Larghos sending to Drak's City to hire assassins."

## CHAPTER FOUR

# Concerning the Power of Phu-Si-Yantong

"See to it, Vanki," I said to the empire's chief spymaster.

"Yes, majister."

His flat and chilling voice was just the same after all this time. His face, pale, composed, held that containment of himself, that inscrutable knowingness, that perhaps he did not realize revealed so much. This was a man who lived in the shadows and was of the darkness. And in contact with people in the everyday run of rubbing elbows they would regard him and know that this man lived within himself. He had proved a master of his trade. Also, and for this I forgave him much, including his part in dumping me under a thorn ivy bush in the Hostile Territories, he was devoted to Delia.

Anyone who tries to run a country, even a ramshackle kind of place as Vallia then was, cannot do it all alone.

You have to learn to delegate.

"And remember, the welfare and happiness of Ortyg and Fransha are more important than a possible advantage on the fringe of Racterland."

Naghan Vanki still wore his trim black and silver clothes, cut in the latest fashion and inconspicuous. Black and white are the Racter colors. He moved his hand over the papers on his desk, the same kind of damned papers that cluttered my desk.

"Once I thought the Racters held the chief hope for the country. Events have altered my appreciation."

With a quick look at his clepsydra—the time was flying by!—I turned to leave. "If Mavindeul does not throw in with us and rise, we'll soon be in a position to attack the Racters from the south, anyway, as soon as Kov Turko has cleared his Falinur."

"My sources inform me that Antar Voinderam will not risk an attack on the dowager Kovneva of Falkerdrin until he is assured of success." Had Naghan Vanki been in the habit of smiling, or of allowing any expression on that chilling face of his, now he might have smiled. Old Natyzha Famphreon, the dowager Kovneva of Falkerdrin, was a holy terror. No one—but no one—could ever be assured of success against her until she was battened down and on her way to the Ice Floes of Sicce.

"We'll do our best to accommodate him." I opened the door, and then thought that Vanki might profit from a little jolt. "You know there is zorca horn rot in Thoth Valaha. We are going to be short of saddle animals if we're not careful. I want a full report of our negotiations with the countries in the Dawn Lands we have approached to purchase airboats."

Vanki said, just a little quickly, "We continue to try in the Dawn Lands, majister." Then he halted himself, about to say something and checking himself. Oddly, I had the clear impression that he knew something, had thought I knew, and had suddenly realized that I did not know.

"Yes?"

He was very smooth. "I will have the report on your desk before the suns rise."

It would have been childish of me to have said, "In triplicate!" as I almost did. We were operating on a level a little above that kind of pettiness.

"We desperately need vollers," I said. Vanki, like most Vallians, called airboats fliers. Voller was the Havilfarese name, coming from the places where they were built. "And we need saddle and draught animals. I shall be going to Hyrklana as soon as I can shed some of this work load. Not that we will get much joy out of fat Queen Fahia. But we must have transport!"

He saw that I was seized by the urgency of this problem. It was vital to the continuing struggle.

"Much of the mergem crop has been planted where the forests were cut down for the sailing ships of the sky."

"We'll just have to forage wider for lumber."

"Yes, majister."

About to burst out, as the old intemperate Dray Prescot would certainly have done, I held my tongue. Spymasters may become two-edged weapons. If that happened Vallia would be in for much bloodshed before we righted the ship of state, so to speak. He watched me with that calm stare as I went out. Our parting remberees were polite, that was all.

But, for all that, Naghan Vanki was an invaluable servant to Vallia.

The urgency of everything was enough to drive a man wild with baffled impatience.

Both Antar Voinderam, Ortyg's father, and Larghos Eventer, Fransha's father, had left the city before I could contact them. Messengers were on their trail. After seeing Vanki, there was one more man I would see, perhaps in this case as in so many others, the most important man of all.

Riding back through the nighted streets of Vondium, passing ruins still sprawled in ugly decay but bright with wild flowers, grim and yet glowing reminders of the Time of Troubles, I relished the scent of moon blooms. She of the Veils sailed the sky above. Her fuzzy golden and rosy glow illuminated buildings and avenues, glimmered molten on the still waters of the canals. Truly, even half in ruins, Vondium was still the beautiful city, proud in her beauty.

At my back rode the duty squadron of the Sword Watch.

Formed out of loyalty to the emperor, formed at the beginning by my blade comrades without my knowledge to protect me against the cunning and viciousness of assassins, the Emperor's Sword Watch kept guard. This was a squadron from 2ESW, for 1ESW was away up north with my son Drak. With him, also, was the Emperor's Yellow Jackets, 1EYJ, helping to finalize our campaigns up there against the clansmen. With them were Seg Segutorio and Inch, and I hungered to see my blade comrades again and talk and carouse and sing and generally forget that I was supposed to be a puissant emperor.

The two second moons of Kregen, the Twins eternally orbiting each other, lifted over the serrated rooftops, and the night brightened with a confusing crisscross pattern of pinkish shadows.

On such a night assassins might stalk abroad. I would have to go and see the Hyr Stikitche in Drak's City, the haunt of thieves and vagabonds and assassins, and see what he would tell me of Larghos Eventer's doings. Not damned much, for old Nath the Knife, the Aleygyn of the Stikitches, was touchy concerning the honor of assassins.

All the same, he had sent many of his fine young men to serve with 1EYJ, and they had fought passing well.

These thoughts as we hurried along brought up the business interrupted by this passionate elopement. The stray thought did occur to me of that horrendous time when Delia had, by mischance, been abducted. "Shades of the Lady Merle and Vangar Riurik," I said to myself. Well, that affair had turned out all right in the end, and I hoped that this one would as well.

Despite the urgency of our ride, the beauty of moons-drenched Vondium, half in ruins, could not fail to stir me. If working for mere artifacts of brick and stone is not simple foolishness, it was in my mind to believe we did right to struggle for the well-being of this city.

New schools had not only to be equipped and staffed and funded, they had to be built. . . .

A flurry of alarm shook a patrol of the Sword Watch forward, their zorcas running with upflung horns as they passed me, grim-faced men surging up to ride knee-to-knee in a compact body around Shadow, my beautiful black zorca. The staccato crack of hooves, the creak of leather and clink of harness, were punctuated by brief shouts, of interrogation and answer, as the forward patrol sorted out the pother.

Jiktar Rodan had the command of the duty squadron this night. His iron-hard face beneath the brim of his helmet looked like a mere mask, carved as one with the helmet itself.

Shadow slackened speed. Rodan rode level with me. Swords glimmered in the light of the moons. Up ahead the shouts lifted.

A zorcaman came hurdling back, pelisse and feathers and plumes flying. He bellowed it out.

"A party of drunks, Jik! Shall we round 'em up?"

Rodan looked annoyed. He had quite clearly mentally braced himself to meet a savage attack upon the person of the emperor he was sworn to preserve with his own life if necessary, and all it was was a parcel of drunks. Yes, one could sympathize with Jiktar Rodan.

He started to say, "Round 'em up—" and no doubt would have gone on to order them thrown into the nearest dungeon and forgotten.

I said, "Who are they?"

The zorcaman bellowed, "Citizens, majister!"

"Then let them fall into the gutter and sleep quietly, we have urgent business ahead of us tonight."

"Quidang, majister!"

Jiktar Rodan looked across at me before he fell back into his position at the head of the duty squadron. He took a breath. We had seen action together. He had taken wounds.

"Yes, I know, Rodan. I am too soft with them."

"Yes, majister." These old hands, training up the youngster, soldiers who had served with me for seasons, know how and when to take liberties with the emperor—not that they were regarded as liberties by me. We all did our jobs for Vallia and that was what counted. He went on, shaking his head, "We need to put a little backbone into them, by Vox!"

I forbore to ask if he meant his youngsters or the party of drunken citizens.

Certainly, the reaction of the duty squadron had been prompt and sharp, and had there been real trouble ahead then these lads of 2ESW would have nipped it in the bud.

Ortyg Voinderam, who had run off with his Lady Fransha because he couldn't wait for the legal bokkertu to be concluded, might benefit by a season or two of being trained up by crusty old vikatus like Jiktar Rodan. Vikatu the Dodger, the archetype of the old soldier, the old sweat, can teach lessons to civilians as well as the swods in the ranks. . . .

When I dismounted in a convenient inner courtyard of the imperial palace—convenient because it hadn't been burned down or knocked to pieces—Rosala, one of Delia's handmaids, was talking to a soldier in the half-shadows of an archway.

I heard her say in a teasing voice, "And here is the emperor now, you famous jurukker, and I must fly!"

She danced across the flags toward me.

Delia knows how to look after her people. Rosala called the soldier a jurukker, that is to say guardsman, and I, perforce, had accepted this nomenclature. I will not belabor the point about my ambivalent attitudes to bodyguards and the like. They have their uses. And the men forming a juruk—a guard—are the important part of the structure for me.

"Majis!" said Rosala, pert, half laughing. "The empress bid me tell you she has gone with the Lady Jilian. She hopes to be back late tomorrow."

Throwing Shadow's reins to the groom who hurried up, and with a pat for the zorca's gleaming black neck and a word or two for the groom, Yando the Limp, for he had taken a wound at the Battle of Kochwold, I went into the palace. Rosala lingered.

"Do not suborn that soldier from his duty, Rosala. . . ."

She knew I teased her.

"Majister!" Her eyes, her lips, her hair, all looked magnificent in the light of the moons. "He stands guard like a famous juruk, like the best soldier in the Sword Watch. Do you think he would desert his post for me?"

I did not answer. Truth to tell, as I went into the palace in search of Khe-Hi-Bjanching, I realized that any soldier with any sense—anyone without commitments—would desert his post for a girl like Rosala. But she was handmaid to the Empress of Vallia. Se was, besides being a girl of remarkable beauty, a girl of immense common sense. She knew the dangers thronging around an imperial palace on Kregen.

And the news she brought that Delia had gone off meant, I judged, that Delia and Jilian were going their own way about finding the Lady Fransha.

Now I am well aware that I am a crusty old curmudgeon who takes delight in foolish notions that appall the more sober-minded, plain Dray Prescot with the weight of an empire in ruins hanging on my shoulders. Yet, I think, and I truly believe, that I was genuinely more concerned for the safety and happiness of Ortyg and Fransha than I was for the political maneuverings surrounding their match. So, as I found Khe-Hi-Bjanching wide awake in the chambers given over to the Wizard of Loh, I felt the leap of gratitude to him and hope that all might yet be well.

"Majister," he greeted me. "I have been trying—but so far my powers fail me."

All my sudden hope vanished like thistledown.

The chamber was illuminated in the mellow glow of samphron oil lamps and was filled with comfortable furnishings. There was nothing of the tawdry bric-a-brac of the common sorcerer here. Wizards of Loh, the most famed and feared thaumaturges of Kregen, as far as I then knew, needed no gimcrack trappings of skulls and bats blood and reptile inner parts and pickled dragons.

"You have been into lupu, Khe-Hi?"

"Yes. I sent my powers out and found nothing. It was strange. Ortyg Voinderam is no sorcerer of any kind, surely?"

"No. Not as far as I know."

I felt the chill. If another sorcerer were at work here, preventing Bjanching from discovering the whereabouts of the runaways by means of his kharrna which gave him the power of observing events at a distance, then that other wizard might be *the* wizard. . . .

Bjanching saw all that on my face.

"If Phu-Si-Yantong is interfering here. . . ."

"Sink me!" I burst out. "I'll have that devil's tripes one of these fine days. He is a maniac and although I have searched for some I have failed to find goodness in him yet."

"I do not know anyone who would say he was capable of an ounce of goodness—"

"Well," I grumped, "I suppose he must have some redeeming features. If we could discover what they were perhaps we might talk to him—" I looked at Bjanching. "Have you contacted Deb-Lu-Quienyin?"

"I was about to do that when you arrived, majister."

Deb-Lu-Quienyin, with whom I had been through a fraught time or two, had remained with Drak and my friends in the north where I fancied he would be of inestimable value to them. He was just about the most powerful Wizard of Loh there was—always excepting that crazed power-mad devil Phu-Si-Yantong.

Even though I had spent much time in company with Quienyin and Bjanching, and had seen Wizards of Loh performing their mysteries, I, like anyone else on Kregen, could never fully feel at ease as they set about their arcane rituals.

Khe-Hi-Bjanching wore a severe robe of a lustrous black. No runes or magical symbols sullied his vestments, and the pallor of his face and the fiery red Lohvian hair seemed, by contrast, all the more striking. As a young—or relatively young—Wizard of Loh, Bjanching might have been excused displays of thaumaturgical fashion. He disdained them. He was able to exert his power and go into lupu—that strange, half-trance state in which his kharrna extended and gave him pictures of people and events many miles away—without fuss and without many of the physical preparations of other Wizards of Loh I had known.

Waiting as Khe-Hi-Bjanching prepared himself, calmed his whole body and psyche, began to infiltrate the tendrils of his power into those arcane other worlds no mortal might tread with impunity, I found my sense of screaming impatience easing. This would take time, and time I did not have, yet I could wait quietly.

Bjanching's eyes rolled up until, in the moment before he placed his palms over them, his eyes glared forth sightlessly in white blankness. The waiting was mercifully short. The Wizard of Loh's breathing lengthened and drew out, softer and softer, shallower and shallower, until it seemed he did not breathe at all. The chambers gave no sound. We were two primeval spirits, isolated in the great mysteries.

Then—Bjanching lowered his hands.

He stared at me, and in his face that *knowing* look told me he had broken through.

I leaned forward eagerly. "Quienyin?"

No answer.

"San?" I gave the Wizard of Loh the honorific of dominie, or sage, and I breathed in a deep draught of the close air.

"Majister—" The voice was Bjanching's. "San Quienyin is there, on the periphery, and he is trying to make contact with me. But. . . ."

I put my teeth into my lip.

For a long space the two wizards sought to reach each other through that timeless, formless, unknowable hinterland of the occult. Sweat began to roll down Bjanching's face. Abruptly, he jumped up, his black gown swirling. He took three faltering steps, beginning to spin around in that dervish-like whirling by which some wizards summon their powers. Instead of going on with the rituals that had been unnecessary for him for so long, he tottered and collapsed into his high-backed chair.

He looked at me, and that look of knowingness had fled.

"What is it?" I asked.

"Majister—Quienyin and I were separated, as by a barrier of enormous force. This is new. We must work and investigate and—"

"Yes, yes. Tell me!"

"We cannot discern a single thing concerning the whereabouts of Voinderam and the Lady Fransha."

"Now the devil take it!" I said, and I swore.

"But, majister—do you not see?"

"I see, San, I see very well. Phu-Si-Yantong—"

"Yes! That arch devil has interdicted our powers, and that means he has achieved a recrudescence of power taking him into an altogether new plane. I think, majister, I believe, we are in for a fight passing anything that has gone before."

"And it's a fight you must win, or all Vallia is doomed."

# CHAPTER FIVE

## On the Day of Opaz the Deliverer

Emder's long, competent fingers deftly pulled the leather straps of my fancy sword belt into the correct position so that I might haul the buckles tight. Quietly-spoken, Emder, an invaluable man who acted as a valet as a mere part of his many functions. His neatness was of that unfussy kind an untidy person does not take as an affront.

"Now the mazilla, majis."

He lifted the enormous collar ready to wrap it around the back of my neck. Now these ornate collars of Vallia, these mazillas, I had had trouble with before. They are stiff with gold wire, heavy with bullion, ablaze with gems. They poke up from your shoulders and enclose your head like a glittering oyster shell.

Emder leaned sideways and took a look at my face. He sighed.

"Today is the Day of Opaz the Deliverer. I know the processions will go on from suns rise to suns set—"

"And the damned speeches, and the ceremonies and all the rest of it. By the Black Chunkrah!" I said, most feelingly, using a hallowed clansman's oath. "I ought to be well out of it."

Emder pursed up his lips and gentled the huge collar down onto my shoulders. Mind you, the thing did give a weird kind of comfort, for it would take a monstrous blow of a sword to cut through that expensive protection. That was how they'd started in the first place, back in the days when Vallia was a motley collection of little nations all struggling for preeminence.

Well, by Vox, we weren't far off getting back to those ancient days now!

Emder began closing the fastenings.

"The people expect to see their emperor on this day, majis. And, as well, it is the day we keep in remembrance of the Battle of Voxyri—"

"That anniversary I'll keep, and with pleasure." The Battle of Voxyri had taken place outside Vondium and inside the city after we'd broken in. It had taken place on the Day of Opaz the Deliverer. That battle had given us back Vondium, the capital of Vallia, and had seen me enthroned and crowned as emperor—for what that was worth.

Then, and I own somewhat petulantly, I said, "And the empress has not returned?"

"Rosala waits in patience, majis, and Floria with her."

I'd left Bjanching beginning the work he and Deb-Lu-Quienyin must tackle to attempt to thwart this new and horrifying power of the arch maniac, Phu-Si-Yantong. I'd completely forgotten about the celebrations arranged for today. And, all the time the processions wended about the city and the bedecked narrow boats glided along the canals, and the bands played and the people cheered, all the time wizards would be struggling and battling, one against the other, on planes far removed from the gorgeous and barbaric splendor of the Day of Opaz the Deliverer. . . .

"The empress didn't forget about the punishments I'm going to have to endure today." I wrenched a buckle tight and the mazilla swayed. My robes glittered. I felt a fool. "She took good care to see she wasn't here to share my discomforts."

"Majis!"

"All right, all right. I'm just in a foul mood."

"Yes, majis."

Good old Emder! A comrade, a friend, and a fellow to make sure the last button was sewed on the last shirt, the boots were polished to mirrors, the swords all held edges.

There was nothing else for it. I had to do my duty this day. This was all a part of being emperor, just as much as worrrying over zorca horn rot and the supply of corn and the new gold mines, and payment of the troops and education for the youngsters. And—all the rest of *that* . . .

I will not go into details of the lavishness of the Day. The twin suns shone, Zim and Genodras, blazing down out of a clear sky. The waters of the canals scintillated in light. The houses were festooned with flags and bunting and draped curtains and streamers. The people shouted. The processions wound in and out, and the priests went through their rituals, earnestly and with dedication, and sweating more than a little.

The bands played. Contingents of various regiments marched. The people pranced through the avenues and crowded the narrow boats so that the canals became solid walkways.

Chanting lines of folk weaved in and out, all repeating over and over those ancient litanies, chief of which resounded all day among the half-ruined houses.

"OO-lie O-paz . . . OO-lie O-paz. . . ." Over and over, rising and falling, Oolie Opaz, on and on and on.

Surrounded by dignitaries and nobles and functionaries, I went as prescribed from place to place within the city. How different this was, by Vox, from those earlier times! Now I was surrounded by comrades, men and women who had fought with me shoulder to shoulder against our common foes. Now I had no fear, not now, not on this Day, of the poisoned frown, the disgusted look, the turning away in contempt.

The Second Sword Watch were there, inconspicuous, but there, ready in case a more deadly threat manifested itself.

Messengers in relays kept me informed on the progress of Bjanching. He had not gained clear contact with Quienyin. The two Wizards of Loh continued to investigate the extent and force of this new power wielded by Phu-Si-Yantong.

Vallia is a civilized country of Kregen, with wild enough parts here and there, as I well knew. But all the same, these processions, the brilliance of jewels and feathers, the caparisoned animals, the uproar with the banging of drums and gongs and the fierce blowing of trumpets, the smells and the scents, the sheer vitality of it all, this was a splendid and barbaric spectacle.

But the luster of the Day was dimmed for me until almost halfway through, just as we were approaching the hour of mid.

"I am parched!" quoth Nath na Kochwold—who remembered his name with the utmost clarity—and he smiled. "I look forward to the meal they have prepared with almost as much pleasure as I look forward to the march past. By Vox! What we have left of the Phalanx is a poor remnant. But they will march with a swing."

"They will, Nath, they will."

We alighted from the narrow boat and burst into the light of the suns and the roaring welcome of the crowds. Above us lifted the bulk of the Temple of Opaz the Judge. Glistening, impressive, floating among the clouds, it seemed, that vision of spire and dome. I looked up. The manifestation of Opaz in the guise of Judge was traditionally linked with midday, the balancing point between night and night. Here the priests would have prepared a mouth-watering repast to tide us over the next part of the Day's events. We were all sharp set.

The marble steps glistened with gold-veined whiteness. Crimson drapes stained the marble with the semblance of blood. Ranked lines of men held back the pressing crowds. The color, the excitement and the heady energy of the celebrations filled everyone with the passionate conviction that it was divine to be alive on such a day as this.

Pausing for a moment to speak to one of the swods guarding the marble stairs, I was aware of his hard, tanned face, the direct look of his brown Vallian eyes. He was a spearman of the Fifteenth Regiment, trim in leather and crimson, his shield with its proud devices angled just so, his stout spear precisely vertical, its steel head polished to a starry glitter.

"Lahal, Kalei." I noticed the absence of rank badges. "You were a Deldar when we fought together."

"Aye, majister. But I got into a fight with a poor fellow out of the Phalanx. They stripped one Deldar rank from me for every tooth he lost."

"Then—" I said, remembering. "Then he lost seven teeth."

Kalei's hard face showed pleasure.

"I will make ob-Deldar again in three of the months of the Maiden with the Many Smiles."

"When you reach shebov-Deldar again send me a message. I will make you a zan-Deldar at once."*

His pleasure increased. I was not being magnanimous. I was not pandering to the men in the ranks. A kampeon is a veteran, a soldier who has received recognition, a man who has won renown in the army. Kalei was a kampeon. Such men are valuable, as precious as gold to an army, for from their experience and war wisdom comes the training of the youngsters. Kalei was too valuable to spend his life carrying a spear as a swod in the ranks.

* ob: one. shebov: seven. zan: ten.

And, at the same time, he had to be subject to the same iron discipline, what the swods call mazingle, as the men he trained up. There was no question of my instantly restoring his rank as a Deldar. That would undermine discipline.

Kalei knew that.

He saluted, an enormous bashing of his spear against his shield, and I nodded and walked on up the marble stairs.

"Remberee, Kalei!"

"Remberee, majister!" And then, unexpectedly, he added in his stentorian Deldar's bellow, "May Vox of the Cunning Sword go with you always, majister!"

The soldier near the foot of the wide sweep of marble steps moved. In neat precision they opened ranks. Their weapons and harness glittered. A sedan chair borne by eight Womoxes swayed up the steps from a narrow boat moored next to the boat in which we had arrived. The chair was sumptuous. It was splendid. Crimson velvet curtains and drapes of cloth of gold concealed the occupant. Tassels of bullion glittered. Feathers waved. The rear Womoxes, massive, bull-headed men from the island of Womox off the west coast of Vallia, raised their carved and gilt-encrusted carrying poles so that the sedan chair remained level.

I turned to look back down the steps.

The chair was altogether more ornate, more regal, than the usual run of gherimcals, for the normal gherimcal of Kregen serves functional needs of carrying people about. This palanquin concentrated glory and splendor within itself.

At the side of the gherimcal walked Rosala and Floria. So I knew.

I walked back down the steps, leaving the dignitaries and the waiting priests above me. I did not run. I do not know how I did not run.

I lifted the cloth-of-gold curtains.

Delia said, "We found not a single sign of them, and I'm late for the Day of Opaz the Deliverer—what a way for an empress to carry on!"

And I, Dray Prescot, laughed.

Neither Delia nor I cared a fig for being empress or emperor. We just wanted to get the job done.

"Whatever you do, my heart," I said, "the people of Vallia love you."

So we went up together to the Temple of Opaz the Judge.

Delia looked superb. She was radiant. She wore a simple sheer gown all of white, with those two special brooches, and

"A sedan-chair borne by eight Womoxes swayed up the steps."

a cape of scarlet and gold, crimson and silver, in an artful blend that combined sumptuousness with good taste in a miraculous fashion. Her brown hair was dressed high, threaded with gold and gems, and those outrageous tints of chestnut lent the perfect touch of natural beauty. Like us all, she carried arms, a rapier and a dagger swinging from jeweled lockets on a narrow gem-encrusted belt over her hips.

"And I am famished," she said as we walked up.

"Jilian?"

"She continues the search. But the trail has gone cold, I think."

When the people saw Delia they went wild.

Fantastic cheering and roaring, shrill cries calling down the blessings of Opaz upon her, a bedlam of love and good wishes broke in an inferno of joy to the clear skies over Vondium.

Delia smiled. The whole world brightened. She looked wonderful. With an incredibly graceful gesture, she lifted her hand, bowing to the people left and right and then walking on, her head high, proud, superb, radiant—Delia—Delia of Delphond, Delia of the Blue Mountains.

And I, Dray Prescot, was privileged to walk along at her side. Yes, it wasn't all bad, being Emperor of Vallia!

The rest of the day passed in something of a blur. All the necessary rituals were gone through with proper deference. Whenever I was called on to give a speech outside the customary rote observances, it was very easy to remind the citizens of Vondium of the perils through which we had just passed, and to harp on the dangers we still faced.

"We of Vallia believe! Our children clamor to be heard. We cannot let their justifiable ambitions go unheeded. The land calls for purification. From all over the continents and islands of Paz our oppressors have flooded in. We have fought them. We have driven them back from Vondium, the proud city, and from many of the provinces."

Standing on an obelisk, or at the summit of steps, or upon some balcony banked with flowers, I would say the same words, or almost the same, telling these people that we had come a very long way, and that there was a very long way still to go.

"The iron legions of Hamal have invaded us. The slavers, aragorn, slavemasters have taken away our loved ones, our fathers and mothers, our husbands and wives, our children, brothers and sisters, taken away to be chained in slavery. The flutsmen wing in our skies, pillaging and slaying. The masichieri march against us with rapine in their hearts—no! No, my friends. I am wrong! These masichieri, all the rest of the scum, they have no hearts that beat in human breasts."

The crowds would yell at this, raging, knowing the awful tragedies that had overtaken us, knowing what we had to do to bring Vallia once more into the light of Opaz.

While I was, as you will see, preaching to the converted, I was uneasily aware that since our successes the hard edge to our purpose might fall away.

After all, many and many a mile separated the hated foemen now from the citizens of Vondium. Despite the ruins everywhere thrusting their harsh reminders upon us, it was deceptively easy to feel the victory had been won. The sounds of the drums were muffled by distance. Yet Vondium remained the heart of Vallia. Nothing less than total dedication could be required. . . .

Delia looked sharply at me as I walked back from the balcony where the last speech had been vociferously received.

"Dray?"

"I was thinking, even as I spoke—we *must* do this, Vondium *must* fight on, nothing less than total dedication can be—" I looked at her, seeing her beauty and the wary look on that face I know so well. "Can be tolerated, permitted?"

"You said required."

"Yes. We run perilously close to deep waters."

"Come away and drink a glass of wine. The suns decline. They have a fine Tardalvoh here which will curl your toes."

We were due to dine this season with the Bankers Guild. Each season on the Day various authorities took it in turns to host the emperor and empress. The Bankers Guild, formed by a number of Companies of Friends to further their own ends, would surpass all efforts at entertainment. Well, I will not bore you with details of what we ate, the golden plates and all that high living. After the feast, the reckoning.

We had changed from the foolish sumptuous clothes of the day to evening attire, with the smaller nikmazillas that are so becoming a part of Vallian costume. Turko and Nath and a few other nobles were talking in a corner when the portly form of Nomile Ristemer rolled up.

"Majister! May I present my son, Mileon Ristemer, of whom I am inordinately proud. He has but just returned home to offer his sword in your service."

I nodded and shook hands in the Vallian fashion.

Old Nomile Ristemer was one of the elite of the banking fraternity of Vondium, immensely rich before the Time of Troubles, still a very wealthy man. His interests extended to many parts of Kregen. He was stout, chunky, with short legs and a strut to his walk. His face was not quite doughy and he had a swab nose. His brain was like a cold chisel. He was nothing like Casmas the Deldy of Ruathytu, right out of his class altogether.

His son, Mileon, partook of that chunky appearance, but he had kept himself in shape and looked what he was, a tough, experienced mercenary. When a mercenary achieves enough distinction, his comrades may see fit to elect him to the august company of brethren who wear the silver mortilhead on its silk ribbon at their throats. He is then a paktun. Of course, the word paktun is more often than not used of any mercenary, as I have said. The silver mortilhead, the pakmort, showed a discreet glitter at Mileon Ristemer's throat.

"You will, I trust, majister, find room and service for my son."

Constantly I was being approached in this way, and I dealt with the applicants as they deserved and in as just a way as I could contrive. Mileon Ristemer looked likely. His father was not a noble but had been given the title of Kyr, a kind of honorific, by the old emperor. The son was plain Koter Ristemer.*

"I shall be glad to have the honor to serve you, majister. I shall not require pay. I have one or two ideas that, I believe, will prove of great value in future campaigns—"

"Where have you seen service, Koter Ristemer?"

"In various countries of Havilfar, and in Loh."

"I am interested in any new schemes. Make an appointment with my chief stylor, Kyr Enevon. I trust we can serve the interests of Vallia together."

Mileon visibly drew himself up, his shoulders going back. Maybe he hadn't been used to dealing with raspy, down-to-earth characters like me before when taking service as a paktun.

"Quidang, majister!"

He rattled that out, and the word, the tone, the very vehemence of that soldier reply, sounded strange in the golden, refined world of the Bankers Guild.

* ("Kyr") is conferred by the emperor, "Tyr" by a high ranking noble. Koter is Vallian for Mister, equating with the Havilfarese Horter. —A.B.A.

I nodded. I fancied Mileon Ristemer would shape up.

Three or four other young hopefuls were introduced to me in the course of the evening, and if I mention Mileon alone at the moment it is not because the others did not serve Vallia well, but that Mileon's scheme—well, all in good time you will hear about that, by Zair!

We fell into a conversation about the army Turko would need to bring Falinur back in to our kind of civilization. He well knew my face was turned against hiring mercenaries. My son Drak had hired paktuns and had won battles with them. There were mercenaries in the army that had marched into the southwest under the command of Vodun Alloran, the Kov of Kaldi. He had taken the Fifth Army down there and had won victories and was now attempting to consolidate what he had conquered. But more than one of my comrades now grasped the essentials of the policy of using Vallians to fight Vallian battles.

The dancing began and there was singing and laughter and much drinking of toasts.

Standing a little back from the main throng, a glass in my hand, talking quietly to Strom Vinsanzo, a small and somewhat wizened man who knew how to make one golden talen equal two in a season or so, I could see Mileon Ristemer laughing with his partner in the dance. The pakmort glittered at his throat.

Vodun Alloran, the Kov of Kaldi, returning to his native Vallia as a successful paktun and wishing to fight to regain his kovnate, did not wear his pakmort. That would be, he had said, too flamboyant. Watching Mileon, straight-backed, limber, most gallant with his partner, I wondered afresh.

And it was perfectly clear that old Nomile Ristemer was enraptured by this soldier son of his, proud and strutting, unable to stop prating about Mileon and the return of the warrior son so dear to his heart. I knew just how he felt. I had to turn away from Strom Vinsanzo with a small word of apology.

Delia, with a graceful gesture and her sweet smile, disengaged herself from the group chattering about her. She walked across to me quickly.

"Dray! You look—"

"Aye. I look the ugly old savage I am."

"Agreed. And the specific?"

"Look at Mileon, there, and old Nomile! I was thinking of Drak, and Zeg, and Jaidur, and—"

"Our three sons make their marks on the world."

"They do. By Zair, but I am proud of them, all of them!"

"I have been thinking that you ought to know what I've been up to in that direction since you went away."

We kept our voices low and we walked together along the terrace, past the serried columns, and the dancers took no notice of us, as was proper.

"And, too," I went on, and I know my voice was troubled, "I am thinking of our daughters. You know the wild she-cat Dayra has become, with her whip and her claw and her black leathers. Jilian, who is much the same, refuses to help because of her vows—"

"And so she should!"

"Aye. You Sisters of the Rose have more secrets than an army of bungling men." I could feel Delia's hand on my arm, a reassuring and invigorating feeling, and that firm hand did not tremble by so much as a spider's eyelash. "And there is Velia and Didi, and they will soon grow big enough to bring more headaches—"

"And Lela?"

I sighed. "Lela. I have not seen her since I came back from my long banishment on Earth. I—it is damned hard, my love, damned hard, when a crusty old father feels his eldest daughter refuses to come to see him—"

"She does not refuse!" Delia's tones were sharp, a rebuke.

"I know, I know. She is busy with the Sisters of the Rose. But you girls of the SoR work her too hard."

"Now if Jilian Sweet-tooth had been our daughter—"

I stopped. "So that is her name!"

"No. Sweet-tooth is what we call her."

"She is ready enough to talk about her banje shop, but not anything about the things we really want to know—no. About the things I really want to know."

"I do not press for your secrets of the Krozairs of Zy."

This was familiar territory. We were a partnership, a twinned one, Delia and I. And we each had our own inner lives, and mostly we shared everything. But there remained these spaces between us that were not empty, distant, repellent but were spaces filled with the light of love.

Then, and Delia astonished me profoundly, she went on to say that she had arranged for our daughters to visit the River Zelph, in far Aphrasöe, and there bathe in the sacred pool of baptism. I turned her to face me. I looked down into her gorgeous face and I saw the love and the pride in our children there, and the defiance—and a little hint of furtiveness?

"Furtive you should be, Delia of Delphond! By Zim-Zair! You take our girls there, all those perils—the mortal danger—why—why—"

"Yes! And this explains where I and the girls have been. Your explanations of where you have been involve your funny little world with only one tiny yellow sun, and one silver moon, and only apims to flesh the world with color and not a single diff anywhere in sight! I think your story far stranger than mine!"

"But the dangers—"

I could feel myself shaking. We had bathed in the sacred pool of baptism, and were thereby assured of a thousand years of life, and our wounds would heal with miraculous swiftness. But the Savanti nal Aphrasöe guarded the pool. There were monsters. I had gone through some parlous times there. And now Delia was calmly telling me . . . !

Well, when I'd calmed down, I saw the rightness of it. Truth to tell, it solved a problem that had been bothering me.

"But that does not explain where Lela is gone to now," I said.

"No. I hope she will not be much longer. She is devoted, to Vallia, to the SoR, to her family—" said Delia.

"Ha!"

"—and to the work entrusted to her."

"Do you know what that work is?"

"No."

"And how many eligible young bachelors has she turned down this season? I believe I could form a regiment from them!"

Delia laughed. "I believe you could! Lela has her heart set on no man yet. There is time."

And, thinking of young men who were in love with my daughters, I felt the wrenching pang strike me that Barty Vessler was dead, struck down by a vicious cowardly blow from Kov Colun Mogper. Well, my lad Jaidur was after that rast, and after his accomplice, Zankov, too. . . . What a tangle it all was! And yet, as always and now with more force than ever, I believed there was a pattern, a grand design, woven by the Savanti who had brought me to Kregen in the first place, or by the Star Lords who brought me here to work for them or hurled me back to Earth on a whim or for the defiance I showed them out of stupid stubbornness.

"It is an unholy thing in a man's life," I said, turning and resuming our promenade along the terrace, "when he does not recognize his children and they do not recognize him."

"But you know them all now, my heart, all, save—"

"Lela."

"She will come home soon, I feel sure. But—"

I saw Naghan Vanki walk out of the overheated room where the dancing and the perfumes and the feathers coiled among the laughter and the music. He looked swiftly along the terrace, turned, saw us, and started at once to walk down. He wore an elegant Vallian evening dress, of dark green and in impeccable taste. Black and silver leaves formed an entwined border. His rapier and dagger swung. His mazilla was the formal black velvet, smooth and fashionable.

"Majister!"

"But what, Delia? Vanki!"

"I have not heard from her in too long. . . ."

"Get Khe Hi or Deb-Lu to suss her out in lupu! By Zair! If she is in danger—"

"No, no! I have arranged all that. If she were dead I would know."

"Majister! News has come in." Naghan Vanki halted before us. His pallid face was as tight as a knuckled fist. "My people report they are on the track of Voinderam and Fransha."

"Who?" I said.

Delia looked at me.

Vanki's face expressed nothing.

Then I said, "I see. This is good news. Tell me where they are and I'll be off at once."

Although Naghan Vanki was the empire's chief spymaster, there were few people in the land aware of that fact. Among the gathered nobility and gentility and bankers here at Bankers Guild, there were, I suppose, not above half a dozen who knew.

So the people, attracted by the intrusion, could leave off dancing and a little crowd gather at a discreet distance along the terrace. Much protocol was relaxed on the Day of Opaz the Deliverer once the formal celebrations were over.

"But, majister—" said Vanki.

"You—" Delia shook her head.

Some of my people walked across. Many of them you know, many have not been mentioned so far. But they were friends, a goodly number ennobled by me. They were concerned for my welfare. I said, "I will go after the runaway lovers and see what they say for themselves. After all, no one condemns them for their actions."

Trylon Marovius puffed his cheeks dubiously.

"You are the emperor, majister. It is not meet you should go haring about. Send men—I will go for you willingly."

"Yes," quoth others, and a whole crowd joined in. "I will go. And I! Me, too!"

They were all well-meaning, anxious, concerned lest their emperor should go chasing off into dangers on the trail of two runaways. I suppose my old beakhead of a face began to draw down into the ferocious expression that, so I am told—tartly—can stop a charging dinosaur in its tracks.

Delia's warning voice reached me. "Dray. . . ."

"Sink me!" I burst out. "Am I not the emperor! Cannot I go and risk a danger or two?"

They didn't like that. Lord Pernalsh shook his head. He was taller than I, broader, a veritable man-mountain.

"Not while I live, majister!"

A chorus of affirmation followed. Vanki whispered close to my ear, his breath fluttering, "My people will handle this." He was not there when I turned to answer. In his customary way he had blended into the background when the crowd arrived. A spymaster he was, Naghan Vanki in his black and silver, and a damned slippery fellow with it.

Delia was making covert signs and the gathered people began to drift away. Something of the sense of petulant frustration that had shaken the old emperor, Delia's father, was going to rub off on me pretty quick, by Vox! I felt caged. I felt as those savagely noble wild animals, caged and chained for the arena, must feel as they are whipped and prodded behind the iron bars.

I, Dray Prescot, puissant emperor, was caged up.

We stood alone.

"It seems to me—" I started to try to express my feelings of being shut off, caged away from the hurly-burly of Kregen.

Delia was sharp with me.

"The trouble with you, Dray Prescot, is that you are feeling sorry for yourself!"

## CHAPTER SIX

# Sword for Delia

The Lord Farris flew in with more problems. As commander-in-chief of the Vallian Air Service, Farris was entitled to fly about in an airboat. But we were desperately short of fliers. A fresh source of supply for the powered airboats had to be found. I greeted Farris warmly, for his dedicated loyalty to Delia always warmed me, and we got down to the latest series of headaches.

Anyway, I'd had the last laugh on that crowd at the dance at the Bankers Guild. The people sent off after the news reported that the eloping couple—whom they found in an inn enjoying themselves—were not Voinderam and Fransha.

So, I could afford a nasty laugh at their expense.

Farris sat down across from me in my little study and sipped his wine, for it was evening.

"It is these slaves we have freed," he said. "They have received their plots of land and their allotments of seeds and implements and animals, and they work hard enough—although if they work as hard now as they did when they were slaves and were whipped for nothing, I cannot truthfully say."

I waited for him to go on.

"They must be protected. The farms on the borders mainly, of course." He saw my expression. Both of us detested the idea that within the island of Vallia there should be borders between us and our enemies. All Vallia was one country, or should be. "The flutsmen drop down from the sky and raid and burn and kill. We have had incursions over ten dwaburs into what we regard as Vallian soil—"

"It is all Vallian soil!"

"Aye. But these damned raiders don't understand that yet. And the truth is, the troops we have on the ground cannot be everywhere. The sailing fliers are subject to the winds. And my force—" He spread his free hand.

"There is one clear answer. The freedmen must be able to defend themselves."

"They fight well enough, given the chance, for it is their homes and wives and children who suffer."

"Right. I shall see to that. Is there any news out of the Dawn Lands on vollers?"

"Nothing. Anyway, down there in Havilfar they are a strange lot. You might stand a better chance in Hyrklana."

"If I ever get away." I told him what had happened at the Bankers Guild. And Farris laughed. I glared at him reproachfully, whereat he laughed the harder.

"I remember when we picked you up in the Hostile Territories," he said. "My Val! If I'd been told then that you would be the emperor who has my undying loyalty, why—" He stopped himself. His shrewd brown Vallian eyes appraised me. He nodded. "Yes, I think I half-understood it, even then."

"And Naghan Vanki was with you—"

Then a messenger announced himself to say that Filbarrka nal Filbarrka had arrived.

"Send him in! By Vox, he will be a sight for sore eyes."

When Filbarrka came in he was just the same. Bouncing, roseate of face, twitching his fingers together, he brought a breath of the clean air of his zorca plains into my study. Filbarrka of the best zorca country in Kregen, he was a man who had organized the zorcabows and the lancers that had so materially contributed to the rout of the ferocious clansmen of Segesthes in the Battle of Kochwold and subsequently.

"What brings you to Vondium, nazab?" I asked.

"That confounded horn rot in Thoth Valaha. They seem to think I can work a magic cureall for them."

"Can you?"

"Yes, majister."

I sat back. Trust Filbarrka nal Filbarrka!

"So I just looked in to see if you were still here."

"And right welcome you are. We need more zorcas. If we cannot obtain sufficient, what do you say to forming a few regiments of men mounted on marlques, or on freymuls?"

"The poor man's zorca!" Filbarrka bounced up and down

and his fingers performed prodigies of entwining. "They are pleasant enough, but—"

"Quite. But we are poor men, are we not?"

"My stock is down, granted, majister. But the colts come along well, some beautiful little—"

He went on enthusiastically, for Filbarrka and zorcas lived together. As the governor of the blue-grass sections of Delia's province of the Blue Mountains, Filbarrka rated the rank of nazab. I valued his wisdom. When, in the course of our conversation he heard of Farris's problems with the freed slaves, he perked up. It was very quickly done.

"Let me at them! I have ideas—"

Well, Filbarrka was a fellow who never lacked for ideas!

As the conversation wended on in the way these rambling discussions do, and I ruefully reflected that this was not the way to clear my desk, I was also forcibly brought up short by the fact that Filbarrka was supposed, when I contacted him, to provide zorcas for Nath Karidge. Instead, here we were reasonably and carefully discussing ways and means of mounting freed slaves on a wild miscellany of saddle animals, and trying to train them up to look out for themselves. . . .

Somehow or other, I had given the job of creating a second-line cavalry force to Filbarrka. He was enthusiastic. He is always enthusiastic. "The trouble will be a lack of maneuvering skills, an inability to get up in the morning and carry out long marches, and a certain liability to panic at the unexpected. But we'll polish 'em up. I'll bring in some of my lads—you know what they are like—and we'll start off with maces and round shields. We'll add darts and lances as these fellows improve. Some of the quilted cloth you produce here in Vondium will be capital for protection, with bronze arm and shoulder bars. We'll keep it simple to start with."

Farris smiled and lifted his wine.

"You convince me, Filbarrka. No doubt of that."

We thrashed that out to Filbarrka's satisfaction. He would be based in Vondium to begin with. Then I said, "I was going to ask you if you could supply five or six hundred prime zorcas."

He lowered his wine. "Five or six hundred? That sounds like a new regiment and remounts—"

"Yes."

Farris, rather incautiously, I thought, said, "We can buy zorcas overseas—"

"Oh, yes," said Filbarrka. "There are other zorcas in the

world, of course. And, there are other mountains besides the Blue Mountains."

We took his point.

"All the same," I said, "we will buy saddle animals from Segesthes. We have to. But—and I own to being selfish here—for this new regiment I would like to have the best. The Jiktar is to be Nath Karidge."

"But he is a Chuktar." They both looked surprised, I did not think they knew of my threat to stuff poor Nath Karidge into a Phalanx.

"He remains a Chuktar, with a step. But this regiment will be a cavalry reserve, the basis for a much larger force, when we can find the zorcas and the right men."

In the end we sorted it all out and I pulled that thin file from under the stack of other files, and wrote down the reassuring fact that soon six hundred zorcas would be taken on strength. I was looking forward to telling Nath Karidge.

Turko and Korero came in and my little study began to fill up. These men had all campaigned together and were comrades in arms, and so I pushed the papers across my desk, put my feet up and let the evening roll. We were joined by other comrades and adjourned to a larger chamber. Pretty soon we started singing. It was a good night.

A good night, yes—but not the way an emperor should carry on when he has a ramshackle empire to run. No, by Krun!

Delia's remark that I was feeling sorry for myself carried a deal of truth. Well, if Delia says something, it usually is true and if it is uncomfortable into the bargain, then that means you must spruce up and see about setting matters right.

Nath Karidge did not join us that night as we sang the old songs. As always, or almost always for the exceptions proved the rule, I started up "The Bowmen of Loh." We all sang lustily.

"I suppose Seg will give command of his Second Army over to someone and return to us," said Turko as the last refrain died away.

Seg Segutorio, the master bowman, the best Bowman of Loh on Kregen in my estimation, was sorely missed.

"Aye," I said. "And as soon as Inch sorts out his Black Mountains—" And then I frowned.

This nonsense with Voinderam and Fransha had put back our plans, and Inch would have to battle on alone in his Black Mountains for a space. Turko spoke up.

"The quicker I can march north and sort out Layco Jhansi the quicker I will be able to hook left and reach Inch."

"They make little progress in the Blue Mountains," said Filbarrka. "That great rascal Korf Aighos told me there are winged devils in great numbers in the mountains, barring off the Blue from the Black."

We all digested that unwillingly.

Then someone started up that silly song, "The Milkmaid's Pail," and we all joined in and, for some of us, drove back the shadows.

Now while these raucous parties we held on Kregen were not your Viking-type carouse, nor yet your Hussar or Lancer shindig, they were vociferous and splendidly barbaric. A couple of aides got into a paddy over a little shishi who had jilted one of them. The cause of the quarrel was not altogether clear. The occasion was turned to jest and merriment as we escorted the wrathful pair to the nearest guardroom where we would find a couple of wooden swords. With the rudis they would settle the matter, get the black humors out, and then with clearer heads—that might be ringing with all the Bells of Beng Kishi—try to solve the problem.

With the wooden swords solemnly carried on a red velvet cushion, we trooped out into a practice yard. The guards on duty smirked with pleasure at the thought of young bloods knocking hell out of each other. We had an audience as we went out under the Moons of Kregen. The stone walls bore the marks of fires. One side of the courtyard was a mass of rubble where the stables of the state carriages had been destroyed.

We were making a din. Yet I saw a man half in the shadows. He carried a long pike. He was going through the manual of drill as taught to a brumbyte in the files. At our noise he turned and dropped the pike. It clanged on the cobbles.

The Maiden with the Many Smiles shone in fuzzy pink glory upon the face of Nath Karidge.

"Nath!" those devils with me chorused, filled with glee.

Karidge just stood there. He wore a brumbyte's kit, a soldier's harness that held a bronze-studded leather coat, a vosk-skull helmet, and he slanted the brumbyte's shield, the crimson flower, in the approved position.

"Majister!"

These frolicsome men with me couldn't understand why Chuktar Nath Karidge, the reckless cavalry commander, should attire himself like this and go through the manual of drill with pike and shield.

I knew.

"Let the two hotheads at each other with their wooden swords," I said. "Let the strict code of the Hyr Jikordur apply." At this there were gales of laughter, for the Jikordur specifies the code of conduct and the rituals of combat in duels—often to the death.

The rowdy part set about arranging the duel in strict conformity with the Hyr Jikordur and I went across to Karidge. I knew why he had dressed like this and was going through the manual of arms of a pike-wielding brumbyte. Karidge regarded me stonily as I approached.

"I see you prepare yourself, Nath." I was very easy with him. "That is as it should be."

"Majister!"

"And, too, that is why I have picked you for your next assignment."

He licked his lips. The vosk-skull helmet shadowed his face, but the glory of the Moons of Kregen spilled down and set that hard, reckless face stark against the bronze fittings.

"I think your wife will approve."

"She was most wroth. She told me that, much as she admires all sections of the Phalanx, she could not really credit being married to a man not in jutman's uniform."

I nodded. If, sometimes, I refer to any of the riders of Kregen as horsemen, forgive me. Jutman is the word, for there are most marvelously varied bunches of saddle animals, and one does not always detail zorcaman or totrixman or voveman.

I told Nath Karidge what I wanted. As I spoke so his features loosened, and then tautened. He smiled. The sparkle grew. His enthusiasm seized him up as a giant winged monster of Kregen's skies snatches up its prey.

"I shall serve to the death, majister—"

"Aye, Nath. Aye, I know that. And it grieves me, as well as affording me intense pride in you. The empress—"

"I shall begin at once."

"You may select your officers and troopers from whatever regiments of the cavalry arm you wish. I do not restrict you in any way. You are to form a regiment of the best, the smartest, the toughest—in short, Nath, you will create a cavalry regiment that is just simply the finest in all the world."

"And this regiment will be the empress's personal bodyguard!"

"Just so. You are herewith promoted instantly to ord-Chuktar. The regiment will be known as EDLG, the Empress's Devoted Life Guard." I gestured in a way I tried to make nonchalant, to hide the guilt I felt at the next words I would say, guilt at the expense of the rest of the army. "Your officers will be a rank higher than customary. Jiktars will command the squadrons. I want the best, the finest, the—"

"Yes, majister."

On a sudden, Nath Karidge's voice sounded soft.

I swallowed.

"This is a thing I should have done seasons ago."

"I can only say that the honor you do me—" He did not go on. I do not think he could. By Zair! But my Delia is loved by her people!

Then a great outburst of shouting and laughter dragged us back from the lip of mawkish sentiment. The two hotheads had laid each other out, their wooden swords clattering onto the cobbles. I barely saw. My Val! My Delia—she demanded everything of me I had to give. Everything. . . .

# CHAPTER SEVEN

## Sacrifice

When Turko and his army were safely on their way north, that, I made up my mind, would be my cutoff point. Then I would take off for Hyrklana to bring back our friends. During my recent absences from Vallia the country had been run by my son Drak, the Presidio, the Lord Farris, with the expert and unstinting help of Larghos the Left-Handed and Naghan Strandar, chief among the other pallans. Yes, that was what I decided.

Jilian had not returned. The Wizards of Loh, although in communication by messenger, had still not penetrated through whatever dark veil of sorcery that arch devil Phu-Si-Yantong had thrown over us. The army needed an overhaul. The harvests remained good. So with a small suite I took myself off to the rocky island of Chandror, off the south coast of Gremivoh. We took one of the sailing fliers and made good progress. On Chandror the new gold mines were yielding ore of a rich red lusciousness. Gold is just a metal; but it has its uses.

Chandror was an imperial island. There was little there, beyond the goats that leaped from crag to crag in the interior, untold millions of sea birds and a few fishing villages with stout stone walls. I suppose none of the nobility in the past had coveted Chandror, and the emperor had simply accepted it as part of his domains.

Now that gold had been discovered—and kept secret—the island figured afresh in our calculations. We had to pay vast sums abroad for supplies, and we had to make sure we did not overly inflate our own economy with what amounted to cheap money.

The old saying in Havilfar has it: "Money does not drop from fluttrell's wings." But it seemed to me, as our sails slanted with the breeze and we began to drift down, that had happened. These gold mines were delivered into our hands by sheer chance; a strayed ponsho, bleating and baaing and falling into a pit. And the shepherd crooking him out and with him, a ponsho fleece of gold. The old stories are the best. . . .

A sudden hubbub of laughter and good-humored chaffing erupted at my back. I did not turn, watching the island grow ahead. I knew the voices. These were two lively youngsters, twins, the sons of the son of Genal Arclay, Vad of Valhotra. One day, Opaz willing, one of these two skylarking lads would be Vad in his turn, the other the vadnich.

Valhotra, a lush land, rich in agriculture and husbandry, lay immediately to the east of Vondium and the southern extension of the imperial province of Hyrvond along the Great River. As a matter of sound common sense Valhotra and other provinces close to the capital were held by nobles loyal to the emperor. These twins, Travok and Tom Arclay, could look forward to a glittering future. But, first, they had to serve as aides, pages, raw-edged young coys sucking in all the information they could. And while they were doing that, they thoroughly enjoyed life, always up to tricks and jests, into scrapes and roaring with laughter all the time. They were devoted to each other.

The sailing ship of the sky slanted down through thin air. The island below spread in grays and browns on the sea. The water rippled silver in lapping waves. From the crags the sea birds soared as we swung down, filling the sky with the beat and flutter of their wings.

Turko was laughing, and Korero was shouting something about its being more convenient to have four hands with imps like these. Still I gazed over the rail at the scene spread out below. There was all the need in Kregen for laughter. . . .

We made a reasonable landing with the sailer of the skies, which meant we got down and threw the anchor out without smashing anything too serious.

The island was garrisoned by the Ninetieth Regiment, a kind of gendarmerie outfit mainly recruited by Naghan Vanki. We wanted to keep knowledge of this treasure trove as secret as we could. An assistant pallan, Noivo Randalsh, welcomed us. A calm, competent man with a habit of moving his head back and forth when he spoke, Randalsh had Chandror well-organized and producing gold. We saw the workings and I made damned sure I talked to the workers, and not a slave within many a mile, and discovered their grievances, if any, and checked on their work conditions. The gold came up out of the pit the ponsho had found with gratfying ease.

Because of the importance of this gold to Vallia, Farris had spared a sizable airboat to ferry the bullion to Vondium. We watched as she took off, turning to vanish into the north.

"You are doing well, Pallan Randalsh."

"Thank you, majister. As a mark of your visit I am authorizing an extra issue of wine—"

"Sore heads in the morning?"

We laughed.

"It will be worth it. Your words mean a great deal to us. The workers understand better now."

I turned away, losing my smile.

Turko stepped in.

"The Ninetieth have prepared a feast. I am sure they do not want death's heads at the table."

So, brisking up, I enjoyed myself at the feast given by the Ninetieth Regiment of Foot. And we sang. Well, swods on Kregen always sing, as you know. . . .

The following afternoon, having seen what we had come to see, we took off, spreading the canvas, hoisting the anchor, letting those magical silver boxes lift us up into thin air. The name of this sailing ship of the sky was *Opazfaril*. She was a fine craft. We waved and shouted down and the Ninetieth in their ordered ranks let rip with the wild war whoop that revealed that all the spit and polish, all the drill, could not entirely conceal their wild warrior origins. The workers shrilled the remberees. So *Opazfaril* sailed up into the glory of the suns.

A moment later the aft lookout called, and we all looked up.

Up there, erratic in the streaming radiance playing among the clouds, a nimble airboat gamboled. We looked closer. Three other airboats circled about the first, catching her up, diving to attack.

The pursuers were trying to cut off the boat which fled madly. And now we saw she was making determined efforts to fly down toward us.

A warning note in his voice, Turko said, "Is it any business of ours?"

"It is taking place in Vallian skies."

"All the same—"

I shouted at Captain Dorndorf. "Beat to quarters!"

The drums began to roll through *Opazfaril*. Men ran to the varters, the snouts of the ballistae frowning along the broadside. Other men carrying bows climbed the rigging. We prepared for battle.

Korero appeared at my side. His four hands grasped two massive shields. His golden beard jutted.

"Yes, yes, Korero," I said, before he could speak.

And then Turko appeared, with his shield uplifted.

Korero the Shield. Turko the Shield. Well, that problem had been solved. But right here and now as we went flying into action, these two comrades might have a little ding-dong among themselves, arguing who was to stand at his back with shields upraised.

"One each side," I said. "And don't get in my way!"

My surprise was perfectly genuine when the both cracked out a "Quidang, majister!"

By Vox! But I must have snarled it at them to evoke that response!

The apparent confusion as the crew of a fighting ship ran to action stations rapidly sorted itself out. The smell of the sea bore in on the breeze Our canvas swelled. Up there the fliers spun, weaving patterns between the clouds. The mingled radiance of the suns fell in an opaline glory.

"Does anyone recognize the cut of their jibs?" I bellowed.

No one replied.

The vollers were of a style new to me, new to everyone else in the ship too, it seemed.

Then, with only a slight hesitation, Korero said, "I think—I would not swear to it—I think they bear some resemblance to airboats from Balintol." He stared up, concentrating. "Not Balintolian, though. But like it."

As the vollers approached it was possible to make out the profusion of carving and ornamentation smothering their hulls. The three pursuing were much larger than we'd at first thought. They were stuffed with men. We could see the round helmets and the thick forests of upraised spears over the bulwarks.

As I had not gone below, Deft-fingered Minch, my orderly, brought the armor on deck and helped me into it. I wanted nothing heavy or fancy for the kind of work I anticipated lay ahead. The supple mesh links of that marvelous coat of mail I had fetched out of the Dawn Lands and a close-fitting helmet would suffice. All the same. Minch saw to it that a tall and waving panache of scarlet feathers sprouted from the top of the helmet. Perforce, I allowed that, seeing it was expected.

Now the fleeing airboat, by the execution of a pretty piece of flying, won free of her pursuers. In a wide skating curve she threw them off to starboard. They swerved around, the pennants and flags fluttering from many flagstaffs. But the smaller airboat slid down and away from them for just enough time to stand a chance of reaching us.

"He'll make it," said Korero with perfect confidence.

"Just," said Turko.

Weg Wegashtorio, the Bowman of Loh I had selected for an important task, glanced across.

"A few heartbeats more, majister—"

"Aye, Weg. Loose when you are ready."

He nodded, turning back to his little rank of bowmen. He had ten of them, ten Bowmen of Loh that Seg had insisted I use. Each man was a veteran, a kampeon who had served faithfully and was now a citizen of Vallia, and no longer a mercenary. Other archers with the compound reflex bows settled themselves comfortably in the fighting tops. The space between the fleeing voller and *Opazfaril* narrowed.

This situation, of course, presented just those kinds of problems that beset me when I was dumped down, naked and unarmed, somewhere or other on Kregen to sort out a problem for the Star Lords. Why should we assume the fleeing boat needed to be rescued? Could not those three grim pursuers be chasing a criminal, a render, say, an aerial pirate of their skies?

By chance it happened that the officer and the duty squadron with me were Jiktar Rodan and his men. I did not need to give him a look. The squadron of the 2ESW waited calmly, not in ranks but taking up good fighting positions about the deck, ready to loose the bow or ply spear or sword as the occasion warranted. The Emperor's Sword Watch was a regiment that fought astride saddle animals, on foot or in the air. Their task was to protect the emperor.

The problem of which side to take in this coming fight, if side we had to take, was rapidly solved.

Jiktar Rodan flung up a hand, pointing to the flags streaming back from the staffs. Wind pressure had concealed their devices from us. Now as the fleeing voller turned in close the banners fluttered bravely into view. By color and symbol, device and design, you can get to know the Treshes of Kregen, and thereby know with whom you are to deal. . . . And just as surely, it would take a lifetime of lifetimes to learn them all!

Staring at those flags as they flew fluttering back I realized I had not instinctively tightened my grip on my sword.

Every flag was green.

Dark green, those standards with purple and gold embroideries, and the tiny little jolt I would ordinarily have experienced was absent.

Rodan shouted, "From Persinia!"

Everybody strained to look, and many stared owlishly across the wind-streaming gap.

Vallia had strong trading links with Persinia, although much weakened now after the Time of Troubles. A deal of that red gold we dug from Chandror was on its way to more than one nation of Persinia to buy supplies and to purchase totrixes and nikvoves.

I looked up at Korero, at his superb face fixed in a trifle of a scowl, the golden beard and moustache bristling.

"Friend or foe, Korero?"

"Who can say? It is like a stewpot there, allied one day and at each other's throats the next. They are always on the go."

"You sound as though you are describing the Dawn Lands of Havilfar!"

"They are something like that in Persinia, although on a smaller scale. Those flags, I think, are Pershawian. The purple and gold nikvove on the green field."

Korero was from Balintol—which remains a mighty mysterious place, by Vox!—and that subcontinent stretches down from Segesthes. Persinia is the southern protrusion of the coastline to the west. It lies to the north of the Undurkor Islands. Because the river which flows in a loop north and west from the mountains fo Balintol reaches the sea far to the west at Zenicce, it effectively cuts off these southern lands from the Great Plains to the north.

The flier looked to be in trouble. Her flight turned into a series of blind lurches through the air.

Rodan said, "She is from Pershaw. And it looks as though she will go no farther."

We had been buying nikvoves from Pershaw. This fleeing voller bore grated openings along her side, two decks of them, and safely penned inside would be a consignment of nikvoves. Those wonderful eight-legged saddle animals, although not as powerful or fierce as the superb voves themselves, were sorely needed by our cavalry. And in the nature of things, they would have already been paid for.

Perhaps that petty financial reckoning made up my mind.

"We must save the flier," I said. "Captain Dorndorf, it is up to you and your helmsman. Maneuver to mask her."

"Quidang—" There was no time for the tiresome majister. *Opazfaril* took the breeze and surged ahead, the silver boxes buried deep in the hull exerted their influence upon the lines of ethero-magnetical force, as the wise men say, and we swung up and past the staggering voller and hurled ourselves full on the three pursuers.

Now your real voller is propelled along as well as lifted by the two silver boxes. These three could pirouette about us like hounds about a stag. Our only motive power came from our canvas spread to the breeze. Well . . . not quite only.

There was one other power, an awful force of nature, that together with the ship designers of Vallia, I had calculated to use in battles of flying sailing ships against vollers. That power had been used to grim effect on the long flight of steps up to Esser Rarioch, the strom's palace and castle on Valka. . . .

Captain Dorndorf proved a fine shipmaster.

*Opazfaril* got in among the three vollers. Then the canvas came in, with just enough spread to give us a trifle of forward momentum, and we settled down to act as a solid fortress and shoot it out. These airboats from Persinia were not too well equipped with varters. Our varter crews bent to their work lustily, twirling the windlasses, drawing back the heavy bows, sliding in the lethal darts or the ugly chunks of rock, letting fly. The Vallian gros-varter is a king among ballistae, and we had four of them among the smaller projectile weapons.

The archers shot. Down in the fighting galleries along the keel the bowmen loosed, up in the fighting tops and the walkways between the masts, the archers showered their steel-tipped death. Return shots came in. Our bulwarks were thick and high, our mantlets arranged just so, and for this kind of work *Opazfaril* was just as well suited as the vollers. If those lean hunting hounds sought to drag down this stag, they found she had needle-sharp horns everywhere and not just adorning her forehead.

The lookouts on special duty posted in a relay chain kept calling the positional information up, along the relay, to Travok, grandson of the Vad of Valhotra, positioned near Captain Dorndorf on the quarterdeck. Travok's twin, Tom, was up in a fighting top, screeching his lungs out.

"I leave the moment to you, captain."

"When the trumpet blows, majister—do you grasp hold!"

"Aye!"

Arrows sprouted from our masts. Our hulls overside must have looked like pincushions. But our varters were striking home in ruthless fashion. Chunks of the vollers splintered stern, bulwarks, hull, beams. One of two lumps of rock whistled across our deck and a young cadet, Dolan the Tumbs, brought one across to me. I weighed it on my palm.

Captain Dorndorf nodded. "Small."

Korero said, "Enough to knock your head off."

Turko said, "That's why—" and stopped.

An arrow stood in his shield.

He broke it off and we looked at it. Not a Loxvian shaft, but long and deadly and tipped with steel. The feathers were undyed, being browny-white from the Oraneflut, a useful bird of graceful body and broad wings.

"I've been shot at a few times with those," observed Korero.

The fight brawled across the sky as *Opazfaril* sailed slowly and steadily on and the vollers swirled like leaves in a hurricane about us. The flier they had been pursuing snuggled in along our flank, grapnels flew and men went across to shoot on that side. A number of crossbow bolts snicked in among the arrows. I began to think the time when the boarding attempts would be made must be near. I told Dorndorf. He nodded, and drew a short, stout, thick and extremely nasty-looking axe. He ran a thumb along the edge.

"Soon now, majister, yes."

"Find out about the voller."

Cadet Dolan the Tumbs ran off, like an alley cat, leaping the cumbered decks, disappearing over the bulwarks to shinny down onto the grappled voller. His freckles had blazed with his passionate enthusiasm.

Travok Arclay yelled.

"One is swinging in below!"

Certainly, there were only two vollers circling above us

and trying to drop nasty objects on our decks. Stationed at the end of the chain of men reporting from the lower fighting galleries, Travok kept looking up at the top where his twin screeched with excitement and hauled up barrels of arrows.

I wondered if these harum-scarum lads were disappointed that the thought that crossed our minds on first sighting the strange vollers had proved false. The island below was rich in gold. Well, then, if the secret got out, wouldn't you expect hordes of renders to come sailing piratically down? Of course. But there was a lot more to this little fracas than mere piracy.

The nearest flier was close enough now to bring a catapult into play that hurled larger and altogether more unpleasant chunks of rock than their small varters. A section of our bulwarks broke in and men staggered away yelling. Portable mantlets were dragged across to give shield cover against arrows and crossbow bolts. Lookouts tried to spot the catapult on the crowded enemy decks and shooters tried to knock out the crew. The fight was becoming personal.

The crash splintered through the uproar and a barrel of arrows burst and showered shafts skittering across the deck. A rock had cleanly severed the rope by which Tom Arclay hauled up replenishment arrows. At once he started to shinny down the line, swinging like a monkey down to the deck, ignoring both the ratlines and the ladder affixed to the mast for landlubberish soldiers.

"He's almost under us!" Travok jumped in excitement. Tom hit the deck near him. They were both wrapped up in their work.

The lookouts below reported the progress of the airboat almost under us. Probably the voller captains were quite unsure how to deal with us, a weird contraption the like of which they had not seen before. They must quickly have realized we had no power and were wind-driven. That made them incautious. No doubt they sought to fly in below and swing up, judging it nicely, and land boarding parties along our keel galleries. They would be in the ship far more easily and quickly that way than by any attempt to land across our mast and rigging-encumbered decks.

If this captain below us wanted to try that, he was welcome. . . .

"Another few murs!" shrieked Travok.

Tom glanced across at his twin.

The bulwarks broke back just by the two lads. Yellow

splinters of wood whirred murderously. A bowman screamed, transfixed by a shaft ten times thicker than those he shot. The two boys were down, rolling on the deck. A trumpet pealed.

The trumpet rang above all the noises of the combat.

Instantly, *Opazfaril* dropped like a stone.

The silver boxes had been thrust apart, the lifting power vanished, the ship fell. She fell crushingly down upon the voller under us. The noise racketed maddeningly. But I saw the Arclay twins, rolling on the deck, sliding toward the shattered side and the awful drop into nothingness.

Somehow I was there. There is no memory of leaping across the planking. I grabbed Tom, who was nearest, and threw him back. He pitched over and reached out, grasping for a handhold.

A smear of blood across the wood told of some poor devil who had been in the way of the flung rock. Travok was over the side, gripping with his fists into the folds of the netting, the tarred cordage biting. He was slipping down. The net was running out, ripped through on its eyelets.

His head vanished below the shattered bulwarks. In only moments he would fall free of the ship as the net and its supporting booms collapsed away.

Four long leaps should carry me to the side and the slipping net, and the grasping fingers of Travok Arclay.

Captain Dorndorf was a fine sailor of the skies. He understood the limitations and the possibilities of his ship. *Opazfaril* lifted a little. I felt that movement under my feet as I left Tom on the deck and began my leap for Travok. No one else was at hand; it had all been very quick. I felt the movement, I leaped, and *Opazfaril* dropped again, dropped sickeningly down. She hit the voller under us and the jar felt as though I had leaped down onto a marble tombstone. I staggered. My balance was gone.

Without a sound I pitched over the side.

Upside down I fell past the side of the ship.

A flailing hand welted out and caught bruisingly in the next net by the one to which Travok clung. His net's supports were broken through and he was slipping down. My net held firmly, and I got another hand hooked into it. I was quite safe. I looked sideways at Travok, to see how quickly I could traverse and grab him.

"Hold on, Travok! We'll soon get you out of this."

"I am not afraid, majister—"

Tom poked his face over the smashed bulwark above us. He looked down.

What followed followed fast.

Tom looked down and saw his twin brother, to whom he was devoted. He saw his emperor. He saw us both and saw how we clung to our nets, and the way the nets swayed and ripped against their smashed eyelets.

He did not hesitate.

That was the thing that got to me, that screwed me up, that made—it is painful.

Without hesitation, Tom reached over and hauled on the net to which I clung, hauling it in until he could reach me.

I yelled.

"No! *No*! Get Travok!" I screamed it out. "*Travok*!"

But Tom Arclay doggedly hauled on.

I put my hand on a damned splinter in the ruined bulwark and I turned my head and looked down. Tom's face was wet with tears and I could not look at him.

Travok's net split. It parted down the middle and Travok Arclay fell and fell, fell away, dwindling to a little spinning black dot with tiny whirling arms and legs.

I could not watch him all the way.

All I could do was haul myself over the side. I couldn't look at Travok as he fell spinning down and I couldn't look at his twin, Tom, as he collapsed on the deck.

Truthfully, I could look at no man in that instant—least of all myself.

# CHAPTER EIGHT

## Zenobya

"Hyrklana!" I said. I shouted it savagely. We were back in Vondium and a lot had happened and I was raw, ravaged, contemptuously intolerant of myself. I didn't want fine young men dying for me, I didn't want fine young men having to make that kind of awful decision—for me. "I'm going to Hyrklana. But before I do I am going to do one thing—send Sans Fantor and Therfenen in. *Bratch*!"

Not often do I use that hard word, *bratch*! It means jump, move, get the lead out. Sometimes, perhaps, I should have used it more.

The messengers bratched.

When the two wise men came in they looked pale. No doubt they had heard that the emperor was in a foul mood. Everyone who could recall what emperors traditionally did when they were in foul moods would tremble. Shoulders and heads would have air gaps. In the old days.

"Sans," I said. My words were hard. "Come in. There is a task to your hands I will have done immediately."

Among the gorgeous ruins of the imperial palace this audience chamber had been refurbished, the roof not having fallen in, and the throne—a mere marble affair with only about a sackful of jewels embedded in golden settings—replaced from where it had been toppled among rubble. It had avoided being looted by this, for although a mere sackful of gems is paltry when embellishing one of an emperor's collection of thrones, it is highly prized and valuable portable property to a reiving mercenary. This was the Chamber of

Allakar, and it impressed the two wise men, who were more used to meeting me in my homely study or their workrooms.

"Majister?" They quavered like little old gnomes instead of acting as they usually did, as wise men and savants of the Empire of Vallia. I frowned.

"Take what is necessary of the minerals we prepare for inclusion in the next batch of silver boxes for vollers. Make up small boxes, in pairs. Attach them to strong leather belts in slides, so that they can be moved together or drawn apart. If anyone falls over the side of a flier again I want him to have some means of saving his life. Do I make myself clear?"

"Yes, majister. . . ." And, "Aye majister. . . ."

I sent them off with their promise of immediate production of the safety flying belts mocking me. If only Travok had had a belt!

The fight had not lasted long after we had come to hand strokes. We had captured two of the vollers—useful additions to the Lord Farris's fleet—and the third had flown. One of those we had captured—the one Captain Dorndorf had smashed his *Opazfaril* down on so ruthlessly—was not much good for anything. She could be stripped for her lumber. It was the silver boxes that were important. We would build a new and better voller around them.

There were prisoners. We in Vallia of the parts that had been liberated kept no slaves. The prisoners would have to be repatriated on flights back to Persinia. These fighting men were from Chobishaw and most wroth they were that they had failed to capture the voller we had rescued. These Chobishaws spoke in fine manly terms, but I didn't have time for their pleas.

"No," I said to their leader, whose impressive plate armor had been taken away, and whose face with its long down-drooping moustaches and thin nose expressed the utmost fury and scorn—baffled fury and useless scorn. "No. I will not yield up to you the Lady Zenobya. She is her own lady to decide her own fate. She asks help of Vallia. She—"

"The king has decreed her death! She has no claim to the throne of Pershaw—"

"I think the lady has a claim."

"If she has—and we do not agree on that—it will be canceled in death."

"Not," I said nastily, "while the Lady Zenobya appeals to Vallia."

"Vallia!" This Chobishaw laughed then, his thin nose arrogant. "Vallia! There is no Vallia any more. It is ruined!"

The damned devil! He was almost right. . . . Almost. . . .

But we had liberated much of the main island and the fringing islands of the coasts, and we would free the remainder.

"King Pafnut refuses to deal any longer with you Vallians. Chobishaw looks to other and stronger empires."

"By all means," I said, "if these can be found. Now go away and wait until we can send you home."

The dark blood rushed to his thin face.

He was wheeled around by my lads of 2ESW and then I called, "I am told you in Chobishaw are very clever with numbers and can make circles out of straight lines and tricks of that sort. But can you make vollers?"

He looked back at me, venom in his face. That thin nose, those down-drooping moustachios, that pallid face with the thin scornful lips—if they were all like that back where he came from no wonder the Lady Zenobya had found no joy of them.

"We do not need to make our own fliers. We can buy them from our good friends."

I resisted the impulse to retort. He was in all probability not speaking of Hamal, for Hamal desperately needed all the vollers she could make herself. Unless, that is, vast new factories had been opened. With mad Empress Thyllis, anything was possible.

All the same, I told Naghan Vanki to begin an investigation to discover just where these folk of Persinia did buy their airboats.

The story the Lady Zenobya told us was charming. She said she ought to have had a few more heads off, and then she wouldn't have needed to stow away in a flier bringing nikvoves to us. Her hereditary foemen from Chobishaw had only got wind of the stratagem at the last moment. Their pursuit had ended with the Lady Zenobya being received as an honored guest in Vondium.

Pershaw, of course, was now firmly under the thumb of King Pafnut of Chobishaw.

"I have many brave fighting men loyal to me, but they lack a leader, they lack instruction, they are bemused by what has happened."

Lady Zenobya spoke in a fierce way, like a zhantilla defending her cubs. A poised woman, beautiful—yes, of course—but she contained within herself a determination one felt gained its own ends against seemingly insuperable odds, and this lent her beauty an aura of power missing from those women who imagine beauty is skin deep. She was not from Loh, but she had red hair, a deep and lustrous auburn that shone splendidly in the lights of the Chamber of Allakar. We got to know the Lady Zenobya better later on—as you shall hear—and we discovered that her charm and politeness concealed a Machiavellian diplomacy and gift of misdirection that, combined with her forthright honesty, gave her a diabolical ingenuity.

Among the nikvoves brought in the voller in which she had stowed away she had contrived to arrange that her own favorite animal should be included. Mind you, his eight legs and powerful body were clad in an odd hide of black and white, with immoderate amounts of hairy mane, tail and hocks. His name was Sjames, and he was, so Zenobya claimed, supernaturally intelligent.

Whether the last was true or not seemed something we would have to wait to find out. For now, the Lady Zenobya looked splendid, riding her Sjames, cantering out into the countryside around Vondium, her auburn hair a flame in the lights of the suns.

The decision to go to Hyrklana was forced on me by that horrific occurrence in *Opazfaril*.

The process was not as clear-cut as that makes it sound. I was still confused. The sight of Tom Arclay hauling me in and letting his twin beloved brother fall to his death. . . . No, I wanted nothing more of that for a space.

The shame crushed me. And, too, the deeply sensed and avoided feeling that an emperor to be an emperor must needs receive that kind of sacrifice, filled me with self-horror. To throw away your life in the heat of battle and sacrifice yourself to save another—yes. Mad though that may be, it is not as rare as the cynics would have us believe. It is a part of that battle rapture of which I hold such strong feelings. I dislike—to use a pale word—the red veil that clouds vision and sanity.

But Tom Arclay had acted coldly, determinedly, unswerving in his devotion to the Emperor of Vallia.

I had to get away.

The two Wizards of Loh had by means of pooled power forced a passage between themselves through the occult realms. The kharrna exercised by Phu-Si-Yantong was not, then, all-powerful.

Nothing fresh came to hand on the whereabouts of Voinderam and Fransha. Our schemes for Mavindeul were perforce frozen. Once Turko got up there with his army, liberated his new kovnate of Falinur, hooked left into Vennar and dealt with Layco Jhansi, we could link up with the Black Mountain Men and the Blue Mountain Boys. After that it would be the Racters of the north. Perhaps we did not really require Mavindeul to rise for us.

I felt we did. It would save lives.

The Lord Farris had promised air support for Turko.

We worked out the army he would take, and the Presidio, with that sense of grandeur I found slightly comic, christened Turko's force the Ninth Army.

The Eighth Army, which had won that battle centered around the thorn-ivy trap, the Battle of Ovalia, I had reserved to my own hand. Many of the same regiments would march with Turko. I held onto the army number.

Nine is the sacred and magical number on Kregen. Turko was pleased.

"It's all a foolishness, Turko," I told him. "You have a Phalanx and regiments of churgurs. Your soldiers are keen. Your spearmen are a little raw. But your archers are first class. Your kreutzin will serve you well. But do not get ideas of glory and grandeur just because this collection is called the Ninth Army. . . ."

"If I didn't know you better, Dray, I'd want to know whose side you are on."

"You're taking a capital adviser in Kapt Erndor. He is an old Freedom Fighter from Valka and as cunning as a leem."

"I'm glad he is with us. I value his advice."

I nodded. Turko might have been made up to be a kov by me, and have fought in many battles, but he lacked the professional experience of a general in command. He'd learn, I made no mistake about that. And the truth was Turko had learned a very great deal regarding campaigning and logistics, strategy and tactics and the all-important field of operations in the wars in which we had fought together.

Units were being sent from both Drak's and Seg's armies to join Turko. I sent a messenger to tell Seg to take over command of both forces, the First and the Second Armies, and another messenger to tell Drak to come home to Vondium.

"I'd like to see Seg before I start," said Turko. "But I don't think it possible. By Morro the Muscle! I miss that man!"

"Me, too."

"And it's a pity Voinderam couldn't cork it until the legal bokkertu was settled. I was counting on him. He is rated as a swordsman—not that swordsmen mean—"

"Quite."

He smiled. "No, Dray. I mean Voinderam took up with the shield; he saw the possibilities early. He has gained a fine reputation as a churgur. I believe he would have put some useful regiments into the field."

"Sword and shield men are still thin on the ground, I agree. But the Vallians are learning."

And so was I. I tried to cram a hundred burs into every Kregan day, which Opaz has decided should hold but forty-eight. Drak and Farris and the Presidio ought to be able to handle affairs while I was away. By Vox! They had done it before, and for all my own long-faced doubts, what we had of Vallia was in better shape than anything seen for seasons. For all the work I did, I was not indispensable as an emperor. And that was the way I wanted it to be.

As always when Delia was in Vondium with me, the efforts proved not only more worthwhile but also much easier. Jilian trailed back to the city, swearing and swishing her wicked claw about, completely foxed. The elopers had run away and vanished.

The Lady Zenobya proved popular in the assemblies and balls. Filbarrka hung about the city, working on plans for the cavalry force of freedmen. Nath Karidge took delivery of his six hundred first-class zorcas and the EDLG grew as prime men came in.

Although I had promised myself I'd leave as soon as Turko flew off with his army, I now delayed my own departure until the EDLG had been properly raised, formed, and put into a reasonable state of readiness. This was one kind of excuse I did not need for myself.

Delia designed the uniform. I was delighted. It carried the brave old scarlet well, with yellow trim and a decent area of darker colors—varying with squadron—to set off the dashing effect. Guidons loaded with bullion were presented to the standard bearers of each squadron. The trumpets were of silver—we vetoed gold on the scores of weight and tone. Yes, the Empress's Devoted Life Guard, glittering, polished, prancing on nimble zorcas, looked a superb regiment. They were not mere ornaments. Each trooper was a kampeon. They would give of their loyalty to Delia; they'd fight for her. They'd fight to the death.

Turko and Korero had agreed to disagree. Turko, as a kov, had a task. But he kept on trying to tell Korero what to do, the better to protect me with his shields.

Korero pulled his golden beard with his tail hand and said, "It is just as well we are leaving."

And then Turko said the right thing, and they were friends again.

"I could do with a regiment like the EDLG with me, up in Falinur," said Turko wistfully, as the guidons were presented. Korero nudged him. At once, Turko went on, "But, by Morro the Muscle! The Empress demands the best there is in all Vallia!"

Because I am weak in some matters, I gravely acceded to Tom Arclay's request to accompany Kov Turko of Falinur.

I had done what had to be done over the death of Travok.

I will not detail the events, but I felt no slackening of my anger, my contempt. The world was not a just place, not Earth, not Kregen. And the fact that I had been in no real danger, hanging over the side of *Opazfaril*, must never be revealed. If Tom knew that he had sacrificed his twin brother's life in vain . . . !

So, in my weakness and selfishness, I was glad to know Tom would be flying off with Turko. That great Khamorro would look out for Tom Arclay, now, with a special fervor.

But he had something else on his mind.

We were sprawled on the mat in the gymnasium, having contorted ourselves in a few falls, and tied ourselves in knots. Turko sat up and blew his cheeks out.

"They don't go in for the martial arts in Hyrklana, Dray? No unarmed combat in the arena?"

I shook my head.

"It's edged and pointed weapons. When you are lucky enough to be given them. Sometimes in the jikhorkdun you are sent against wild beasts with your bare hands."

"Well . . . ? That would be—"

"Ghastly. I have seen it."

So he said, "So, my old dom, you keep well away from the jikhorkdun in Huringa—"

I found a craggy smile. "Deb-Lu-Quienyin told me that our friends are involved with the jikhorkdun again."

"No!"

"I shall gather more details before I go. It's not the arena in the jikhorkdun that bothers me so much. I just hope fat Queen Fahia and her neemus do not get a scent of me."

Then we indulged in a few more falls, the skills and disciplines of the Khamsters pitted against those of the Krozairs, and both learning from each other. Queen Fahia's pet neemus, feral, treacherous, black as a night of Nortor Zan, decorated the steps of her throne. I was not enamored of the idea of seeing Fahia again or renewing acquaintance with her pets.

The moment Drak arrived I knew I'd be surrounded by an orgy of back-slapping, arm-wrenching, uproarious hullaballoo as my comrades of the First Emperor's Sword Watch renewed their acquaintance with me. I knew they felt pushed away from me, almost slighted, but I'd impressed them forcibly with the notion that their duty lay with Drak, seeing that he was the one fighting the war up there. Now nothing would keep those ruffians of 1ESW from standing watch over me, as in the old days. Certainly, 2ESW would not. Nor would the Yellow Jackets, who would return with Drak. These kampeons felt they had a divine right to put their own bodies between me and the deadly shaft, the murderous sword. I was not happy about that, as you know; but I had to accept the needle, as they say on Kregen.

An interesting strand of the past was revealed to me at that time. Among the many people I saw every day on business of one sort or another there were always a score or so who came offering their swords, seeking a particular favor. I tried to accommodate them all, according to their merits.

One limber fellow was wheeled in during the bur I put aside for this purpose—the waiting room was always filled and Enevon would allow no golden corruption to seek preference—and I sized him up. The pakzhan glittered at his throat. His pakai was coiled around his shoulder three times, that mercenary's record of trophies, the string of victory rings. His face was hard—as it would be, it would be!—and he held himself alert. He wore a tufted goat-like beard. He looked at me forthrightly.

"Koter Ian Vandrop, majister! Known to myself as Ian the Onker, for not having returned to Vondium sooner."

This could be flannel, of course. But he looked likely. More than likely. He was hyr-paktun, experienced, with his tally of kills.

I quizzed him on his service and learned he had served all

over Paz, our grouping of continents and islands on this side of Kregen. He would find employment with me.

"But not as a mercenary. You are a Vallian."

"I almost forgot that, majister. But my father—"

"Vandrop?" There was the Bower of the Scented Lotus, a middling establishment at a crossroads of Southern Vondium, a fine place to take the Baths of the Nine. It had been smashed to smithereens in the Time of the Troubles. And Koter Vandrop had worn a goat-beard just like this strapping hyr-paktun.

"If I mentioned the names of Urban the Gloves and Travok Ott, Fat Ortyg—and the Bower of the Scented Lotus? Your father wore a goat's-beard tuft as you do?"

He shook his head. "My father was clean-shaven, except when he awoke in the morning, a red-faced, serious, swearing man."

I was about to brush this misplaced episode from the past aside when the hyr-paktun Ian Vandrop went on.

"My grandfather, may Opaz light his days, had a beard like mine, so I am told, and he patronized the Scented Lotus."

Well, time flies, time flies. Grandfather. . . .

"For the kindness shown by your grandfather, koter, I shall appoint you to the Emperor's Yellow Jackets, if you so desire. An ob-Hikdar to start with. You'll be a Jiktar in no time. There are recruits to train up—" I stopped as he looked puzzled.

"I thank you, majister, it is munificent. But—grandfather never said he met the Emperor of Vallia!"

"He is well, I trust?"

"He is with Opaz, majister, and well, I sincerely believe."

"He will be. He was a kind man. Opaz will have him in his keeping."

I mention this incident because it closed a past chapter—well, half-closed it. There were many men willing to serve. Vallia's prodigal sons were returning home. The word that Vallia no longer employed mercenaries had spread. Also, word that the Vallian army gained repute also spread. The lads who had gone overseas to seek their fortunes, adventures and gold now flocked back to Vallia to stem the invasions of her foes.

Everyone was needed. Ian Vandrop was worth a regiment, because he would train and command a regiment in the bloody battles to come.

What I had visualized when those happy maniacs of mine returned to Vondium with Drak transpired.

Oh, yes. . . .

Talk about a riot. Carouse, bender, splurge, debauch—the uproar went on for a sennight, at least. Mind you, during the day I worked, as usual, and they went on parade, staying upright by the simple force of will. Their names you know—many of them. There were new faces in the ranks. The two corps, the Sword Watch and the Yellow Jackets, were not just pretty, dressed-up guardsmen or tough fighting men, they were very much cadres for teaching warrior skills and for infusing the spirit of the emperor's jurukkers into the whole army.

But that worthy objective must be seen in its true perspective, for the Vallian Army now possessed its own traditions and spirit. Created from nothing, building on courage and devotion, growing from guerrilla bands, the army flowered as experience matured it. Certainly the job would have been immeasurably harder had we not been able to call on the services and advice and training skills of my Freedom Fighters of Valka. And returning mercenaries, scarred with seasons of campaigning, added to our cadres. But the job would have been done. The Vallian Freedom Army was of Vallia.

That was the lesson and the victory.

The daylight never lasted long enough; the lights of Kregen's moons shone upon our labors. And through it all, I began to see the approach of the day when I could leave for Hyrklana. Deb-Lu-Quienyin returned to Vondium with Drak and was long closeted with Khe-Hi-Bjanching. When they saw me they looked much more relaxed than I would have expected.

"We are now convinced that the interference of Phu-Si-Yantong—for it was he—had no connection with the elopement of the Lady Fransha and Ortyg Voinderam."

I stared. "Then, why did he exert all that force?"

They both started to speak, halted, and I said, "Deb-Lu?"

"We are aware of Yantong's insane desire to rule all of Paz, rule it physically, that is. Mad, mad. He has to try to break down the occult shield we have erected. The concepts are difficult for one who is not a sorcerer—"

"One who," put in Bjanching, "is not a Wizard of Loh."

"True. We are engaged in a battle on the ethereal planes, to put it crudely, and this attack was a reconnaissance in force."

"And there is no news of Fransha and Ortyg?"

"A Wizard of Loh needs knowledge of those he seeks in lupu—personal acquaintance, some artifact, a portion of themselves, the proverbial lock of hair, for instance—"

"But you discovered the whereabouts of my friends—"

"Yes, yes, majister. But they were sent to their destinations by sorcerous power." Here both Wizards of Loh looked uncomfortable. Well, I knew that the Savanti nal Aphrasöe scared hell out of any sorcerer. "I could follow that. We thought Yantong had had a hand in this elopement and that we could follow his trail. But he did not."

"So Voinderam and Fransha are gone—and no one knows where?"

They nodded.

I said, "I shall reinforce Kov Turko's army. We'll have to hit Layco Jhansi so hard we start him running clear across Vennar and rush him up and into Racterland. And Kov Seg will attack from the east. It'll be a fine old argy-bargy while it's going on. But I'll be back from Hyrklana by then."

The sheer size of Vallia and our limited transport would give me ample time down south in Hyrklana to get our friends out and see about vollers before we hit Jhansi and the Racters.

It was at this time that the question of Barty Vessler's will came before the courts.

He had left everything to Dayra.

He had been the last of his line, the Strom of Calimbrev, and, as far as the courts could see, any other heirs there might have been were all dead. I sent three men to the island of Calimbrev to hold the place in trust for Dayra. Also, I arranged with Tom Tomor in Valka to send a few regiments as security. I sent Pallan Nogan Westmin, a loyal member of the Presidio. Although folk do not change much over their better than two hundred or so years of live on Kregen, there is an odd strain, probably non-hereditary, affecting hair. Some people, men and women both, go gray and then white. It has nothing to do with senility. Pallan Westmin had shining silvery hair. It is not particularly common.

I sent an imperial justicar, Nazab Vantile, an energetic man bucking for a bigger province in the imperial service.

I sent Chuktar Logu Le-Ka, who as a Pachak had given nikobi, the Pachak code of loyalty. He was now a Vallian citizen, with an estate and a fair income, and as a commander in the army would take control of the forces in Calimbrev.

All this I did for my daughter Dayra, yes, to keep her inheritance intact from those who might seek to snatch it away from her. But I truly think I did it as much—even more—out of remembrance of Barty Vessler. He had wanted this. I would do my utmost to make sure his wishes were carried out.

There is a theory or philosophy—to dignify the notion—sincerely believed in by those who hold to it that all problems will solve themselves. They can point to planning and interference by government or whomever and call attention to the resultant shambles. They appear to have a strong case. Laissez-faire, as a system, has been discredited but the tightly planned economies that have attempted to replace that way of going on have fared no better. Dictatorship, where one person wields the chop, or democracy, where everyone gets to shoot his own arrow, as they say on Kregen, is not to everyone's taste. That old debbil power rears his ugly and fascinating head.

A whole lot of folk just want to carry on drinking and singing and laughing and having a damn good time, and get paid fairly for what they work at, and leave the headaches of sorting it all out to somebody else.

Another slew want to get in the driving seat and crack the whip.

I suppose, as was forcibly pointed out to me by the good folk of Vallia—and before them of Valka and Djanduin—you have to have some Joe Muggins to blow the whistle.

If that was what I was, a work-burdened, worried, run-ragged referee, then that was what I was.

Oh, they called me an emperor and I had a lot of land and chests of gold and jewels and a few palaces—many of them burned down—and that collection of objects is no recompense. I did have good friends and blade comrades. And—there was Delia.

So the full circle was completed. I was the emperor and I was stuck with it, at least until Drak took over. I told him, this tall, serious, intense son of mine, "Drak, my lad, I'm off to Hyrklana to fetch our friends—Naghan the Gnat, and Tilly and Oby—and you'll run Vallia while I'm gone."

"You recall, Father, what I told you in the flier over Ba-Domek on the way to Aphrosöe, before you disappeared as you so frequently do? I said I would not be emperor while you or mother lived—"

I was brisk. I thought I knew this strapping son of mine

and I didn't wish to make an issue of this now and harden attitudes.

"If your mother and I want to go off for a holiday, and I place the empire in your hands, will you refuse?"

"We-ell—no. But—"

"I was born a plain and ordinary fellow. I've been a sailor, a soldier and here and there an airman and a flutsman. I've done a heap of things. I've been slave. But you—you are born of a line of emperors, the son of an empress, and you are clearly not an ordinary sort of fellow at all. Your destiny is to be an emperor. I do not think that mine is."

"Father!"

"Your brother Zeg is now King of Zandikar. Well and good. He is a splendid man, a Krozair of Zy, like you and me. He will not challenge you for Vallia—will he?"

"I do not think so. But—"

"And your brother Jaidur. He is a tearaway, reckless and feckless. He hates my guts—"

"No!"

"And he has other fish to fry. I don't think he would seek to dislodge you from Vallia—would he?"

"No. But—"

"So that leaves you."

Drak's nostrils pinched in. He is sometimes an old sobersides, but he can be just as wild and barbaric as anyone whose name is Prescot.

"If you will let me get any words in at all," he said, "I will say that I will go to Hyrklana. I went to Faol and fetched back Melow and Kardo, and—"

I was very nasty to him. I screwed up my eyes and I said, "And Queen Lush?"

He did not flush. He stared at me. "Queen Lushfymi—"

"Oho! So it's Lushfymi, is it? Have you spoken to your mother?" I was well aware of the treacherous ground I trod. Delia and I wanted Drak to marry Seg's daughter Silda, for we had seen how Silda had behaved, and I had seen how Silda would have given her life, willingly, to save Drak.

But at the slightest hint of parental maneuvering, Drak would act—well, he'd be just as stubborn and pig-headed as I am, Zair forgive us both.

He said, very quietly, "I have the greatest respect for Queen Lushfymi."

"Good." I wasn't fool enough to ask, "And is that all?"

We were interrupted then by Delia coming into my study.

She saw Drak's face, and my ugly old beakhead, and she sighed, and—how it was done remains a marvel and a mystery—we were all talking about the fancy dress ball that night and planning costumes. I ask you. Costumes for a fancy dress ball! And we'd been discussing the dynasty of an empire!

There is no need to go into a description of the ball. It was sumptuous, superb and splendid. Everyone seemed to be there. The thing of note, the event that rocked me back on my heels, took place as I was taking my leave with Delia radiant on my arm. I looked at the crowd, and every face was smiling and glowing, and every face belonged to a friend.

Ah! There is the wealth that no empire can give!

"I'm off to Hyrklana day after tomorrow," I said. "So I shall take the remberees of you now. Everything is arranged."

They let Korero be their spokesman. He stepped forward.

"That is good news, majister! A little adventuring will not come amiss. We are all ready—"

"What?" I said. An awful suspicion dizzied me.

"Oh, yes, majister. We're all coming. Why, you don't think we'd let our emperor go flying off into danger all on his own, do you?"

# CHAPTER NINE

## "You'll be just that, Dray Prescot! Arena fodder!"

The argument went on all next day.

"But," I said, "I'm the emperor. You're supposed to do what I say."

That was a laugh, of course, in a matter of this seriousness.

"You just cannot fly off to Hyrklana all on your own!"

That claustrophobic feeling of being trapped in a cage of invisible iron bars engulfed me. Hitherto when I'd been flung about Kregen by the Star Lords I had hungered to return home. Now that I had a serious task to perform, rescuing our friends, I was being mewed up and allowed out only with a great gaggle of nursemaids to hold my hand and wipe my nose. Talk about a cage!

They all wanted to come. 1 and 2 ESW. 1 and 2 EYJ. Nath Karidge insisted on bringing EDLG. Most of the slate of Vallian nobility were lining up. Applications poured in from all the regiments.

"Think of fat Queen Fahia!" I said. "She'll think we're invading her island!"

With a judicious air, Lord Farris said, "I can spare you enough fliers to take a thousand men. They'll have to draw lots to see who goes."

"Well, I'm going," said Korero, "and I'll fight anyone who tries to steal my place."

"And me!" "And me!"

"By Vox!" I said. "This isn't like the old days."

"No," said Delia. And she smiled, the cruel and heartless woman. "No, Dray Prescot. You are the emperor now."

I groaned. Were the brave old days gone when I'd wrap

the old scarlet breechclout about myself and take up my weapons and board a voller, richly stacked with wicker hampers provided by Delia's loving forethought, and fly off to find adventure, hurtling across the face of Kregen under the Suns of Scorpio?

"By the disgusting diseased liver and lights of Makki Grodno! I'm not having this! If I am the damned Emperor of Vallia then what I say goes! How can I work my way into the jikhorkdun in Huringa and rescue our friends if there's an enormous lollygagging army of ruffians hanging around my neck?"

"Oh," they said, "you'll think of a way."

Sink me!

Turko, who hadn't left yet, talked darkly of sending north for Seg and Inch to come down and knock some sense into my obstinate vosk skull of a head.

"And then," I snarled, "I suppose they'll want to come, too."

"Probably," said Turko, and he flexed his muscles.

Despite all the lightheartedness of this there was a darker side. Oh, it wasn't anything to do with questioning the authority vested in me as emperor. If folk didn't want me to try to be an emperor, I'd quit, instanter, and they knew that. I'd told them enough.

But just suppose—just suppose the Star Lords took it into their superhuman heads to whisk me up out of Vondium and hurl me down into some other part of Kregen, all naked and unarmed, to sort out a problem for them? The Everoinye had been silent of late. I'd not even seen their spy and messenger, the Gdoinye, flying high and looking down mockingly on my doings. If that happened now, what would be the reaction of the people of Vondium, of Vallia?

This time, my disappearance would be viewed in an entirely different light. In, I could see, an unfavorable light.

I said to Delia when we were alone, "Look, I can't manage the jikhorkdun with that crowd along! Surely they can see that?"

"I am not sure you should risk the arena at all."

"But—we want Tilly and Oby and Naghan back, don't we?"

"Of course! But, dear heart, there has to be another way. An embassy to Queen Fahia—"

"She'd laugh at them. She thinks she is the leem's claws. Hamal won't bother her now because Hamal is so tied up with Thyllis's mad schemes of conquest. Hyrklana must be doing very well, very well indeed. And their agents will be scouring the world for human fodder for the arena."

"And you'll be just that, Dray Prescot! Arena fodder!"

"Better me on my own than a great gang of—"

"No!" Delia put a hand to her heart.

After that, for a space, we were occupied. But, all the same, nothing was solved regarding my expedition.

The same difficulties that stopped Hamal from invading and conquering Hyrklana—as mad Empress Thyllis probably longed to do—prevented us from flying there in sufficient force to do what was necessary. We were overstretched and our resources were committed. Hamal had invaded north and south, although her invasion to the west had withdrawn. We were fighting to regain Vallia. Both empires grappled with problems that overtaxed their strength.

"All right," I said, "then I shall not go to Hyrklana."

I said that. I did not mean it. I had a plan.

In all this furor the Lady Zenobya continued on in her serene and yet enthusiastic way. She was a many-faceted individual. She clearly expected Vallia to give her assistance to regain her lost lands in Pershaw and kick out the Chobishaws. The Presidio was in sympathy with her. All the evidence we had, supported by reports from Vanki's spies, indicated that the right of thc casc lay with thc Lady Zenobya. But how, in our impoverished state, were we to help?

Certainly, our gold would buy mercenaries.

"Yes, and I thank you," said the Lady Zenobya. "I shall avail myself of your kindness and use the gold, and you will be repaid, in full and with interest, in specie or in kind, when I am firmly established in Pershaw."

So that was decided. The Lady Zenobya had very definite views on the type of warrior she required.

"The men must be well-armored," she said, with that toss of her red-haired head that indicated she knew exactly what she was talking about. "They should have lance and mace. Under the armor they need a good thick cloth and where it shows, divided and out of the way above the legs, it should be heavily embroidered for the battlefield."

We stood with a group of my rascally henchmen from 1ESW bellowing unkind orders at a bunch of coys, out on Voxyri Drinnik. The recruits were riding marlques and they kept tangling out of formation. It was lucky for them the spears were blunt. The Lady Zenobya had given the recruits a comprehensive look and, no doubt, dismissed them from any consideration for a season or so. A zorcaman rode slowly toward us from Voxyri Gate. The suns shone, the breeze blew, the dust and animals and oiled leather filled the air with familiar odors.

"The trouble with a cataphract with a kontos is that he's a bit slow." The Lady Zenobya was staring at the approaching zorcaman. "Cataphracts are a delight, of course. But you really need lights for scouting, and air, if possible. I'll have to find flutsmen I can at least trust while they are paid. Their crossbows ought to keep them out of trouble with the Chobishaws—although their crossbows are wicked."

The zorcaman turned out to be Filbarrka na Filbarrka.

His beaming face was a welcome sight. He was incredibly smartly turned out. His zorca was tremendous.

"Lahal, majister!" he called. And then his cheerful voice changed in tone to a remarkable degree. "Lahal, my lady."

"Lahal, Filbarrka," said the Lady Zenobya, and her voice, too, held a different, huskier note than the voice in which she spoke to me or anybody else.

Some poor wight out on the parade ground dropped a spear and the wrath of his Deldar was awful to behold.

"They won't drop their kontoi in Pershaw when I'm through with them," said Filbarrka.

I raised one eyebrow at him.

"I have asked Filbarrka na Filbarrka," said the Lady Zenobya, her laugh exquisite, "if he will command my forces."

Filbarrka's fingers grasped the reins, otherwise they'd have been entwining like a nest of rattlers. "I have set up the whole organization for the second-line cavalry. My lads from the Blue Grass country are training 'em hard. You'll have a good, dependable—if a trifle brittle—force there in no time at all."

"Thank you, Filbarrka," I said. "And so you are off to Pershaw with the Lady Zenobya?"

"Aye!"

And, of course, there was more to it than that, as was very obvious. Later on, Delia told me, "They make a superb pair, do you not think, my love?"

"Oh, aye! Filbarrka is getting all the fun, going off to adventures overseas, and I'm stuck here—"

"Hush!"

For just about the first time on Kregen I had the hankering for the damned Star Lords to seize me up and dump me down somewhere. I'd sort out their nonsense for them and then I'd be a free man, able to go to Hyrklana on my own, able to do what I wanted. Of course, there was Delia. . . .

She would welcome the return of our friends from Hyrklana. And I did not want, most certainly did not want, my Delia risking her life anywhere near Queen Fahia's jikhorkdun!

This plan was typical of Dray Prescot. It was simple. When necessary I can invent complicated plans of fiendish subtlety; I prefer them simple. Although I am told my face is of that fierce damn-you-to-hell kind, I am able to assume an expression of near imbecility. This has served me well in diverse escapades. Now Deb-Lu-Quienyin was able materially to improve on nature.

"It is all a matter of muscle control," he told me as we sat privately in my study. "You have attained a fair degree of control. I think I can improve on that."

He made me do exercises with my ugly old beakhead. Also, without doubt, he exerted some of his supernatural powers. I do know that after a sennight he had me so composing my features that I did not recognize myself in the silver mirror.

"It is a miracle, San—"

"Not a miracle. A matter of tone, of muscle, of enhancing features and of reducing them. With practice an adept is able to suggest what his face is like. People do not see what they look at; they see what they expect to see."

"True. So—?"

"So they see your clothes and they fit the face to them. Where are you going?"

I half-turned. "I'm going to test this out."

He let his laugh ripple out like a tree branch splitting from the main trunk. "Beware lest Folly and Pride lead to Perdition!"

"Aye—and Hunch and Nodgen have been saying that they're going to Hyrklana with me. I ask you! Can you imagine our Hunch in the arena?"

"The mere thought leaves me cold—and also—amused."

Wearing a simple gray tunic, with a leather belt from which one of the long thin daggers of Vallia swung from plain bronze lockets, with sandals on my feet, I put on a new face and stalked from the study. I passed along corridors and soon people were there, passing me without a second glance. People I knew! People who knew me!

Diffident about how long this would work, how long I could keep my facial muscles holding the new face, I returned to my study. One or two people looked at me more closely as I walked back, and I had to duck into a cross-corridor and let my face relax. By Zair! It was hard work. I ached as though I'd been stung by a hive of bees. But, with practice, I'd be able to hold these new faces for longer periods.

Deb-Lu studied me as I walked in.

"Hurt?"

"Yes?"

"That will pass."

"I hope so. If I'm to get out of the palace without one of my rascals spotting me, the face I put on has to last me. The security system here is now first class. No assassin would last a couple of heartbeats."

"And you mean to leave? Just like that?"

I nodded. "By Zair! Do I not!"

"The empress . . . ?"

I glowered. "She will be left a message and she will understand. . . . I know that to be so."

Then Deb-Lu-Quienyin shook me. "I am a Wizard of Loh, and all men fear us. And rightly so. But I think I might be tempted to relinquish all my arts and all my knowledge for the love of a lady like the Empress Delia."

"You old devil!" I said. But I spoke in affection.

I was sure, absolutely hell-fire sure, there was nothing in two worlds that could tempt me to abandon Delia.

By this time along I was shedding the work load as fast as was seemly. Ever since the first days when I'd realized there was work to do for Vallia I had, as you know, arranged for people to take over when I vanished. On Valka the Assembly was able to run the island stromnate perfectly. And, as my tasks sensibly lessened, with the people appointed by the Presidio shouldering more of the burdens, another little part of the puzzzle about power fell into place.

If you have an emperor who is not allowed to do anything, has no job to do, then he will, like anyone else, become bored. And he'll start looking around for something to get up to, to while away the time. Well, by Djan! And hadn't I looked around, when bored, for something to do in Djanduin, and wound up king as a result? Keep an emperor busy and he will discipline himself, that was the theory.

In order to reward the many folk who had worked so hard

for Vallia, the Presidio had instituted a whole fresh ranking of minor nobility, whose standing was a little below the already existing minor nobility. The main difference between this new hierarchy and the older minor nobility lay in the absence of lands or estates attached to the titles. The titles themselves had resounding names, which you will hear when a recipient enters my story, and usually a generous pension. By this means a non-endowed but wealthy peerage was established loyal to the country and to the emperor.

Again, I took the selfish pleasure of rewarding men and women, and seeing their pleasure. Maybe this is petty, maybe it is just another manifestation of the power syndrome, all I know is that when a fellow who had done well for the country received his new title of spandar or chornuv and his five or ten thousand golden talens, and started thinking about his new coat of arms, I felt his happiness as my happiness. And this despite my profoundly held ridicule of all titles and pomp.

The simple plan I had concocted—simpleminded, probably—demanded that I get to Huringa, the capital of Hyrklana, and then simply join the throngs flocking to the arena. Once there I would find out which of the four colors in eternal competition now commanded the allegiance of my friends. We had fought for the ruby drang. Then, once they had been located, I'd just boldly go in, carrying disguises, and have them out of it and into a borrowed voller and whisk them away home. Simple.

The major problem, as I saw it, was stealing a voller from the Lord Farris. He was not as young as he had been—by Vox! who is?—but he was just as punctilious in his duty, the perfect emperor's right hand, a treasure, and a confoundedly difficult fellow to steal a flier from.

Barty Vessler had taken a voller. True, it had been his own. I let my eye fall on the Lady Zenobya's cage voller. But that was too large. Anyway, she and Filbarrka would require the use of the craft. She'd said that Pershaw had bought fliers from Hamal before the supply dried up, and the pesky things broke down, a familiar story. Where Chobishaw was buying vollers from now she did not know.

So I put on decent Vallian buff, the wide-winged tunic and the breeches, and drew on a pair of the tall black boots. The broad-brimmed Vallian hat, with those two slots cut in the forward brim and the jaunty feathers flaunting, shadowed the new face I assumed. I sallied out and tried to bribe an attendant at the vollerdrome.

Well!

After they unchained me and stood me on my feet and dusted me off, I had to invent some rigmarole about checking security of the flierdrome.

My face had slipped during the dust up. It was a miracle nobody was hurt.

It happened to be the 1EYJ on duty at the flierdrome that night. Now Clardo the Clis and Torn Tomor stared suspiciously at me. As you know, the two corps forming the emperor's guard ran themselves, their officers alternating as to duties and leaves. Now these two looked at me as though I'd tried to make off with the crown jewels.

"Yes, majister," they said, and, "Certainly, majister."

But they knew!

The devils, they guessed right away what I was up to.

So, after that contretemps, I was faced with the problem of finding alternative means of transport.

It really was a bit thick. When an emperor can't quietly sneak off for a spot of adventuring, hurtling along under the Moons of Kregen, life tends to be dull, dull. . . .

Not that life was dull, as you have heard and will hear. Naturally, much happened I have not so far apprised you of. The son of Trylon Lofoinen, for example, being enamored of a certain lady, hired a band to serenade her outside her father's villa. And his rival, the son of Strom Nevius, got to hear of it and arranged for a dung cart to run down the hill, all over the band, Lofoinen's son, and whoever else was in the way. That whoever else happened to be a solemn procession of adherents of Mev-ira-Halviren, going chanting to see their idol open its mouth and give forth prophecies.

The resulting uproar, not to say scent, enraptured the neighborhood.

The two lads were sent packing up north to join Seg's Second Army. He wrote that they were being kept buckled down to their duties—and had each found a little shishi already. This was an unsavory story—pungent ibroi was in short supply in that neighborhood for a sennight—and not necessarily typical of the amusements afforded by Vondium. Crude—of course. Funny—possibly, depending on your station vis-à-vis the wind. Perhaps it is best to leave the story to molder where it lies.

The crusty, bearded kampeon who had bossed my field quarters in the Eighth Army, Deft-Fingered Minch, possessed what was to me an amusing and endearing habit. He had fought with tremendous gusto in the ranks and had made shebov-maztik, before coming to my notice. He ran a field quarters with a competence I recognized as being akin to what was expected of a first lieutenant of a ship of the line in Nelson's Navy. I ought in parentheses to say that junior noncommissioned officers in Vallia were maztiks. Matoc is a Havilfarian name. And, anyway, they aren't like N.C.O.s or noncoms; they are more like those special privileged fellows in the legions of Rome. More or less. Minch's endearing habit was simply this: Every time he encountered Emder in the course of his duties he would draw himself up and deliver himself of a chest-crushing salute. Emder, quiet, gentle, courteous, was treated as though he were a Jiktar at the least, and more probably a Kapt. Minch was serious, I fancied, but Emder wasn't quite sure how he should receive these military honors.

This was a case of the rough diamond respecting the cut and faceted gem.

One day Minch fairly cracked his fist against his chest, as Emder appeared in the corridor. Neither man saw me. I started to smile and then Minch broke with tradition.

"Jen Emder! A word!"

I will not attempt to reproduce the conversation word for word. What it boiled down to was Minch's desire for more information on my civilized habits. Emder did everything in the palace; Minch was the out-of-doors camp-king.

"For, Jen Emder, when we get to Hyrklana the emperor will be living in surroundings much like this. Is it possible you will accompany him as well as me?"

Emder made some reply. I just stood there. This was getting right out of hand. Plans, plans—how could I just go off and leave them all now? There was left to me one person, and one person alone, who could cut this knot.

So I went to see her.

"Delia," I said, "this nonsense has to stop!"

"Yes, dear. How?"

"That's for you to tell them all! By Vox! You are the empress, daughter of the old emperor! You know about these things. Tell 'em. Or, I swear it, I'll just take off one dark night and—"

She smiled. "The Sword Watch and the Yellow Jackets have very good eyes."

"Maybe. But when my mind is made up, my mind is—"

"Like a weathervane. We must hold a conference."

I groaned. "When did chitter-chatter solve anything?"

"You'll see. I promise."

So Delia called her famous conference. As I say, she is not only the most beautiful and most wonderful person in two worlds, she is also the most clever, the most tactful—the most downright cunning.

The decision was this: Farris would supply vollers to take a reasonably sized party, lots would be drawn, I would not be allowed to travel alone. When they started politely putting forward reasons why the speakers in turn had a special and undeniable duty to be among the participants, I left. All that reasonableness and fair-speaking frightened me. These were hairy warriors, as ready to slit your throat if you offended them as to wait for an apology—and they were all sitting neatly in rows discussing the point like a girl's grammar school debating society. But, you see, they were sitting there so docilely under the eye of Delia, Empress of Vallia.

These incidents did make me form a resolution. In future when I wanted to go off somewhere to get something done, I'd keep the fact to myself, and just go.

Delia would be told, of course. She had lived for far too long in the shadow of these mysterious absences forced on me by the Star Lords.

The thing was settled and I had to put the best face on it I could. So I took myself off and stood before the silver mirror in private and put on more than one best face. The bee-sting pains attacked me less and less, and I could hold a face for gratifyingly longer periods. Two things happened, and then we could leave.

Young Bargom, an old comrade, a Valkan, requested the pleasure of my company at the reopening of the Rose of Valka. By Zair! How that took me back! So, dressed to kill, I went down to the Great Northern Cut and took part in the ceremony consecrating the new inn and posting house. We had a right old night of it, and we sang that song "The Fetching of Drak na Valka" until the stars paled in the sky.

Among the singers a couple of Pachaks were, despite the presence of the emperor and the joyful ructions, far more interested in themselves. This was right and proper. They were Donal Em-Da, a Hikdar on leave from one of the Valkan regiments, and his affianced love, Natema Na-Pla. They sat in a corner—there were no quiet corners—with their right arms and two left arms each entwined. Their tail hands took care of the wine. I like Pachaks. I was told they planned to marry before Donal Em-Da marched out to rejoin his regiment, somewhere up north at the front. Then I learned something that brought me across to stand before them, finding a smile, hushing them back into the seat as they began to stand up.

"Now, Kotera," I said to the Pachak girl, giving her the full title of lady of Vallia. She was charming, blooming with health and youth, dressed in a simple laypom-colored gown and with only the brooch that was the badge of her fiancé's regiment as ornament. "Natema Na-Pla. The Pla from your father's name is that of Planath, is it not?" I was teasing her, for I had been told just this moment.

"Yes, majister—" She did not flush but her eyes were wide.

"Did he not tell you of the standard he bore?"

"Oh, yes, majister. Many times. He was proud."

"And I promised Planath Pe-Na that I would dower his daughter." That wasn't quite the word, but the idea was much the same. I remembered Planath Pe-Na. He had been my standard bearer at the affair of the Burned Man at Twin Forks, and at the Battle of Tomor Peak. So I bumbled on and the meeting somehow heartened me. Many fine men, apim and diff, had sought and succeeded, sought ways of serving Vallia and succeeded in giving their service to the best of their ability.

That was made my first duty next day. I gave Enevon instructions to present a seemly sum—not trifling, and yet not stupidly embarrassing, for Pachaks have that berserk streak, true or false does not matter, and their honor means much. Then the day's work could begin and Naghan Raerdu, Naghan the Barrel, was first on the agenda. Turko was present.

"Majister—word from Chuktar Mevek. The gold we sent has been well used. But it is detestation of Layco Jhansi that matters more." Naghan's laugh broke out, and he shut his eyes and the tears squeezed forth. "By Vox, majister! Jhansi seems to have taken leave of his senses. His mercenaries show no mercy and grasp the whole of Falinur in a grip of iron, trying to squeeze blood."

Turko looked grim, and it was easy to guess what he was thinking.

"So I march?" was all he said.

"Aye, kov. The time is now."

I said, "Have a tenderness for the stromnate of Balkash. Kov Turko. It acknowledges you as its legal lord, or will when Jhansi is thrown out. But, well, you know."

"Aye," said Turko, easily. "Balkash remains the stromnate of Dray Segutorio. I count it a joy to me to have Seg's son as a friend. And he will be home soon, so I believe."

"The quicker the better. Silda wants to see him."

Now there was nothing to hold me back. Turko was all ready. We stood to see him off. I own I half wished I were going with him, but by the time he had his army positioned and Seg had swung across, I'd be back from Hyrklana.

Farris provided a medium-sized voller to take the hundred who would go. Delia was there. So, thank Zair, was I. With the remberees thundering in our ears, we lifted off. Flags fluttered. The suns shone. And the flier turned over Vondium and headed south, south for Hyrklana, and Huringa, and the jikhorkdun.

I was the emperor of Vallia, and constrained by these hundred stalwarts who had drawn the luck in the lottery. But I just could not see how I was to organize them when it came to the arena. But, also, I was Dray Prescot. I fancied—I hoped, I prayed—that the old Dray Prescot, Lord of Strombor and Krozair of Zy, might turn a trick or two to get himself unlumbered.

Then, why then it would be a skip and jump and some headlong action before the game was played out.

"By Kaidun!" I said to myself. I looked calculatingly at these hundred companions of mine. I looked at Delia. "By the glass eye and brass sword of Beng Thrax! Now I'm not a cunning old leem hunter if I can't fashion something out of this!"

# CHAPTER TEN

## Unmok the Nets

Standing right in the eyes of the flier with the wind rushing in our faces, Delia and I grasped the rail and stared at the sea far below. Splinters of silver light rayed back and the streaming mingled radiance of ruby and emerald added touches of fire and viridian to the scene. We could see no ships down there.

"Listen carefully," I said. "If I am—taken—as I may well be—"

"Those dreadful Everoinye?"

"Aye. If I am, promise me you will not fret—well, that may be foolish. Promise me at least, that. . . ." And I stopped, too muddled to go on.

Delia gripped my arm. "I know what you mean. It is hard, it always has been hard and it always will be hard. But I know. If you have to go away to your silly little planet with only one tiny yellow sun and one tiny silver moon and no diffs at all, only apims, why, then—"

"By Zair!" I shivered in the windrush. "I don't want to be sent back to Earth!"

"No. But if you go away, I will understand. But that is all."

I swallowed. "Promise me you will not go to see Queen Fahia. She is fat and unhealthy; she is also dangerous. Our hundred wild men will not stand against her army forever."

"You mean you may be sent somewhere else?"

I spoke the truth, for if I was called by the Star Lords they would send me somewhere else about their business.

"Yes. You must promise me not to go to Huringa."

"Very—well. But—"

I looked at her.

She sighed.

"Very well, my heart. I promise. I see the sense of it. It is so unfair, though, so damned hard!"

"Life is unfair. It is always hard."

So, you can see into what kind of low-class skullduggery I had fallen, what a proficient liar I was forced to become. But I wasn't having Delia going anywhere near that horrific arena. No, by Zim-Zair! For I and our friends had been lifted to safety from the blood-soaked silver sand, and Delia was all naked and chained to a stake at the center. I shuddered. That had been an experience I would not willingly repeat. Enough of that horror was enough.

Then she said, "You have seen the golden and scarlet bird?"

There was no need to lie. The big one had been put across, all else merely followed. "No. But I sense that I may be called. Try not to let this—" Stupid, stupid! Of course my going away would upset her! "You'll have to convince this gang of cutthroats who invited themselves along."

"They will listen—"

"They'll listen to you. I expect Turko will find them of use." I glanced back at those fighting men crowding the decks. "It seems to me whoever rigged the lottery was a master hand."

Delia laughed. She was determined to throw off all cares until the causes of those cares arrived. "I do not care to inquire too closely into the legality of the lottery. But I agree, there are a suspiciously large number of. . . ." She hesitated.

"To find the right word for them is difficult."

They were all our staunchest comrades in this voller. If the lottery had not been fixed, then Five-Handed Eos-Bakchi, the spirit of luck and good fortune called on in Vallia, had answered a goodly number of calls from the ripest fruits of the ESW and EYJ and EDLG. By Krun! And from the sprigs of the nobility whose business had brought them to Vondium at this time.

Looking at them, I considered my plans had just about matured. All that was necessary now was the timing.

Looking back as I relate my narrative I suppose I can afford a wry smile. It must be clear to you listening to my words, as it is clear to me—now—that I was living in a dream world.

Even my Delia was a part of that dream, for she had promised me without overmuch demur. But I was wrapped up in my own schemes. Onker, as they say on Kregen of that particular kind of idiot, onker of onkers, get onker. The Gdoinye liked to call me an onker, and I'd call him one back, too, in those slanging matches which, I suspect, if the stakes had not been so high I'd have enjoyed as much as he did, the onker!

Southeast we flew, out over the Sea of Opaz which separates Vallia from the island of Pandahem. We would not fly over this latter island, for the Pandaheem, besides their longstanding antagonism to Vallia, were now in the merciless grip of Phu-Si-Yantong. Ever southwards we flew across the Southern Ocean, passing just clear of that lonely island group, Astar, where once the Leem-Lovers, the ghastly Shanks from over the curve of the world, had set up a base to raid and harry and kill the peoples of the shorelines of Paz. A garrison held the islands now.

"Do we fly direct to Hyrklana, across Hamal?"

I shook my head. "No, Delia. We avoid Hamal like the plague. We will fly around the coast, out of sight of land. I think we can risk crossing the Risshamal Keys." These stretch out like skeletal fingers from the northeastern corner of Hamal. Hyrklana lies due south of them, past Arnor and Niklana. To cut across them would save time.

So that is what we did. Perhaps, had I been less cocksure, less confident and taken us all the way around, well—then it would have been a different story, by Zair. . . .

Any Kregan needs his six or eight square meals a day and we were capitally provided for. I refused to blink when Deft-Fingered Minch produced a delicacy that was a particular specialty of the palace kitchens. He had spoken to Emder, that was clear.

Down below us the Keys passed, gray and brown, narrow and humped, some barren and some choked with jungles, for we flew with the equator just to the north of us. On those strings of islands lived among a multitude of races the Yuccamots, a web-footed, thick-tailed race of diffs who lived by fishing and were kind and friendly by nature. And that made me think how Vad Nalgre Sultant, of Kavinstok, who had proved so unpleasant a character down there, had rallied around the Racters when Vallia herself passed through her Time of Troubles.

"Look at the weather up ahead," said Korero, flicking his tail hand.

"Aye. It looks murky."

The horizon ahead held that brazen copper look, as of a furnace glowing with the fires of hell. Black clouds boiled. If we were in for a twisting blow we'd best batten down, or get down. I measured the extent of the gale—typhoon, hurricane, call it what you will. It pounced with monstrous speed. One moment we were apprised of its presence, the next we were starting to descend and in the third we were caught and shaken like a ponsho in the jaws of a leem.

The blackness enveloped us like the cloak of Notor Zan.

The wind shrieked about us. We were hurled across the sky, blown like a pip from the mouth of a giant. End over end, whirling, we were buffeted and deafened, crushed by the violence of the elements.

The voller was well built, one of those we had secured from Hyrklana, that being throught a clever notion as we were flying to that island realm. She was broken in two as a child breaks a reed boat. Chunks fell off. Men fell. We were all wearing the safety belts produced just in time by the wise men of Vondium, and as the voller broke up and we were cast adrift, so we went sailing independently across the sky, mere helpless chips in a millrace of wind.

The suns might not have been shining in the sky. The darkness blustered about us. For a few moments I caught sight of other hapless wights being hurled and tossed about and then I was swept away into the blackness. Night was not far off. The wind tore at me, filling my mouth and ears, screaming. The twister curled a tail around and the hurricane of wind coiled devilishly, spinning me away—somewhere.

The time passed in this nauseous inferno of black noise. The howling went on and on and on. End over end I pitched away, one of a hundred separated and scattered leaves in a whirlwind.

The chances of making a safe landing in this were practically nil. Anyway, I'd probably come down into the sea, for my bump of direction told me I was being hurled toward the south. How long it all lasted was easy to calculate after the event. While I was being driven hither and thither, swung up and belted down, the time stretched so that it seemed I'd spent all my life being tossed about in the black gullet of that blow.

That blow!

Afterward I learned that a whole fleet of argenters, stout, beamy craft, had been lost. A squadron of swordships had been tossed onto the rocks of one of the Risshamal Keys and thoroughly reduced to flinders. And a wing of the massive skyships of Hamal had been contemptuously smashed into the ground. The gale broomed sea and sky and swept them both clean.

The end of it for me was a sensible lessening of the wind and the sight of a flake of the Maiden with the Many Smiles, gleaming fuzzzy pink light through cloud wrack. For the rest of that night and the following day I was tumbled along southward. Sea, and only sea, stretched below me. I was hungry and thirsty—I was thirsty, by Krun! But there could be no hope of letting down to the sea. All I could do was hope to last out and put the thirst torturing me out of my mind and so let the wind hurl me on.

The second night was unpleasant.

If these wonderful belts we'd invented had possessed the power of independent movement through the air. . . . But, then, that was the secret we still had not fathomed, the prize Hamal and all the countries who manufactured vollers kept close.

I tried not to worry overmuch on the fate of Delia. My friends were a hundred tough and resourceful desperadoes, and if I'd been chucked off by the wind, I trusted that some of them had been able to link up with Delia. Korero had been with me when the voller broke up. But I was alone, singled out, a tiny speck in the vast sky above the vast ocean.

When the island came into sight, far to the south, a mere black smudge upon the glittering sea, I heaved a sigh of relief and then started paddling desperately to strike a course for that haven. If I missed it. . . .

The fates, or whoever has charge of handing out favors or black marks—certainly not, I fancied, either the Savanti or the Star Lords—guided me near enough to the island for me to slide the silver boxes apart along the belt and drop gently into the sea. Then it took me a couple of burs to swim in.

The beach was white sand, smooth and inviting, and only twice I was forced to lift up on the safety belt to avoid gaping jaws and serrated teeth from some hungry predator of the sea. I lay on the beach, spouting water, breathing easier, and then rolled over and surveyed what I'd dropped and swum into.

Practically every coastline on Kregen—not all—is festooned with islands, large and small. It was perfectly possible that this little beauty appeared on no maps anywhere at all. But the ground was solid underfoot as I rose. Then I realized the wind was still strong, still blowing half a gale, and I went running up the beach, half propelled by the wind and half drawn by the fruit hanging on the trees.

That fruit tasted good, by Krun! My thirst tended to be fierce, and my face was smothered with fruit juice. Water was a prime requisite, and I struck along the coast looking for a stream. Tropical islands are veritable paradises—if certain things are available and certain things are absent.

Well, I found water, and drank—cautiously. I bathed the salt off my skin. I perked up. A craggy mass of rock chopped off the next bay and, after a time, I rolled along to have a look-see.

An argenter floated in the bay, bold as brass, real, no mirage, four anchors out, and the rocky headland giving her beautiful shelter. I studied her most carefully before I walked down to the waterline and hullooed across.

She bore the colors of Hyrklana. Mainly green, of course, seeing that Queen Fahia was a fanatical follower of the Jikhorkdun and her chosen corner was the green, the emerald neemu.

"Ahoy!"

A head poked over the bulwarks. A spear point glittered.

No doubt they wouldn't be surprised to find a cannibal. After all, desert islands are desert islands and have a reputation to keep up.

In any event, they took me aboard *Pearl of Klanadun* and instead of killing me out of hand fed me two square meals and a gallon of Kregan tea. If I treat this whole episode matter-of-factly, that is the way I tried to treat it while it was happening. But, it was a fraught old time, I can tell you.

Drifting over the sea, nothing in sight save sea and sky, slowly starving and thirsting to death—no. No, I do not believe I enjoyed that.

Because I did not usually wear a Krozair longsword when not engaged in something strenuous, I was not carrying one with me now. I'd been talking to Korero, digesting a good meal, and dressed in a light tunic for the tropics. Naturally, I had a rapier and main gauche. Well, they—the Jiktar and the Hikdar—tend to grow on a fellow after a time, so it seems. I was extremely careful to let these folk in the argenter see that I had no intention of drawing weapons against them.

*Pearl of Klanadun* held a smell, a wild-animal smell that wafted up through the gratings in her wide decks. Down below in her capacious holds the owners of that wild-beast smell were caged in iron bars.

"Yes, Horter Jak," said the captain, bluff and genial, rotund of belly and purple of nose. "This is what I am reduced to." A vein throbbed alongside his nose. "I cannot lay the blame at the feet of Havil the Green, for I am a religious man, and mindful of the obligations a sea master must never forget. But, all the same—" And he gestured in a manner at once helpless and comical at the gratings. "A mere freighter of wild animals for the jikhorkdun! Is this my reward for a hundred years of sea apprenticeship?"

"But, Captain Nath," I said, "there are many men engaged in this work. The jikhorkduns of Hyrklana are never satisfied."

"True, true. My brother, who commanded our late father's ship, was gored to death by an Ilurndil—the second horn went clean through here." And Captain Nath the Bows jabbed a thumb into the side of his stomach.

I didn't much care for Ilurndils, six-footed battering rams with leather hides you could make roof tiles out of—that roof tiles were made out of—and a pair of horns superimposed between piggy eyes. As for Nath the Bows, as he said, his father's name was Nath and what was good enough for him was good enough for his boys. They were twins, Nath the Bows and Nath the Stern. It wasn't new.

*Pearl of Klanadun* was a natty enough argenter. Her topmen were Hobolings, among the best in the business. She had a lot of Brokelsh in the deck hands. Her marine guard consisted of half a dozen Undurkers with their canine faces and snooty looks and smart bows and notched arrows. We sailed along as soon as the storm abated enough to make pasasgeway comfortable for the wild beast cargo.

Down in the saloon I met the owner of the cargo. I was fully prepared to dislike him on sight. After all, running animals in for the arena, where they would first of all chomp up criminals and condemned slaves, and then be cut to bits by kaidurs who knew how to handle weapons, is not the kind of occupation guaranteed to endear any man to me.

But it was extraordinarily difficult to dislike Unmok the Nets. He was an Och. He did not, however, have six limbs like Ochs are supposed to have. As he said, "There was I, minding my own business—I was in selling beads and bangles at the time, not much but a living—and this chavonth came at me. Chewed out my middle left. Still feel it twinge come rainy days. Took sinews outta my lower left, too. Dratted chavonth. All teeth and claws and that mess of blue-gray and black hexes."

Unmok the Nets limped. As an Och he stood shorter than Hunch, who as a Tryfant had to stand on tiptoe to look over the big guy's bar. His Och head was the usual lemon shape, with puffy jaws and lolling chops, although he favored a kind of heavy woollen muffler.

"Since that danged chavonth got me I feel the cold."

We were only a few degrees south of the equator here.

He liked to talk. I cannot repeat most of it, all small talk larded with dollops of Och wisdom, which might suit a small race of diffs with six limbs; it's only marginally applicable to an apim with only four limbs. I tried to remember some to tell my Djang friends.

He started to tell me how he'd got into the wild-beast catching business when we went down to the dinner table to eat, and he went right on, interrupting himself and going off into unrelated subjects and getting back to the point. He never did finish. I gathered, more as a matter of guesswork, that after his mauling by a savage big cat he rather wanted to get his own back. For a little crippled Och, well, that took some doing, petty and vindictive though some folk might take it.

There was always a demand for wild animals in the arena. And for human fodder. We sailed on down south toward Hyrklana and, despite some of my chaotic feelings, Unmok the Nets and I got along famously.

And he told me about the animals.

He had a team of harum-scarum diffs and apims to assist. Some knew how to handle the beasts; others simply used the whip and the torch and lived scared half to death most of the time.

"Get rid of them as soon as I can, Jak," he told me. "Poor trash. You have to know how a beast feels to trap it, and then how to keep it alive. Some just curl over and die if you don't treat 'em right."

"You're making for Huringa, of course—"

"Gotta pick up a consignment of thomplods first. Had 'em shipped in to Hyrklana South. They'll fetch a fortune."

He said thomplod, which is the vernacular for the animal I always think of as a haystack on feet. Twelve feet, six a side.

And the smell—well, I can't smell it, not many men can. But other animals—well, now. That dung cart of the son of Strom Nevius that ran away with the band and the son of Trylon Lofoinen and the solemn procession of adherents of Mev-ira-Halviren, that didn't create half the stir among the neighborhood that a single thomplod could churn up among the animals of a sizeable town. No, sir!

Not all the animals. Mostly saddle animals. Some riding animals seemed to be immune to the smell; most are not. Unmok was going to have to arrange transportation for his menagerie. The carts would be pulled by Quoffas, and those huge-faced shambling hearthrugs would patiently haul and not care a fig for the thomplods. But no one was going to ride a totrix or a marlque or a hirvel, not with a thomplod within sniffing range.

Well, Unmok and I got along and pretty soon he was suggesting I might like to throw in with him. This often happens to me, on Earth and on Kregen. Delia and I had taken a few handfuls of golden deldys, one of the more usual currencies of Havilfar, and I had a walletful. I thumped a purseful on the table and Unmok sniffed and allowed that Havil the Green or some divine spirit had answered his prayers. He was a little short, did I see, and we were partners. We shook on it, in the Kregan way. As I say, I was surprised myself.

I was to be a working partner.

Captain Nath the Bows kept well out to the east giving the coast of Hamal a wide berth. Sailing direct to Hyrklana South was not so much out of our way, after all.

"Those devils of Hamal can't pay for animals for their jikhorkduns now," observed Unmok. "That stupid war they've got themselves involved in. Oh, they have plenty of prisoners. But they're short of prime cargoes of animals."

A few days later a voller passed high overhead, traveling fast toward the south. Unmok screwed his chops up and stared aloft, tense, hopping on his one good foot. Then he relaxed. A single glance had told us the flier was Hyrklanian and not Hamalese.

"Thought it might have been a cage voller." Unmok visibly relaxed, and the breeze blew the feather in his cap askew. "That'd mean tough competition." He admitted, seeing I was now his partner, that he had been a trifle strapped. He had planned on selling a few beasts at the wharf side, and damn poor prices, too, to pay for the passage. "One day," he said darkly, "I'll have me my own cage voller. Then you'll see!"

As soon as we reached a stylor, he said, the bokkertu could all be written up in due legal form.

"And if that was Maglo the Ears, why, I'll—I'll—"

"Who's he?"

"The biggest rogue unhanged since Queen Fahia grew her moustache." Then he looked about swiftly, to see if anyone had overheard this flagrant example of lèse majesté, as they say.

"Maglo the Ears preys on honest traders like me. He is welcome in the jikhorkdun because he can sell at cut prices. Of course he can, the yetch! He steals what honest men have worked for."

No matter what trade or profession you go in for, it seems on two worlds, there are always the fly-boys, the get-rich-quick merchants, the unscrupulous to twist a profit out of villainy. Unmok heaved up a sigh and cut phlegm.

"And the jikhorkduns can afford to pay. Hyrklana has never been richer. Hamal pours out her treasure for war and we profit. Mind you, they drive a hard bargain when it comes to selling a few hundred people for the arena. They have a good supply, as I said, and we still have to send out parties and scratch and scrape to find men suitable—"

I started to interrupt, harshly, unpleasantly, and forced myself to calm down. But for his trade and its singularity, Unmok the Nets was a simple ordinary trader, wasn't he? Hyrklana needed men like Unmok. Others like him, probably much more unpleasant in their habits, would be out now scouring foreign countries for arena fodder.

Korero and I had been talking up in the prow of the voller when she smashed and I could only hope the others had been able to stick together. Certainly, if some slaving rast from the arena tried to capture my hundred lads, he'd be eating his teeth, and digesting a length of steel through his guts.

If there exists a demand men will be found to supply it.

That is no excuse, never has been. But Unmok cared for the splendid wild animals in his charge, mindful of not only their physical comfort but seeking ways of easing their rages at confinement. He disliked the whip. He checked a shaven-pated Gon who slashed a strigicaw, and the Gon sulked. Unmok heaved up one of his feather-whiffling sighs, and promised me he'd discharge the useless lumber, as he called them, and hire fresh beast handlers in Fanahal, the chief port of Hyrklana South.

Unmok's chief assistant, a strong-bodied Fristle, whose

cat's face was missing a sizeable portion of fur so that the membrane glistened pinkly, provided the strong arm necessary. This Fristle spoke little, spat often, and was called Froshak the Shine.

Froshak saw my sailor knife in its sheath snugged at the back of my right hip, and asked to examine it. I let him hold the knife, and he turned it over, and felt the heft. Then he handed it back and whipped out his own blade. The knives were very similar.

"Good," said Froshak. "Good for slicing guts."

I agreed. Out of politeness.

He gave no trouble that I had been taken in as a partner. As I say, I was a working partner. Unmok's system was simple and neat. One empty cage at the end was cleaned and swabbed out and provided with fresh litter. The gate to the adjoining cage was opened and the occupant of the second cage enticed, cajoled—whipped—into entering the first. Then with the gates shut the second cage was cleaned out. The process was repeated until the end of the line, when on the following day the end cage was prepared and the process repeated in reverse.

I took my share. I cannot say I came to be overly familiar with the wild animals; but the education was formidable. Mostly I'd been on the receiving end, with a sword in my fists.

Unmok had three leems. He was proud of them. No one else relished the idea; but they were valuable, and we needed to eat.

Pens up on deck held tame livestock. Preparing them for the beasts' dinners was not a pleasant job. On a long sea voyage rations were tightly arranged, anyway. Unmok had lost only two of his stock, as he told me sorrowfully, a fine graint and a chag, which had been weak anyway. He took particular care of the four splendid specimens of neemus. These black, vicious, treacherous beasts with their round heads and flat ears and slanting slits of lambent golden flame for eyes were to be sold to Queen Fahia. Unmok was confident of that. I could just imagine them, scented, pampered, chained with silver links, sprawled on the steps of her throne.

And I must mention the werstings. These white and black four-legged hunting dogs were just about trained. They remained savage. Unmok owned five couples, collared with bronze, bearing his mark. I doubted if even a wersting would be able to check these wild animals if they broke free, but

Unmok informed me that these werstings, toward whom he held an ambivalent attitude, were as much for his own protection against grasping rogues like Maglo the Ears as against escaped stock.

He had no Manhounds, and I was not sorry for that, I can tell you!

The Suns of Scorpio blazed down, the breeze blew, we made a good passage and came up beautifully to our landfall, making boards in to Fanahal, and we saw not a sign of another craft until we were in the coastal sealanes.

The port gleamed pink and green over white in the blaze. The water glittered. A busy confusion of ships and boats congested the roadway. We were hauled in by a ten-oared tug manned by Brokelsh, and the local dignitaries came aboard to the ritual wine, bribes, and signing of papers. The noise of the wharves and the smells had to be adjusted to after the long windblown reaches of the ocean.

I had arrived in Hyrklana.

## CHAPTER ELEVEN

# A Shot at a Swordship

One thing you could say for Unmok the Nets—he was a businessman. He discharged the useless lumber—the shaven-headed Gon would have been a nuisance, but Froshak the Shine clicked his sailor knife up and down in the sheath. The Gon departed. Unmok worked at a high pressure. The thomplods were loaded into a second vessel, little more than a sailing steerable raft for coastal navigation, fees were paid, bribes were distributed, stores taken aboard, and we set off northward around the west coast of Hyrklana.

Everyone was jumpy.

Hyrklana is a large island shaped rather like a pear, or a flint arrowhead. From north to south it measures around thirteen hundred miles and across the broadest part just over eight hundred. The coast of Havilfar to the west curves in a bow shaped to fit the bulge of Hyrklana. The Hyrklese Channel is approximately three hundred miles across.

These waters, wide though they were, were infested with pirates. Renders from the coastal countries of the Dawn Lands, ships searching for plunder, attacking and looting anything else that sailed the seas, the brethren were an odiferous bunch. A deal of policing had been done; but the current wars had made supervision too costly. It was every ship for herself.

So we had taken aboard Unmok's hired guards at Fanahal to reinforce Captain Nath's Undurker marines. We made as fast a passage as we could, giving the contrariness of Whetti Orbium who under Opaz's beneficent hand runs the weather on Kregen. Propitiations were made, of course, and the low-domed temple with the ships' figureheads set up outside in ranks and rows took in another tidy little heap of gold coins to the old-age pensions of the priests.

Money began to figure now. My store of gold, although mere handfuls, as I have said, was in these circumstances considerable wealth. All the same, it would not last for ever.

Unmok had been careful with his hired guards. They were mostly Fristles and Rapas. He had contracted to pay them five sinvers per sennight. Although, contrarily, I give the word sennight for a week of six days, it seems to me to fit. Across in the Dawn Lands I'd hired out for eight broad strebes a day, and even there a Fristle or Rapa could get the standard one silver coin per diem. Unmok, as I say, was shrewd.

There were no Pachaks or Chuliks in the bunch we hired. Ten of them, and one Khibil. His fox-like face drooped instead of bristling with the natural arrogance of a Khibil. He had been given a nasty—a very nasty—blow in the middle at some time and it had broken some spiritual spring deep within him. He was an archer; but his bow, although compound and reflex and an admirable weapon, pulled lightly. But, for all that, he remained a Khibil.

"I am a Khibil," he said, as he stood before the table where Unmok sat with the leather bags of silver sinvers, some spilled casually out across the wood, glittering. "I hire out for nothing less than eight."

Looking at this Khibil, Pondar the Iumfrey, I was forcibly reminded of the time I'd hired out over in the Dawn Lands, and of Pompino demanding more because he was a Khibil. The contrast between this Pondar before me now and my comrade Pompino could not have been more marked. And, by Zair, where was Pompino the Iarvin now?

"The Rapas and Fristles have settled for five," pointed out Unmok. "But, yes, you are a Khibil. I will pay you one silver sinver a day. No more."

"Done."

Pondar the Iumfrey affixed his mark.

Men were not easy to find. Good men were scarce. But they still existed, carrying on in the old ways and refusing to be drawn into foreign wars. Hyrklana liked to be an island and cut off from the rest of Havilfar.

So we sailed up the Hyrklese Channel and kept our eyes skinned for renders. Pirates are a pain in the neck. When we saw our swordship, her single bank of oars driving deeply, surging on toward us, sheeted in spray like a half-submerged rock, the old wailing cry went up, filled with horror.

"Swordship! Swordship!"

We were, therefore, in for a fight.

I said to Unmok, "Is there a spare bow and a few shafts?"

He lifted his shrewd Och head up above the companionway coaming. He waited for no man on his descent below decks.

"Bows? Shafts? Jak, what are you dreaming of?"

"We have to fight them off—"

"*They* do, the hired mercenaries. *We* don't!"

I didn't blame him for scuttling below. He was better off out of the coming fight. It wasn't even as though he had all his limbs, was it, now? But he shouted that there was a bow of sorts in his cabin and I was welcome to it.

The bow proved to be a compound job of wood and sinew, with a little horn, and the reflex curves made only a half-hearted stab at the double-reflex curves of the bows of Valka.

But I took it up and strung it and heaved on the string. The shafts were iron-tipped and fletched with the yellow feathers from hulfoo birds, a kind of Hyrklanian goose. They looked to be reasonably straight.

On deck, having seen Unmok stowed away safely below, I found the Khibil, Pondar, arguing with a heavyset Rapa, whose red wattles congested and whose dark eyes snapped anger.

They were arguing as to who was to be Jiktar of the mercenary guard. Of course, Jiktar was just a name, a kind of Kregan relative to saying the captain of the guard.

I said, "You know your posts. Take them. Pondar, take the stern. Randalar, take the bows."

The swordship looked as though her captain meant to hit our port bow. The Rapa and the Khibil wanted to continue their argument, but I told them to get on with it, and they did.

We possessed but one varter. It looked as though it might fall to pieces the moment the windlass was wound, even before the missile was discharged. Captain Nath stood looking at it and pursing his lips.

"Well, I don't know. . . ."

Without a word I started to wind the windlass. The old wood creaked and groaned. But the plaited string inched back and the bow bent. I did it cautiously, I may add, out of respect for my own hide. A broken varter string can whip out your eye better than a diving blood-lance.

I won't go into the details of the fight, mainly because there were so few. Even this antiquated and dangerous varter could out-range a bow. Before the two ships closed the range for archery I swung the varter on its swivel and lined up the ugly beak of the swordship. We were going up and down and the renders' vessel was pitching like a maddened totrix.

Froshak the Shine dumped a chunk of rock into the chute. I waited until *Pearl of Klanadun* rolled, and pulled the trigger. The rock flew.

Just what it did I do not know. But the swordship stuck her bows under the next wave and the sea washed back in an unbroken green tide and she didn't right herself. She just went on and in, with all her oars driving lustily.

We sailed on, and it was as though the swordship had been just a bad dream.

We didn't even stop to see. That would have been very difficult with a plunging, wide-beamed and unhandy argenter.

The outcome of that was that the men started calling me Jak the Shot. I'd given the name Jak, for obvious reasons. I made no demurral on the Shot business, just let it ride.

Swordships are cranky craft at best, and seem to spend as much of their time under the water as above it. "Now if that had been a Vallian galleon. . . ." I said to Unmok.

"Oh, them!" He sniffed. "I've been married a couple of times and one of my sons went off to Vallia. Never got to be a paktun, got himself killed somewhere in Pandahem, so a comrade told me. My lad said the Vallese are a strange lot. Haven't got a soldier among 'em. All pot-bellied money-grabbers. Then he laughed. "Like me—with pot-bellies!"

I forbore to bring Unmok up to date. But I warmed to his honesty. What he did he did because that was the way he made his living. Among his chatter he spoke often of buying a cage voller, of making his fortune and going into a new line of business. This varied with each recital of his dream.

Froshak the Shine came up. "Varter's busted. We were lucky."

We looked. That ballista would never loose again. One of the arms was cracked through, and the wood was black rotten for three-quarters of the crack, and pale yellow the rest.

"Lucky," said Captain Nath the Bows. "I'll have to replace her. Money, money, money . . . !"

"Praying again," I said, and—refreshingly—we all laughed.

Huringa, capital of Hyrklana, stands on the south bank of the River of Leaping Fishes, some thirty dwaburs up from the mouth. The river is not navigable past about the halfway mark, so we had to hire quoffa carts to take us the remainder of the journey. Hyrklana is a civilized country. As civilized, that is, as any civilized country on Kregen.

"We ought to be in the city in good time, Jak," said Unmok as *Pearl of Klanadun* and the coaster unloaded, the carts carrying the cages lumbering along, the men yelling and the whips cracking, we started. "But there is the Forest of the Departed to pass through."

In these gloomy woods uncounted numbers of past inhabitants of Huringa and the surrounding country had been interred for centuries. The place was a forest, yes; it was also a giant mausoleum. Froshak picked his teeth, spat, and said nothing. I eyed Unmok.

"Maglo the Ears?"

"Him, and a score of drikingers almost as bad."

Bandits are bad news anywhere.

Those drikingers I had employed in Vallia, clearing out aragorn and slavers and the iron legions of Hamal, had been driven to banditry against their foes. Your hardened, throat-cutting, purse-slitting bandit is a different matter.

Naturally, the mercenaries demanded extra pay. Unmok started to chitter-chatter, and I said, "Pay 'em," and so we did. We were eating bread sliced thin already. No sense in throwing the loaf away because of that.

Our ten thomplods lumbered along, thomp, thomp, thomp, their twelve legs apiece shaking the ground. The carts groaned, the wild beasts screeched and yowled and spat. We walked on, weapons in hand, staring every which way. In the Forest of the Departed are many grassy rides and wide open spaces lined with long-abandoned tombs. The shadows dropped confusingly down. The leaves rustled, a tiny hot wind blew, the smell of the forest fought the stinks of the caravan. We plodded on.

Looking at Unmok the Nets as he limped along, occasionally agreeing to ride aboard a cart, I reflected that this was one way to earn a living that was not for me. But we neared Huringa and the jikhorkdun and the reason for all this.

The bandits hit us just as we were thinking about making camp.

We were crossing a wide grassy expanse where there was no hope of our seeking shelter among the trees, and the drikingers came howling and yelling along a ride at right angles. They carried spears and swords and axes, and they urged their totrixes along with spurs. They would have cut us into little pieces, gone slap-bang through us and then turned, pirouetting, to finish us off at their leisure.

Instead, they went careering madly across our front, swerving away. Men struggled to stay in their saddles. Spears fell to the grass. Men fell, too, to be trampled in the stampede of maddened totrixes, their six hooves battering helmet and breastplate and pulping out the red ooze.

"The thomplods!" screamed Unmok. He danced in ecstasy. "I hope that's Maglo the Ears, may his guts dissolve into green slime!"

The bandits could not control their mounts. The attack was a fiasco. Perking up, our guards loosed off a few shafts and this finished the business. Yelling and swearing, the drikingers vanished among the trees.

"If they come back," I said loudly, "we will serve them steel stew!"

"Aye!" shouted the mercenaries. They were almighty puffed with the victory. But not one had the temerity or stupidity to mention a jikai. There are limits. . . .

Although our hired guards had not yet been offered the opportunity to display their quality as fighting men for us, they were not slow in behaving as any good paktun will and doubling across to loot the corpses. This is a mere part of life and death on Kregen, a facet of the economy.

The idea of perfectly good swords and armor being allowed to rust uselessly away goes against the grain.

Wandering across, I found myself a useful-looking thraxter, the straight cut and thrust sword of Halivar. The grip was plain, the hilt unadorned, and the blade not too heavy. One needs something a little more robust than a rapier in a nasty little fracas of this kind. As for armor, two kaxes I looked at were both pierced through by arrows. I retrieved the arrows from the corselets; one was broken and the other I stuffed back into the quiver I had kept after being dubbed Jak the Shot. In the end I found a leather jerkin with bronze studding. It clothed a dead apim and by letting the thongs out to their fullest extent I was able to get it around my shoulders. Had it been the slightest tight on me I'd have not touched it with a bargepole. But the dead man was of a goodly breadth across the shoulders. He had died of a totrix hoof in the head.

The mercenaries were busily hacking off fingers and ears to get at rings. I wasn't particularly interested in *that.* In the normal course I wouldn't have bothered any further, but Unmok and my partnership was a trifle strapped. A Rapa lay pitched onto his vulturine nose, and the gleam of a fine scarron necklace attracted me. I went across and turned him over and nodded. The gems were valuable, loot, no doubt, from some unfortunate woman trapped in a destroyed caravan. I started to unhook them.

A Fristle wanted to dispute my claim. I pointed to the arrow through the Rapa's eye. The feathers were yellow from a Hulfoo bird, that Hyrklanian goose. "Mine, I think."

The Fristle spat a little, ruffled up his fur and then went off farther into the trees after easier pickings.

Unmok was delighted with the scarron necklace.

"You could make a play about that," I said, and I found my ugly old beak head itching, almost as though I smiled at a jest.

Shadows now cloaked the clearing and occasionally the last of the twin suns shafted a smoky twinkle between the trees. Myriad insects whirled and gyrated, chips of flickering light in the rays. We set about pitching camp and came alert again, quivering with fresh alarm, as the jingle of harness and the clip-clop of hooves heralded more jutmen. But they were zorcamen, a regiment out from Huringa and not caring overmuch for the duty of bandit-chasing. They'd be back inside the city long before midnight.

Unmok spoke to their Jiktar, graphically describing the bandits' attack. The soldiers poked around among the remains. They took a few of the bodies with them, so as to look good on their report, I judged. I kept away from them. They were smart and could march with lances all aligned; but I didn't trust them.

What had been going on in Hyrklana that bandits could exist, and with impunity so close to the capital city? Even in a dense and gloomy place like the Forest of the Departed?

The ominous growls from the big cats and that whiffling, snorting, bubbly hullabaloo from the thomplods cut short my theories of political upheavals. Dripping hunks of meat were served out, and the growls changed to grunts and snarls and digesting noises of pleasure. Thomplods eat a good deal, naturally, giving their size. Luckily they eat almost anything and we shepherded them under suitable trees where they quickly ripped and stuffed, ripped and stuffed, until the tree was as bare of leaves as high as the muzzles could reach. Then on to the next tree. As for grass, that went down by the mawful.

Unmok, like most folk standing in those parts of Kregen not so far converted, kept a slave or three. His camp chief, Nobi, was a little Och with a villainous face and no teeth. He kept a little mincer on a string around his neck. Now Nobi pushed and harrassed the other two slaves into serving the evening meal. Fragrant scents wafted. The wine was poured. After a hard day we could relax.

Then a dratted strigicaw broke free.

Absolute bedlam. Pandemonium. We all ran this way and that, banging gongs and old brass trays, yelling and screeching, and scared right down to our toenails.

One thing about hunting-big-cats in captivity is that being fed by chunks of meat flung at them, they are half tame and half wild, and will eat meat they haven't killed themselves. We found the strigicaw with his head buried in the intestines of one of the Rapa casualties of the bandits' attack.

His brown and red hide glimmered splendidly by the light of our campfires and the scattering light of She of the Veils, pink and golden among the trees. Striped in the foreparts and double-spotted in the rear, with six pumping legs shading to black at the clawed paws, the strigicaw is a powerful and fast-running carnivore. We lassoed him from a respectful distance, and hauled, pushed and prodded him back to his cage. He kept his talons fast sunk into the remains of the Rapa.

"Still hungry," commented Froshak the Shine. "Meat no good."

"Then lucky we are it's all gone," said Unmok. "Tomorrow we'll be asked to pay good money for supplies. And if I know that camp manager, he'll cheat us rigid."

Froshak touched his knife. "Let me talk to him."

Unmok laughed, and then winced, and cradled the stump of his left middle. "What, Froshak, you leem hunter! And have the queen's guards lock us all up on that pretext, and drive us out into the arena to be gobbbled up by our own stock?"

"She would too," said Froshak. "She-leem."

And he didn't even bother to cast a guilty glance over his shoulder.

Next day a bur or so after the hour of mid we rolled up to the gates of the transit camp. A slope of a hill ahead cut off any view of Huringa. I should have expected this. But I had been firm in the belief that we'd just drive the stock up to the jikhorkdun and be let in. Easy.

The formalities were formidable. Paperwork threatened to bog us all down. Certificates had to be produced. The medical men checked the animals thoroughly. Some were put to one side as being second-class specimens, and these would find their way to other jikhorkduns. Only the best were good enough for Huringa.

Perforce, I sweated it out as Unmok drove the hardest bargains he could. The managers and the inspectors insisted on everything being done correctly, which meant being done their way. An attempt at bribery was met with an impossible demand. There were other wild-beast purveyors to be thought about. There were a few of the inevitable fights. I stayed well and truly clear.

But, slowly, we and our stock were processed.

We received permission to take the thomplods in to Huringa. Enough nobles were interested. Money was paid over. Unmok was able to discharge the mercenaries, who would soon find fresh employment. Froshak was left in charge at the camp. Unmok looked me over.

"Best foot forward, Jak the Shot. Best clothes. We have to create an impression."

"My wardrobe consists of the tunic in which you found me, after I was washed overboard, as I told you. And a jerkin from a dead drikinger."

Unmok guffawed. "We'll outfit you, Jak."

"One thing puzzzles me. What happens to the totrixes and the other juts when these thomplods enter the city?"

He winked, in that foolish yet extraordinarily knowing way Ochs have. "The managers of the jikhorkdun know all about thomplods, and all the other animals you care to name. They will give us a phial or two at the city gate."

So, and with an excitement I did not bother to mask, I went with these meandering haystacks down toward Huringa, which is the capital city of Hyrklana, where they joy in the jikhorkdun.

# CHAPTER TWELVE

## Beasts for Huringa

Huringa had grown another enceinte since I had last seen the place. The outer lines of walls were not, to my perhaps too-critical eye, quite tall enough. We thomplodded along the dusty road and left everything smothered in the white dust as we passed. The new walls stretched out of sight on either hand. Built of a gray-white stone, they looked impressive, curtains relieved by towers in a long sweeping curve to north and south out of sight. Beyond these walls rose the older walls. Beyond them the remains of the old walls were visible here and there. The city jumbled. Dominating it all, of course, the high fortress of Hakal.

Rearing from the solid rock, tall, dominating, the high fortress of Hakal brought back a host, a flood, a tempest of memories. The lip of the jikhorkdun was visible, and a hint of the many walls separating off the practice courts, the smaller arenas, the secluded gardens, the ball areas.

During the day the gas jets along the four main boulevards would be extinguished. Vollers crisscrossed through the air above the rooftops. The sense of bustle and urgency, of people about their daily business, of life being lived, gave a zest to the scene—a spurious zest in my view.

Slightly offset from the old Boloth Gate in the inner walls—what were now the inner walls—the gate giving ingress through the new walls lofted immensely. Massively serrated architecture allowed many arrow slits to frown down and murdering holes to dominate the gate's main tunnel. The thomplods passed through the opening with room for two more at each side and above and to spare.

"The Gate of The Trompipluns," said Unmok. He sniffed.

I gathered that though he valued his thomplods, he would dearly love to have brought a dozen trompipluns into Huringa.

Officials, backed by blank-faced guards, halted us. The arrangements were made and a boskskin bag containing golden deldys changed hands. The phials, buckets and water were brought.

Then we emptied the phials into the water and sloshed the resulting mixture all over our perambulating haystacks.

A few casual inquiries, a coarse joke or two, and the chingle of deldys brought me the information that the phials contained jutblood mixed with a variety of herbs. I let my memory jot down the names and descriptions. Unmok's tame slaves jabbered and scurried and the buckets were emptied. I could smell nothing fresh, but when we went on a string of calsanys and a group of totrixes took no notice of us at all.

Unmok had brought just one couple of werstings with him, two dogs he particularly favored, and they stalked along, black and white terrors from which people automatically shrank to allow their sharp white teeth plenty of passageway.

The noble with an interest in the thomplods turned out to be Noran. A strom no longer because his father had died, he was now Vad Noran. He did not recognize me. Why should he? He had seen me for perhaps a couple of burs many seasons ago.

Noran had lost that first bright flush of youth. Lines indented his forehead. He was thicker in the gut. But still he retained the awareness of his position as the leader of his particular set.

"By Gaji's bowels! And these are the famous beasts I have waited to see! They are a mangy lot."

The thomplods stood with drooping heads in the walled courtyard of Vad Noran's villa. Missal trees lent a merciful shade. The sanded area was neatly raked. Watchful guards, mostly blegs and Rhaclaws, stood at the gates. Noran was bright and contemptuous and he did not deceive Unmok.

"The queen . . ." said Unmok, and paused, artfully.

"Yes, yes, I shall buy them. But the price—"

Casually, I eased away and walked a little space as though to examine the ornate well in one corner. A slave—she was a Fristle woman much bent over—hauled up the gleaming copper bucket and poured water into a copper bowl for me.

I placed an ob on the stone coping. The small coin vanished into her ragged slave breechclout like a fly on a lizard's tongue.

The haggling could be left to Unmok. That was his trade. As a beast purveyor he had no real need to wear one of the colors of arena allegiance. Just about everyone in Huringa wore a favor. A man sauntered across to me. He wore fancy clothes and his thraxter in an embroidered scabbard thumped his thigh. His face was over-red, filled out and petulant. But he was still Callimark. Again, I had absolutely no fears that he could possibly remember me, a man seen for a few burs one evening seasons ago.

"You wear no favor, horter." His own red cockade shone.

"Lahal," I addressed him, and by omitting the double L indicated his lack of politeness. His eyebrows drew down, but I went on smoothly, "I have had my red so long its stitching has quite worn through. It lies somewhere now, no doubt being trampled upon by a green, or a blue or—"

"By Clem! That is not to be borne!"

Instantly, by reason of this exchange, we were on friendly terms. He rummaged around in his scrip and produced a red favor, small, crumpled, but wearable.

"You would do me the honor—" he began.

I found that grizzly old smile and nodded, and took the red favor.

"I am in your debt, Horter . . . ?"

"Callimark."

"Jak."

Unmok had completed the preliminaries, and Callimark, looking across, called out cheerily. Noran and Unmok joined us and there was mention of sazz or parclear, depending on one's preference for white or colored sherbert drinks, and palines, and perhaps banber sandwiches. Unmok winked at me. The atmosphere was genial, and that augured well for our partnership's financial well-being.

Here in Hyrklana we were somewhat closer to the equator than we would be in Vallia, but because of the enormous spread of Kregen's temperate zone the temperature remained comfortable. Noran's villa proved to be the sumptuous palace one would expect. We sat in cane chairs in one of his refectories and drank our sazz and talked. The conversation quickly turned on the execution—in the arena, of course—of the criminal lunatics who had attempted to burn one of Noran's voller factories.

I perked up.

"By Gaji's slimy intestines!" exclaimed Noran, flushed, vindictive. "They may not like the queen, but that does not mean they have to destroy my livelihood!"

"No, indeed, Noran," said Callimark, sipping parclear.

Now, seasons ago I had told these people I was Varko ti Hakkinostoling. The name was mouthful enough, the land far to the south had been ravaged; no one was going to bother overmuch about it. I had learned enough to pass muster, and indeed, had told Unmok that I was from Hakkinostoling.

So it was that I could venture an informed opinion.

I said, "Surely they do this, vad, as much in resentment of Hamal as of the queen—"

"Yes. You have it right, Horter Jak. But it is I who suffers!"

"The vad is constrained to sell to Hamal," put in Callimark, acting perfectly the part of the confidant to one in high position. "The Empress Thyllis is quite mad, of course, quite unlike our own dear queen. We must stay out of the insane war she wages."

"Yes." Noran exerted his own authority, overriding his friend. "We profit by her stupidities. But the thought of Hamalese skyships over Huringa—no. Better to sell to Hamal."

Now a vad is a very high rank of nobility, and Noran was being very gracious and condescending in his manner. This, I judged, was to impress Unmok and to bring down the price. So I risked another shaft. . . .

"I agree with you absolutely, notor." I spoke in a soft, almost philosophical voice and trusted he would take no offense. "This, I am told, is the queen's wish. The only trouble is that this makes Hamal stronger."

Noran nodded. He didn't like it, but it was the truth.

"If only—" he said, and stopped.

I went on, "If we could sell to other countries we would benefit Hyrklana immensely."

"I know that! By Flem! It is enough to make a man take up sword himself!"

"Perhaps one day you will be afforded that opportunity."

Both Noran and Callimark looked sharply at me. I saw their reactions, transparently reflected in their faces. The next moment might see a little hop, skip and jumping. . . .

Unmok was a mere beast purveyor, but he had standing.

Slowly, Noran worked his way around to what he fancied might be an answer to my manner.

"You speak as though—" he started, and then: "You do not talk like a beast handler, Horter Jak."

"The queen—"

"Ah!"

Unmok was looking at me as though I'd started spitting fire like the Spiny Risslacas.

I said, "A man has to turn his hand to many things in life, and must do what those in authority demand, in loyalty and affection. This is so, is it not, Vad Noran?"

"This is so, Horter Jak. But if you are not here as I had thought, have you anything specific to ask?"

This was brass-tacking with a vengeance.

"At the present moment, no. But your sentiments do you credit—and I mean no disrespect, as I hope you will understand."

"Go on."

Go on! I was fishing around desperately as it was, filling the air with noise. Go on. . . . I'd had a hard time getting here! So I leaned back in the cane chair and sipped my drink and looked wise—emperors are good at looking wise when their heads are empty—and told him, "The time will come, and I hope soon, when the queen will make her decision."

That appeared to satisfy him, for he banged a little silver gong, and we all rose as the slaves advanced to clear the tables. We went out to the courtyard and the business of the thomplods was concluded. As Unmok said to me, "Whatever was going on in there, Jak, he didn't haggle afterward."

So I said, "That's what partners are for, Unmok."

# CHAPTER THIRTEEN

## Of an Encounter in a Skyship

During the considerable time I had spent in Ruathytu, capital of Hamal, I had rarely visited any of the arenas there. Huringa was not so large a city as Ruathytu, and life was to a far greater extent dominated by the arena. Everywhere were reminders. Folk wore their colors of allegiance as a matter of course. They might live cheek by jowl, the baker being a follower of the diamond zhantil, and the cobbler an adherent of the sapphire graint, but always they were aware of the corners in the arena for which they shouted.

And they shouted. By Krun, but they made a din!

When the games were being staged the noise was clearly audible all over the city.

"For my part," said Unmok the Nets, during the next games when we could not bring in any of the remainder of our animals, "I do not care to choose a color. I do my work, and although it does not please me, it gives me a living." We were heading for an open-air eating place where we looked forward to roast vosk, momolams and enormous helpings of squish pie. "Now, when I get me my cage-voller. . . ."

The people moving slowly on the boulevards and sitting at the tables all wore a pinched look, a grayish cast to their gizzards. They spoke in high-pitched voices, and laughed a great deal, with exaggerated gestures. They fooled no one. They were not in the jikhorkdun, and therefore were, for the time being, out of the main pulsating current of life.

We sat down to eat. This was a good time for service. Nothing much happened outside the jikhorkdun when the games were on.

The jikhorkdun itself comprised all the inner courts and practice yards, the barracks, the cells, the animal cages and, as the focal point of all the effort, the arena within the great amphitheater. My job was to get Tilly, Oby and Naghan the Gnat out safely. Before that, I must make sure of a voller. Despite the importance of airboats to Vallia, I would not jeopardize my task of freeing my friends for the sake of a single flier. First things first.

"I am not an overly religious man, Jak," said Unmok, leaning back, "but sometimes I question the judgment of Ochenshum in arranging my life for me. As for Havil the Green, I think his days are numbered."

"How so?"

"Why, did you not hear that Vad Noran and his crony, Callimark? It was Flem this and Glem that, and anything-lem, all the time."

I knew exactly what Unmok was talking about. I felt the hateful repugnance for the evil cult of Lem the Silver Leem. I looked hard at Unmok, hoping he was not involved with that blasphemy. Right or wrong, my friends and I had determined that Lem the Silver Leem should never sully Vallia.

"Some secret religion of theirs. I've heard of it vaguely." Unmok's middle left stump twitched. "I know nothing of it and wish to know nothing. But there's a lot of it about."

"From what I know," I said, speaking with caution, "I fancy even Havil the Green is preferable."

"Every week you hear of babies gone missing."

I buried my face in squish pie. My thoughts were far too black and my face would have expressed my murderous feelings for the monsters who butchered babies to the greater glory of the Silver Leem.

We had managed to rid the martial race of Canops of the cult of Lem the Silver Leem, and the whole nation had been peacefully resettled on the island of Canopjik, situated at the mouth of the Gulf of Wracks which leads from the Ocean of Clouds into the Shrouded Sea. The island was considerably larger than their original home of Canopdrin and they flourished and maintained friendly relations with Migladrin, among other peoples and nations of the Shrouded Sea and the Dawn Lands.

When our meal was finished, Unmok said he would go to see a client who, because of an indisposition, was confined to his bed and unable to take his reserved seat in the amphitheater. I excused myself with a vague comment that Unmok would make a better fist of it than I. I sauntered along the boulevard with the infernal din from the arena booming like the thunder of the Ice Floes of Sicce. The noise rose and faded away and each punctuation marked the end of some poor devil on the blood-soaked silver sand.

Vollers cost money.

After my adventures the money remaining would not buy me the kind of voller I required, even if I could find someone to sell the craft. Production was tightly controlled, and the information that Vad Noran was engaged in voller manufacture came as a revelation to me.

So that meant I would have to liberate an airboat. I have done this before and was to do it again. All the same, I fancied in this case I'd recompense the person from whom I borrowed the flier. That seemed only fair. Vallia was not at war with Hyrklana. Ludicrous though the notion may be, it does have weight, this idea that stealing from one's enemies is not stealing in the true meaning of the word. Well, it is not, true, but you have to ponder the question and, sometimes, come up with unpalatable answers.

While the blood-antics went on in the arena was as good a time as any and better than most for work of this nefarious nature. The flierdrome I selected lay beyond the Walls of the Sapphire, between them and the new walls. The suns burned down as I walked gently along. Unmok had been as good as his word, and I wore decent Hyrklanan clothes: a blue tunic, a gray wraparound and high-thonged sandals. I wore only the thraxter—and my old knife, of course—and had left the rapier and dagger at our camp.

Many roofs jumbled below me in a little valley. On the flat ground to the side rested many airboats, of different descriptions but all of a moderate size. It slowly dawned on me as I approached that this was now a factory as well as a flierdrome.

Large numbers of slaves were in evidence as well as men of the artisan class, those they call guls in Hamal. The place looked busy. Here they built airboats for Hamal. Guards patrolled, mostly Rhaclaws and Rapas; but I fancied I could elude them for the vital amount of time required.

The blue tunic and gray wraparound were detestable garments. But they had their part to play. Passing through the shadows of an outlying block with a gate and a guard before me, I stopped. Because there are two suns in the sky of Kregen everyone expects everything to have two shadows. So the word for shadow, umshal, is a plural, rather naturally. In a room where there is a single lamp, or at the times of solar eclipses, when a Kregan wishes to talk of a single shadow, he will say a nikumshal, half-shadows. In the shadows I put on a new face, as Deb-Lu had instructed me. The bees began to sting, but I would have to endure that. I marched briskly on.

"Lahal, dom," I said as I came up to the guard. He was a cat-faced Fristle, bored and yawning, wishing he was in the jikhorkdun—as a spectator! My use of the familiar word dom, pal, half disarmed him. I rattled on. "Vad Noran sent me, urgent word within—you know how it is with these notors."

"Aye, dom, I do know. What is the latest?"

I had my wits enough about me to know what he was on about. I improvised as only an old kaidur could. I told him that one bout had seen off twenty Brokelsh coys and not a hair of the heads of their opponents scratched. This Fristle wore a blue favor. So I added to flavor the dish, "And the blues are doing well so, as a red, you will pardon me from laughing."

He laughed and opened the gate and I went through.

Strutting along with the importance of the petty official about business, I penetrated between the buildings, and penetrated is a good word, there, by Krun! The place was alive with men and women scurrying about. The slaves ran. The guls walked to show their free status. The sounds of hammering and sawing floated from various buildings. This was Sumbakir on a large scale.

If I knew nothing at all about voller production, I knew that the silver boxes would not be made and filled here. They'd be freighted in for fitting to the vollers. Rhaclaw guards prowled. I ignored them, and my nose went up a few inches. The right petty bureaucrat, me!

My face was beginning to sting uncomfortably, but I did not want to relax in case I did not put on exactly the same face again.

Rounding a corner I looked up at the edge of the flat area. Steps led up. Only one Rhaclaw guarded them, and he was more interested in the lines of slaves hauling half-built vollers up to the finishing sheds crowning the edge. The slaves made a din. I judged that the valley had been chosen as the site because it was thought easier to defend against aerial attack. Towers studded the place, and archers moved in the fighting tops. They'd shaft an aerial attack, and they'd shaft runaway slaves. And—they'd shaft clean through anyone who attempted to steal a voller.

My lips drew down in that new face. This was not looking good.

Well, as long as I was here I might as well see how far I could get.

Now the weird thing was, and I swear this is absolutely true, as Zair is my witness!, the fact of stealing a voller and the story I had told, or rather hinted at, to Vad Noran brought vivid impressions into my mind. As I started up the slope I was thinking of Prince Tyfar and of Jaezila.

Prince Tyfar and I had gone through a few adventures together and he was a good comrade. Also, he was a Prince of Hamal, which was unfortunate. The son of Prince Nedfar of Hamal, Tyfar was intelligent, studious, a lover of good books, honorable and upright. Also he was a superb axeman. He'd gone back to Hamal after our last adventures and, I confess, I missed his company.

As for Jaezila—well, now! That commanding and beautiful woman, mistress of the bow and the sword, had plagued Tyfar cruelly with her manner and her willfulness. She worked for Hamal, although I was not certain she was Hamalese, and had been attempting to obtain fliers for the Empress Thyllis. She was a marvel, that girl, ravishing, alluring and damned temperamental, as Tyfar had discovered. When we'd been forcibly parted she could easily have gone with Tyfar back to Hamal, and there made the shattering discovery that the ninny she so contumed was a noble prince and highly thought of. I'd have liked to have witnessed that revelation, by Vox!

Maintaining that brisk gait I ascended the stairs. The Rhaclaw half turned to look. His leather armor was liberally studded with bronze and he carried a stux, one of the throwing spears that can burst clear through you. He was a Rhaclaw, a race of diffs more commonly found in Havilfar, with the enormous domed head fully as wide as his shoulders. He looked at me suspiciously.

I started my rigmarole of bearing a message as I neared him. As I reached the top, I paused, theatrically holding my side and gasping for breath.

"My Havil! That climb takes it out of a fellow."

"You have no business here—"

Beyond him and beyond the edge of the finishing sheds I could see row after row of vollers. These were all the same, over at this end of the field. Six-place fliers, they were military craft, most useful for scouting purposes with enough punch if they got into a tight squeeze to scrape clear.

"Wait a minute, dom, till I get my breath."

"You have no business." He didn't bother to finish talking to me. He half turned and opened his letter box of a mouth. He was going to holler for the Deldar of the guard.

So, unwillingly, I leaped forward and laid him down gently enough, and then ran on leaving him slumbering.

Security at this voller factory was not so slack as I'd assumed.

A hell of a racket began. As I ran I realized this was a bedlam of bells and gongs and ratcheted clackers, all kicking up their own brand of inferno. A file of Rapas doubled around the end of the finishing shed. Evidently, each sentry post was overseen by the next. Some system of checking could alone account for the rumpus.

If I could reach a voller. . . .

Guards were running from every which way. They sprang up all over the field like dragon's teeth.

I'd never reach a voller now. . . . The finishing shed was the only cover. Instantly, I turned and hared off for the shadows.

Once aboard the voller and the girl is mine. . . . The silly jingle kept running around in my head.

For a factory, the finishing shed proved to be a handsome building. Its eaves projected. I went into the shadows like a fish diving under a weir. Inside the shed the dimness could not be allowed to hinder me. Slaves started to yell, and the evil sound of whips and that hateful word "Grak!" burst out. I straddled three overseers who would awake wondering what had hit them. I hared on, running flat out, making for the far end.

Down both sides of the shed the bulks of vollers lay waiting for the final touches. No doubt here was where the silver boxes were fitted. If I got out of this in one piece it might pay to return here and investigate the mysterious silver boxes. A Rapa leaped at me, his thraxter a glimmering bar of steel. I slid his brand, chopped him in the wattles, jumped and ran on.

The pack hullabalooed after me.

If this was an example of how Dray Prescot liberated a voller, then Zair help him!

Out the far door, no time to blink at the blaze of suns shine. The next shed's open door gaped an invitation.

Inside this one they were building a very large vessel. Very large indeed. Although not as huge as a Hamalese skyship, she towered up to the beams of the roof, and her bulk swelled to allow an alleyway at each side. Here slaves and guls labored to put the finishing touches to the hull.

There was no time to stop.

Then the thought occurred to me. Up to now thought had played little part. . . .

I went up the nearest ladder and dived into the ship.

She was a fine craft. No doubt of that. Even in this uncompleted state, with holes in the decks and planks and ladders everywhere, sawdust and shavings strewing the decks, paint pots and buckets and all the bric-a-brac of ship construction lumbering the clearways, she still held a good line, still conveyed the sense of the power she would wield in the skies.

Noises inside echoed like gongs in a cathedral. Light fell confusedly. I hurried along. My face was now a blazing pain. To hell with it! With a feeling of enormous relief I let my new face disappear, and my own old beakhead of a face glowered out. Disguise is all very well. But there are limits . . . !

The gray wraparound had served its purpose. I unwrapped it and chucked it into a waste bin among oily trash. Now I looked like any horter, with a decent dark-red breechclout and a blue tunic reaching to mid-thigh. I hitched up the thraxter. The weapon had not yet been drawn.

A deal of noise spurted up from aft and below. This was noise not of slaves arguing among themselves or guls telling the slaves what to do, but of guards searching around for their quarry which had—for the moment—eluded them.

One thing I was certain of: I'd done the right thing in running. I'd never have talked my way out of that mess.

Down a corridor that was just about finished, apart from a lick of paint, I marched on smartly. At the end there would be a companionway down and I could emerge from any of the holes being filled with varters, or reach the lower fighting galleries and descend to the shed floor from there.

Voices reached me from ahead. I did not stop. Now I could bluff from an entirely new hand. News would not have reached this far yet.

Light shafted down from a broad opening in the deck

above. People stood in a group in the center of the radiance. Some held plans, which they slanted to catch the light. A big fellow with a mass of dark hair was gesticulating around and jabbing the plan. Another man was standing a little to one side looking at the carpenters' work on the near bulkhead, and he turned back to speak to the big fellow with the plans.

". . . Not good enough," said this young fellow. He spoke in a pleasant enough voice. He wore decent clothes, of a neat cut and of blue and gray, with gray trousers. I saw those trousers. At his side swung a rapier, and a main gauche would match it on the other, of that I felt sure. He looked lithe and limber, with a handsome, keen face, and I sighed.

As I said, I'd been thinking as I ventured in here of Prince Tyfar. . . .

I walked forward boldly into the light.

One or two of the group looked up as I appeared.

The woman—the girl—was there, this time dressed in dark blue, and a rapier swung at her side, too.

"Lahal," I said cheerily. "I am sorry for my lateness. But there was some disorder, something about a man running down there. I trust you are well?"

I used no names.

Prince Tyfar gaped at me. Jaezila stared.

Then she smiled. "Lahal, Jak. We are pleased to see you."

# CHAPTER FOURTEEN

## I Amuse my Friends

As I was a member of the delegation with Prince Tyfar of Hamal there was no trouble about my leaving. He had with him two grave-faced men, high officials of the department in Hamal charged with voller procurement. Also he had Barkindrar the Bullet and Nath the Shaft. With Jaezila was her retainer, Kaldu. They merely nodded to me and smiled. They took their lead from their master and mistress. Anyway, we had been comrades together, blade comrades. There was much between us.

So we went down the steps and the furor continued as the guards hunted the fugitive. The wildest of rumors flew about.

As we walked together, Jaezila smiled. "You, I suppose, Jak the Sturr?"

"Aye, my lady, me. And my thanks—"

Prince Tyfar half turned, the epitome of a handsome young prince.

"You observed the skyship, Jak. Your opinion?"

"A fine craft, Prince." I'd heard the others address him thusly, so that was one hurdle out of the way. He was here with the delegation officially from Hamal buying fliers. "She will serve admirably once she is completed."

"My thought, exactly, except—"

I chanced a shaft. "The varter positions on the upper deck?"

"Precisely."

A little technical discussion ensued, in which I was able to insert my oar from time to time. Tyfar was a right tearaway in that he'd chanced dropping me in it. But, I fancy, he had taken the measure of my mettle as I'd taken the measure of his down in the Moder, among other fraught places.

The big fellow with the hair and the plans appeared anxious to please. He was the manager, Nalgre Orndalt, and he heaved up a sigh just before we said the remberees.

"The ship will be only two weeks behind schedule, Prince. You can't get the quality of workmanship like you used to. And I'd as lief be in the stands of the jikhorkdun as working this afternoon."

Rather sharply, Tyfar said, "You perhaps object to working for Hamalese paymasters?"

Nalgre Orndalt's thick fingers clenched on the plans. The paper ridged and creased. Then, slowly, he said, "No, Prince. There are some, as you know, who. . . . No, I do my work and take my wages, and leave politics to the queen."

With her brilliant smile, Jaezila said, "Well, Nalgre, perhaps you could hasten the work. Improve on the two weeks?"

"I will try." He did not say, "For you, my lady." But the impression of his having said that remained. I did not wonder. Many men would move mountains for Jaezila. I did not think she would treat them like dirt beneath her sandals, but if she did they'd be grateful for the attention.

When we were safely outside the gates and walking slowly toward the lines where the zorcas were stabled, Tyfar said to the officials in his delegation, "I believe you expressed the desire to witness the games? There will still be some games left. Of the more barbarous kind." His face expressed his distaste. He had told me he did not care for the jikhorkdun in his native Hamal.

"Thank you, Prince." The officials and their aides mounted up and rode off. We looked after them, waiting for them to leave. Kaldu, big-boned and powerful, his brown beard trimmed to a point, kept away from me. He would not look at me.

I moved to stand at his side. "Do not blame yourself, Kaldu. You did right—"

"But we left you to certain death—"

"The death was not certain. For I am here. Now, for the sake of Havil, cheer up! Your duty was to the lady Jaezila. You did right, and you would do the same again."

He had forcibly taken Jaezila aboard the voller and lifted away to safety as I had been ringed with steel.

"Aye, Jak. Aye. I would do the same again."

"Queyd-arn-tung!" I said, which means no more need be said on the subject.

And Kaldu passed a broad hand across his beard and smiled.

Then it was Tyfar's turn to attempt to apologize for leaving me. In all the kerfuffle of the attack he had not been in any position to contribute. I told him so, and added, "And now that you are here and I am here, in Hyrklana, we have a lot to do."

"And Deb-Lu? And Hunch and Nodgen?"

I moved my hands. "I assume they are safe. They lifted away in good time."

"I pray they are safe. I set much store by Deb-Lu-Quienyin. And as for Hunch and Nodgen—"

"Hunch, at least," put in Jaezila, with her laugh, "would have trembled in his shoes up there."

We all laughed. Even I laughed, for that seems the right thing to do when Hunch the Tryfant comes into the conversation. And he had been a good companion to us, with his comrade Nodgen. . . .

I was not going to tell Tyfar or Jaezila that Quienyin and Hunch and Nodgen, and the Pachak twins, Fre-Da, had reached Vallia. Tyfar and Jaezila were Hamalese and thought I was working for mad Empress Thyllis as were they.

That was the explanation I gave them for my presence. As I expected, it worked like a charm. If you understand that I felt a twinge of guilt at telling that kind of untruth to two people for whom I entertained the highest respect, admiration and affection, you understand aright. But as with Rees and Chido, personal friendship beclouds the supposedly greater issues of patriotism. And I had already vowed that patriotism, for all the demeaning postures now understood by that word, would not be allowed to harm Tyfar or Jaezila.

Not while I lived, by Vox!

As we mounted up—I've no idea to whom the zorca I so airily made use of belonged—I thought if only these two were not Hamalese!

We had a deal of mileage to make up. Through downright cunning use of my supposed secret assignment from Empress Thyllis I was able to bypass most of the awkward questions. I let them understand I'd got out of that scrape back there in Absordur with the Vajikry-mad trylon by telling the truth. When I mentioned that infuriating game of Vajikry, Tyfar threw back his head and laughed uproariously.

"You, Jak! Vajikry! But you're a Jikaida man."

"Surely. I was hard put to it to survive." Then I told them of the gambit I'd used to win free, whereat they laughed the louder.

I could see the funny side of it well enough, but I said, "It was a good laugh afterward. But at the time, and what with that oaf singing his damned dismal song, the "March of the Skeletons," well, it wasn't so—"

Jaezila interrupted swiftly, turning to me from her saddle. "Jak! We are thoughtless and cruel to laugh so!" And then she couldn't stop bursting out with a snorting laugh she tried to stop and only made worse.

Comrades. Blade comrades! I warmed to them.

And their adventures had been a trifle fraught, also. They'd had a few fights and helter-skelterings of that kind winning free and reaching Hamal. Kregen offers unbounded opportunities for skull-bashing if you have a mind to that kind of frolic, which I have not. Then it was my turn to laugh as they described Jaezila's surprise—her consternation—when she discovered the ninny she so put upon was a prince, a real live prince of Hamal.

"Ah, but Jaezila," I said, "you should have seen him down the Moder. He was like a zhantil."

"Oh, now, come, Jak, really—" protested Tyfar. But he gave a glance at the girl—the woman—who rode so straight and proudly at his side. And I, nodding to myself, fancied the future held prospects there that would have astonished just absolutely everybody when we were crossing the Dawn Lands.

"And the quest for vollers proved negative there," they told me. "And we were ordered to speed up production in Hyrklana."

I made a face. "But can you order another country like that? You know they do not like the Hamalese."

Now it was Tyfar's face which changed. He looked at once savage and dismayed. "I know. I deplore what we are doing with our army and air service. We attack, it seems, at the whim of the Empress Thyllis—may Havil forgive me if I speak out of turn, Jak. But I cannot much longer remain still. My father keeps his own counsel. But—"

"You know my opinion of Prince Nedfar," I said. "He is a great man. He will always strive to walk the path of righteousness." I did not use those exact and somewhat mawkish words; the sentiment remained true.

"Aye." Tyfar's eyebrows drew down and his forehead wrinkled. "Aye. I pray he does not run into trouble."

"If the iron legions of Hamal are stopped," said Jaezila, and she spoke on a breath, "what will Thyllis do then, d'you think?"

We didn't know. But we all felt it would be something exceedingly dire.

I forbore to inquire who was going to do the stopping. Up in Vallia we had made a good beginning in that direction. . . .

They asked me where I was staying, preparatory, I guessed, to inviting me to stay with them. I said I was living outside the walls, and doing very well. I did not particularize.

There were three or four small townships, not quite suburbs, outside the walls, and all at least two varter shots from the walls. This was a common-sense precaution. They assumed I was staying in one of these suburbs.

"We have been put up in regal fashion with Pallan Mahmud nal Yrmcelt," said Tyfar. "He is the queen's chief pallan."

"Ord Mahmud," I said, thinking.

Tyfar looked surprised. "Why, no. Orlan Mahmud. You have his name wrong. Beware, he is high in the queen's favor."

"I believe I have heard," said Jaezila offhandedly, "that Orlan's father's name was Ord."

I nodded and let it pass. Time flows, time flows. . . .

It seemed to me he would not remember the descent of a slate slab and a scarlet breechclout. He might. If he did I fancied he would wish to forget. After all, at the time he had been involved with a group plotting the downfall of Queen Fahia. Perhaps, I surmised as we jogged along, perhaps Orlan Mahmud nal Yrmcelt was still opposed to the queen, and taking over his father's position as chief pallan, sought to work from within the establishment. It was a possibility.

Also, it was quite likely to be mere wishful thinking. Men as they grow older, on Kregen as on Earth, often change from being red-hot revolutionaries to straitlaced pillars of the community. The thought, the fact, is not new.

The games still proceeded and the beast roar of the crowd swelled over Huringa. Tyfar declared his throat was as dry as that infernal desert we had marched through together and so we reined in at a convenient hostlery and, dismounting, saw that the zorcas were led off by slaves. Then we sat around a table, with the retainers at a respectful distance.

This was nonsense for us, for we were all comrades-in-arms. But we had no wish, for our various reasons, to attract undue and unfavorable notice.

As we sipped the wine, for it was just time, I reflected that this was all very fine and wonderful; it brought me no nearer to securing a voller for the escape I planned.

Overjoyed though I was to meet up with Tyfar and Jaezila, I could not, must not, allow them to deflect me from my purpose in Huringa.

We had a deal to talk over. Prince Nedfar, Tyfar's father, had reached Ruathytu safely. I was relieved to hear this. Tyfar, again, expressed his unease over the policies being followed by his country. Jaezila, her color up, her splendid eyes fierce, observed that, by Krun! Hamal trod a dangerous path. But she, like Tyfar, would not commit herself to any definite statement. They worked for Hamal, as I worked for Vallia. The thought saddened me.

My explanations, although lame in my ears, satisfied them when I said I would have to return to my quarters. We enjoyed a slap-up meal before the jikhorkdun turned out and the taverns became choked with excited patrons discussing the details of the games. I gathered that the yellows had lost their place of preeminence, and the blues had, as I had told that guard, achieved the highest position.

Mentioning the lady Ariane nal Amklana, Tyfar said he had not seen or heard of her since entering Hyrklana. The lady Ariane had not, in our opinion, biased though we might be, turned out too well in the Moder. Much might be forgiven her, but Tyfar was too much the gentleman, the true noble, to dwell on that. She was, he said he had discovered, well-known in Huringa, visiting there from time to time. She was a vadni, the Vadni of Amklana, and her husband, like Queen Fahia's husband, King Rogan, was a nonentity.

"I heard once—oh, a mere whisper—that King Rogan might seek to take the reins of government into his own hands." I said this in the quiet expectancy of immediate and incredulous disbelief. My expectations were not disappointed.

"He is a nothing," declared Tyfar. "Poor fellow."

"It is true. I do not know where your whisper came from, Jak," said Jaezila. "But it is surely false."

"Aye. It was probably a pious hope. A wish that he might prove a better sovereign than fat Queen Fahia."

No one outside our circle heard me, which was just as well.

Pleasant though it was to sit in the radiance of the declining suns and eat and drink and talk with my comrades, I had work to do. I stood up. Tyfar instantly stopped my attempts to pay the reckoning, with princely grace quietly insisting he would settle. I made an arrangement to meet them on the morrow, expressed my regrets I was called away and walked off. My twin shadows preceded me as I walked along, heading for the jikhorkdun.

In that warren of evil and horror and high courage three other friends awaited—all unknowing—the chance of escape I trusted fervently I was bringing them.

# CHAPTER FIFTEEN

## Of Questions and Reminders

"No. Never heard of him."

"A little fellow. Very cheery. The best armorer you could hope to find."

"Sorry, dom."

I turned away. This was the fifth dead end. Around me the familiar—hatefully familiar—sounds of the practice rings rose into the evening sky. The bulk of the amphitheater cast deep and imposing shadows. The smaller courts blocked off the last rays of Zim and Genodras, which in Havilfar are known as Far and Havil. The clink of steel on steel, the swift stamp and scrape of foot, the hoarse intake of breath, all these blood-quickening sounds served on this evening only to depress me. The jikhorkdun was vast. It was a labyrinth.

This maze might not be quite as dangerous as that labyrinth within the Moder, down which we had ventured, braving monsters and sorceries; it held its own evil brand of danger. There had, it seemed to me, been nothing else for it but to ask for Naghan the Gnat by name. Yes, there was inherent peril in this. He might be using another name. Strangers who asked around for one particular person would be looked at most carefully. But—how else was I to find Naghan?

Deb-Lu-Quienyin had assured me my friends, although of the jikhorkdun, were not involved in the arena. Tilly, that beautiful golden-haired Fristle fifi, might be anywhere in the immense barrack blocks. Oby, who was no longer a young tearaway and who might now prefer his name in full—Obfaril—had given up all desires to be a kaidur. In Valka he had become obsessed with fliers. He was an expert in vollers. Now, I trusted he had not been given the chance to fulfill his youthful ambitions.

As for Balass the Hawk, that doughty fighting man would have been sent back to his native land of Xuntal. I did not expect to find Balass here.

The promenades were crowded with folk come to see the kaidurs at close quarters. Even a day of surfeit in the arena could not satisfy many of the aficionados. Time would never dull for me the impression, the emotion, the passions of the arena. I'd been through the mill. I thought I knew.

Partisan devotees would come to admire and to shower gifts on the kaidurs who had been victorious. Wagers were arranged, and the bets were enormous. The trainers would display their new men; the backers would look and whisper behind their hands, pomanders well in evidence. It was a flesh market, of course, but at the same time the young sprigs of the gentry and nobility would take up a sword and set to with a renowned kaidur. The steel rang and scraped. I knew no kaidur was going to use all his skill to show up some popinjay. All the same, nasty knocks could be taken—aye, and given!—in these pretty little private matches.

The jikhorkdun has its four color corners, plus the area reserved for the queen's kaidurs, and I went first and naturally to the reds. And, again naturally, I sought the armorers and made my inquiries. After the fifth dead end I changed my tune about Naghan being the best armorer you could find. It was true. I have mentioned other armorers who had worked for me and who were comrades, and there were many—particularly in Valka—who were superb. Naghan the Gnat took his place among the finest. But my questions would be met with scowls and black brows.

So that little man with the great heart became just Naghan the Gnat, an armorer.

And still I found no trace at all, not even a memory. Well, that is passing foolish on my part, for by the nature of its trade, being a kaidur means you do not make friends. They tend to die off quickly, and you take your turn in that dismal procession.

About to chuck the reds and try my luck with the blues, for unless you volunteer to walk into the arena you do not often have the chance of choosing what color you fight under, I saw Cleitar Adria talking to a pot-bellied man loaded with gold chains. I thought it was Cleitar Adria. I stopped, looking without appearing to stare.

By Kaidun! It was Cleitar.

We'd been captured as slaves together, and given the opportunity to fight in the arena, and taken it. Cleitar had prospered as a kaidur as though wedded to it. It had become his life—and I own I was glad to see he was still alive. He had the marks of the jikhorkdun upon him.

The dead tissues of the scar bisecting the left half of his face glistened like white ceramic from Loh. That scar started at his hairline and finished at his chin. His left eye socket was simply dead scar tissue.

I fancied no one called him Ob-Eye Adria.

He had not been a particularly close comrade. I had rubbed along with him out of pure self-interest, to avoid a fracas, and cheered his victories because he fought for the ruby drang.

It seemed to me he would not recognize me. But, just in case, I moved to one side and began to compose my features as Deb-Lu had instructed me and started to put on a new face.

Something soft and padded, and containing something hard and edged, thumped me in the middle of the back. I did not fall. Balance is important to a fighting man, even when he is in the middle of half bending over to change his face. I straightened as a bull roar broke out, a bellowing, hectoring, vicious torrent of words.

Some pot-bellied, swag-jowled, bloodshot-eyed, gold-bedecked oaf had bumped into me. The objects I had felt had been his guts and his sword. I will not repeat what he said.

The tide of invective poured on. I did not know who he was. The uproar attracted attention. He clearly felt himself to be an important man.

Even as I plucked my fist out of the air and slapped it down, opening my hand out to clamp around my thigh, I turned away. Hitting him would not help my three friends. And, somewhere in the limbo of the unborn, that new face of mine howled for a body.

By Zair! But I know my own face must have looked a sight—that devil's look that stops a risslaca in its tracks.

I dodged down a side alley. Toward the end a cage held half a dozen werstings, and the black-and-white killer dogs prowled around and around, tongues lolling. Poor old Unmok the Nets had been in a quandary about his werstings. He put great store by them, and pampered them, and did not want to sell them and, because the rest of his merchandise was of top quality, had received offers. The quandary lay in this—his werstings were now soft. Pampered, overfed, overweight, perfumed and silk-ribboned, they would not last a heartbeat against real killers.

Mind you, I hold no brief for werstings. They have taken the seat out of more than one pair of breeches before I could jump clear. They and stavrers, both. . . .

The noise rose into the sky. The suns were gone and the gas lights jetted. Under the arcades all manner of unholy trades were going on, fruits of the excitement of the arena. The crowds jostled, taking the opportunity for a last look at famous kaidurs before the evening's entertainments took on their more familiar aspects—taverns, theaters, dopa dens, girls all beckoned the raffish sets of Huringa.

In the shadows under the wooden swell of tiered seating of a small private arena I halted. Footsteps padded after me. Three drunks passed in the opposite direction, and I used their stumbling bodies as a shield to turn to confront whoever it was who stalked me. A man stepped forward.

"Lahal, Drak the Sword!"

"Lahal," I answered firmly. "You would do yourself a good service, Cleitar, if you omit the Sword from my name."

His one eye disappeared as he winked—or blinked—who can say in a one-eyed man?

"I understand. I thought you dead. You left—I recall it as though it were yesterday."

"And, when that fat oaf bumped into me, you saw . . . ?"

"Aye, Drak. One does not easily forget that look—"

"So I am told."

"By the brass sword and glass eye of Beng Thrax! I am glad to see you. These young coys are all flatfish these days."

I digested that. So much came out there. Cleitar must know we had not been blade comrades. But we had been comrades fighting for the ruby drang. I nodded. "Can you . . . ?"

"Oh, I am a cheldur now and may come and go as I please."

As I try to explain it, a cheldur is not quite like a Roman lanista. He is a trainer, above all, responsible for his barracks and for the production of kaidurs. He does not really possess the lanista's privileges of arranging affairs.

Cleitar gestured to his face.

"This was a blessing in disguise." He went on to describe in gory detail the fight in which he had received his wound. We walked on to where he said we could find wine or dopa. "After that they said I could be a cheldur and no longer fight. Well, by Kaidun! I have done well—"

"The ruby drang sits at the bottom of the staff."

He looked savage. "Aye! The sapphire graint lords it now!"

So, weirdly, weirdly! I was back thinking and passionately thirsting for the ruby drang to be triumphant. I recalled how we reds fought and shouted, cat-calling the other colors, contemptuous of them all alike, how we crowed at our victories and screamed and rattled weapons along the iron bars at our defeats. Oh, yes, I had been a hyr-kaidur and one does not easily forget that, by Kaidun, no!

And, the other weird thing was, here we were, walking along and talking almost as though so many seasons separating our last meeting meant nothing, had never existed. . . .

He wanted to know all about that dramatic escape in which a monstrous skyship had descended into the arena and plucked us from the silver sand. I told him a little—very little, as you will easily imagine. Then it was simple to go on talking about Oby and Tilly and Naghan the Gnat, for they, with Balass the Hawk, had been rescued along with me.

He had not heard of them, any of them, from that day to this.

So, I said to myself as we went into a vile-smelling place filled with wooden benches beneath a training ring, that means Naghan *has* to be armorer to another color.

"In here, Drak—" Cleitar said, ducking his head to pass under the lintel. I took his arm and held him back.

"It would be a good idea to call me by my name," I said. "I am Chaadur, sometimes called Chaadur the Iarvin."

He looked nonplussed for only a space, then he nodded, and we went in. He well understood that Queen Fahia would like to get her hands on me. Her pet neemus would have a feast then. And I was aware that he had to be watched.

As for the name Chaadur, this was a name I had used once in Hamal. And Iarvin—well, Pompino wouldn't mind if I borrowed that, would he now?

The impression I took that Cleitar Adria hankered after the old days when he had been a hyr-kaidur strengthened. He spoke offhandedly about the new men he had to train up. Not one, he said, banging his fist on the table, not a damned one was fit to latch the sandals of the coys in our day!

It occurred to me that, as the ploy had been successful already here in Huringa, I would try it again. By innuendo and hint I got across to Cleitar that, far from the queen being angry with me and seeking to have me killed, quite the contrary was true. I even went so far as to suggest the skyship had been a part of the plan.

"And I am here in Huringa, and Fahia—" I said Fahia and not the queen or Queen Fahia to impress him "—has been graciously pleased with my work for her. So, Cleitar, keep the old black-fanged winespout stoppered. Dernun?"

I said dernun in a nonviolent, inquisitive way, and his immediate response of "Quidang" carried also that note of conspiracy. And, at that, he got a thrill out of feeling in touch with skullduggery for the queen.

Dopa, that fiendish drink, was being drunk by other men in this malodorous cavern. Cleitar bellowed for purple Hamish wine and I was quite startled when it was forthwith produced.

He nodded, slyly. "This is more like it, Dra—Chaadur. We do ourselves well, out of sight, like. Better than Beng Thrax's Spit, yes?"

"But you are surely allowed into the city?"

"Of course." He poured. "But well—I have grown used to the jikhorkdun. It is my home now. Far more than my real home ever was, when I was a quoffa handler."

We talked over the old days, remembering past kaidurs and hyr-kaidurs, and the great kaidurs they had performed in the arena. Just how much he really believed of my story about the queen I wasn't too sure. But I fancied he wanted to believe. He was a very lonely man in these latter days.

This dopa den was not patronized by kaidurs, of course. Here congregated the men involved in the ancillary details. Here sat and drank beast-handlers and slave-managers, cheldurs and armorers, the quasi-privileged of the arena. If they wanted to sing or fight, as is the habit in dopa dens, I did not care, being in the mood to oblige either desire. I gave Cleitar to understand that my reason for being here this evening was to pick up a few tips. I'd been away, I said.

He gave me the names and rankings and running odds of various of his kaidurs. The reds were down in the mouth these days.

"We have a new batch due in, coys as green and raw as uncropped corn. Maybe out of three hundred I will find three who will do. Eh, Chaadur! You remember how we began, me and you and Naghan the Gnat?"

"I do."

By Kaidun! I did! And I had to get about finding Naghan and not sitting like a putative sot drinking purple Hamish wine.

So, with excuses and promises to return, I took my leave.

And, and I say this with all sincerity, it had given me quite a jolt to meet Cleitar Adria again and talk over the old days. Quite a jolt. As I say, when you have been a hyr-kaidur in the arena, you never lose the cachet, odiferous though it may be.

The partnership with Unmok proceeded splendidly, but he wanted to save the incoming money. I agreed. So instead of buying ourselves zorcas to ride about we purchased urvivels. These are sturdy animals, although not in the same class as zorcas. I walked across the patio toward my urvivel, patiently awaiting me, and two shadows closed in under the lights. We went outside the jikhorkdun. The people had mainly streamed away along the boulevards. Suddenly, this patio was deserted of all save me and these two.

"By Rhapaporgolam the Reiver of Souls!" quoth one, very merry. "I do believe we have a chicken to be plucked!"

"By the Resplendent Bridzikelsh!" chortled the other, very darkly. "I do believe you have the right of it!"

They bore in, bludgeons upraised. One was, as you will perceive, a Rapa, and the other a Brokelsh.

I turned to face them. "A chicken, my friends? Oh, you famblys, I have no feathers left!"

So, joyfully, we met in combat—they to take my gold and slit my throat or bash my skull in if they had to, and I to prevent them. The first bludgeon blows hissed through air instead of rattling my brains in my skull. The first knife was drawn in exasperation. They were a right comical pair—I've no idea what their mothers called them—and they went to sleep, slumbering like the babes they once had been. I looked down on them and shook my head, in sorrow rather than anger.

"Thank you, my friends," I said to their unconscious bodies. "You serve to remind me that life is mutable and that the suns may rise over Kregen as ever—but not for everyone."

And with that, I mounted up on the urvivel and ambled off to our camp outside the city, and to a fine old argument with Unmok the Nets.

# CHAPTER SIXTEEN

## An Armorer Raises an Echo

The argument erupted into a rip-roaring row.

"But we're partners, Jak!"

"Yes. But—"

"The animals are sold. There is nothing to detain us here. I do not like the jikhorkdun—"

"No more do I!"

"Well, then! What ails you, Jak? Let us clear out. I have good suppliers lined up and we can fetch in a fresh consignment—"

"What about your cage-voller?"

Unmok lifted his upper left and middle right. His upper right held a goblet of cheap wine.

"Not yet. I do not have the cash. But our money is safe with Avec Parlin, who has banking connections—"

"Yes, yes. But—"

"And this voyage will see it, Jak. It will! Then we can buy a cage-voller and set up properly in business."

"I thought you were giving up? What was the last scheme—totrix breeding in Haklanun? Or was it a return to the beads and bangles on a vast scale—?"

"You mock me! We are *partners,* Jak!"

It went on for some time. I couldn't leave Huringa now, of course not, and Unmok couldn't see why not, and I couldn't tell him. We went to sleep in an uncomfortable silence that all our attempts to come to an understanding only made worse.

In the morning we breakfasted with only the stiffest and politest of words between us. Froshak the Shine kept well out of it, and so opened his mouth as to yell more than twice at the slaves, which clearly indicated all was not well with his world.

"I have to see Vad Noran," said Unmok. "No doubt you will be about your business—whatever that may be. I will see you tonight?"

"Yes. I will not—yes, I will see you tonight."

I'd been about to say I wouldn't leave without saying the remberees. But that would only arouse a fresh storm.

Riding the urvivel into Huringa, I pondered the problems. Today I intended to try my luck with the blues. The sapphire graint was the top color these days. Maybe Naghan had a hand in that. The guards at the Gate of the Trompipluns let me through—trompipluns means yellow feet—and I cantered to the inn where I would leave the urvivel for the day, preferring that to a public stables. The inn was The Queen's Head. That has ominous overtones, if you like. It was situated right next door to the Arbora Theater where all this month of She of the Veils they were presenting *The Vengeance of Kov Rheinglaf*, from the Third Book of *The Vicissitudes of Panadian the Ibreiver*, by, as you are well aware, Nalgre ti Liancesmot. These ordinary events went on, the inn was patronized, the theater attended and all the time the jikhorkdun lowered its shadow over all.

The noise of a busy city arose on the morning air. Slaves were hard at it. Guls were earning their hire. The gentry and nobles were thinking of getting up and facing the day. Carriages were already abroad. The hectic activity of the night in which the country carts trundled in with the produce to sustain the city's life had ceased and given way to the equally hectic business of the day.

And I had a Gnat of an armorer to find, and a beautiful Fristle fifi, and a right tearaway who passionately loved vollers.

This early in the morning the environs of the jikhorkdun held an exhausted, gray, hungover look. The guards shuffled. I had scrounged a piece of blue cloth from our camp and had replaced the red with the blue. I walked up as though I owned the place.

Well. . . .

At that time of day it was not too hard to find a way to let a gold coin change hands; a wink, a smile, and I was into the outer courts. Nothing—or very little—would get anyone into the inner courts. You had to be of the arena to be allowed there. I began my inquiries.

"Naghan the Gnat?" said a Khibil guard, his burly body straining his leather armor, his alert foxy face shrewd. "Well, now. . . ."

Another gold coin changed hands.

Always fancy themselves a cut above the ordinary run of diffs, Khibils. I get along with most of them. Their ruddy whiskers, their bright eyes, their keen fox-like faces, have been a comfort to me on many a battlefield. The gold vanished.

"Yes, dom. Naghan the Gnat—" He hesitated.

"Yes!"

"Aye, dom. Yes. I know him."

I quieted down. Maybe there were two men with the name of Naghan the Gnat. I nodded and the Khibil went on.

"See this thraxter?" He drew his sword and showed it to me. He pointed. The rivets of the hilt were indeed beautifully forged and fitted. I thought—I would not, dared not believe—they were Naghan's work. "He did that, the little feller, after I wrecked the blade on the armor of that bastard of a Rapa who—"

"Where is he?"

"I'm telling you, aren't I?"

"Yes." I made myself speak meekly. "You are, dom."

After all this time I was really going to find Naghan!

"He wanted to work for the reds. Course, the managers wouldn't have that." The shrewd fox face lowered on me. "I c'n tell you that we're doing well now because Naghan's armor is the best in the world. That's why. Course, he works hard. Has to, d'ye see? They whip him if he don't."

My fingernails bit into my skin, but I held still.

"Where is he?"

"Where? Why, where d'you expect him to be?"

I suppose, just about then, this smart Khibil more or less took a closer look at my face. He swallowed. His stiff red whiskers bristled. Then he said, rather quickly, "Why, he's in his forge, of course. Where else would an armorer be?"

Of course. The blue section might not be laid out in the same way as the red. I caught my breath, and then in what I considered a neutral voice, I said, "Tell me where the forge is, dom."

The Khibil jumped.

He pointed. "Down that alleyway between the barracks

and the second training ring. You can't miss it—stinks of charcoal and smoke and oil—"

I walked on.

The sound of a two-pound hammer in that particular rhythm: chang, ching-ching, chang, ching-ching, met me as I walked along. The smells were there, charcoal and smoke and oil. The furnace glowed cherry red. Three miserable-looking slaves cowered out of my way, carrying baskets of charcoal. I walked on. A man stood at his anvil, half-bent, striking neat, tidy blows, working with the utter absorption of a master craftsman.

This was no dramatic confrontation. There was no hectic rescue amid showers of arrows, no smiting away of sword blades to snatch Naghan to the saddle and gallop madly into the sunset.

I just walked up and said, "Lahal, Naghan, my name is Chaadur and—"

He whirled. He was just the same, thank Zair.

The hammer fell from his nerveless hand.

His stained leather apron with the marks of the fire on it, his small body all gristle and bone, his lively face, with the soot marks of his trade, sweating already, and his whole astonished gape endeared him to me all over again.

He began to stutter, and swallowed, and: "Dray!" and he would have gone on.

I said, "I am Chaadur the Iarvin. Best you mind that."

"Aye," he said. "Aye." He shook his head, and bent to retrieve his hammer.

"Talk later, O Gnat. Are Tilly and Oby here?"

"No." He wiped his nose and left black smudges. "Oby is with the yellows. I am not sure about Tilly. But, but . . . !"

"Later. Does anything detain you here?"

"Not a damn thing."

"Then bring your hammer and a few tools. Walk casually. We are on an important task for a great lord. Dernun?"

"Aye, and thanks be to Opaz—"

"Come on."

So we walked along the alleyway. We did not pass the way I had come, for gold would not have quieted that Khibil guard. When Khibils hire out as guards they hew to their own codes of honor.

"I can't just walk out, Dr—Chaadur!"

"You can and you will."

We went along past the second training ring, briskly, Naghan two paces abaft me.

The gate I chose for the exit was guarded by a Rhaclaw. Rhaclaws possess immense domed heads; that does not mean they have any more brains than any other race of diffs.

"Hey, dom," I said brusquely. "Here is a pickle. The kov needs an armorer at once—at once, mind—and if I do not fetch him a miserable slave I, and you, will rue the days we were born."

"Kov?" said the Rhaclaw. He looked at me vacantly. "What kov?"

"Rast!" I bellowed. "Do you bandy words with the kov! You are a fool if you do. Out of the way before the kov has you strung upside down and your head in the fire."

He blanched.

He lifted his spear and I brushed it aside, as one would brush aside a hanging branch in a garden, and walked on. I bellowed at Naghan.

"Yetch! *Grak!* The kov will have your tripes for harness points if you don't jump!"

"Quidang!" yelled Naghan, playing up nobly, and we hurried past the Rhaclaw and left him trying to regain the balance of his spear.

Mind you, the moment we passed beyond the angle of the wall we both did a quick right turn and darted into the shade of a few dusty tuffa trees, all wispy and drooping and springy.

"What—?" began Naghan.

"See that fellow walking toward us?"

"The man with the striped apron and the tray upon his head?"

"Yes. Fall down and writhe. Yell—but only a little."

Naghan immediately dropped to the ground, curled up and kicked his legs. He shrieked—but only a little.

The butcher's arm came over balancing his tray. He looked down. "What ails him? Is it catching?"

"Yes," I said, and put him to sleep. I caught the tray as he fell. Naghan put the lad's clothes on—they were not too big to pass muster—and he balanced the tray on his head.

"Throw the meat away, for the sweet sake of Opaz!"

"Aye, aye." Naghan tipped the tray over. "You wouldn't take meat out of the jikhorkdun, now, would you?" And he laughed.

"Walk a little ahead. I am not with you."

"Aye. How did you—?"

"Two things, O Gnat. One: gold. Two: a kaidur's knowledge. Talk later."

We walked on in the bright morning, just a butcher's man, probably a slave tricking himself out with a striped apron, and a hulking great fellow who'd as lief knock the butcher's lad over as not if he got in his way. We went along smoothly until we came to an area where the stalls and booths were shuttered and quiet. When the gas jets were lit this place would teem with people on their way to visit famous kaidurs, perhaps idling for a few moments and spending money on knickknacks. At least, we were clear of the inner precincts. Then I noticed that Naghan, balancing the tray on his head with one hand, kept a fast grip upon his leather toolbag with the other. The head of his hammer protruded at one end and the business end of a pair of tongs at the other.

Before I could hasten my steps four Rapa guards rounded an emporium which, although shuttered, proudly proclaimed on bills and hoardings that here the mysterious potions that gave love where it was sought might be purchased. The four Rapas were quarreling—well, that was their privilege. But perhaps because of their quarrel they chose to pick on the butcher's delivery lad.

"Hey! C'mere!"

And then, of course, they saw the leather tool kit, and immediately diagnosed the situation. This thieving rast of a butcher's slave had stolen a valuable bag of tools!

Because of the very ordinariness of the tool bag being picked up by Naghan, I had not noticed. Mea culpa! Again I considered that if this was the way Dray Prescot went about rescuing his friends, Zair help him. . . . And then it was all a flurry of action, and skipping and jumping and of skull bashing.

The four Rapas, out to earn their hire, clearly expected Naghan to run. They began to race toward him and, as I started off, so Naghan whipped the hammer from his bag, the tray going clattering into the Rapa's running feet. The hammer circled once and slogged into the first Rapa's middle. The second slashed his sword down, and then I slid the blade on my own thraxter and, regretfully, turned my wrist over and let the sword strike through.

The third and fourth yelled and plunged in and Naghan dropped to his hands and knees and chingled his hammer against the next Rapa's kneecap. I felt that for the poor devil of a Rapa. . . . Very nasty. My thraxter revolved in the air, the blade swept the last Rapa's weapon aside and the flat thunked down against the side of his head, spreading the feathers, and spreading the Rapa, too, sending him sprawling across the stones. Naghan stood up.

"Run," I said. "Yes, I think we should run now."

So we ran.

We got to the next courtyard and then slowed our pace and walked out across a roadway where they were exercising a gaggle of totrixes. The lumbering six-legged riding animals went clip-clup-clop past. Totrixes are used in the arena. No true lover of the marvelous saddle animals of Kregen cares for that.

We squeezed along out of the way and crossed the road and went toward the gate where only a Fristle stood guard. Most of the outer sections, open to the public, needn't have been guarded at all. But this passion for posting sentries everywhere is quite practical. For one thing, it impresses the common folk. And, for another, it gives the bodyguard something to do.

The Fristle was brushing up his whiskers with his little personal brush, all smothered in tawdry imitation jewelry, and twisting his head about the better to get just the right angle he wanted. He had taken off his helmet. His fierce cat's face was contorted with the effort of seeing his whiskers in his pocket mirror. When we hoved up he cocked an eye at us, in annoyance. I suppose, logically, that Fristle was near to death, in a cold and calculating way. Had he spoken out of turn, had he tried to stop us, had our blows just missed being nonlethal, then he would have died. Instead of all that unpleasantness he waved the brush at us and went back to his cat's whiskers. We walked through the open gateway.

That Fristle possessed remarkably fine whiskers.

"They're a poor lot of mercenaries, aren't they, Naghan?"

Naghan kept the striped apron. He wanted to skip and jump and I put a hand on his shoulder and pushed him down.

"Yes," he said at last. "Outside. But, inside—!"

"I know."

Halfway to The Queen's Head Naghan discarded the striped apron. He wore shabby old clothes, a holey tunic and a pair of sandals that were falling to pieces.

"Shove the tools into the bag, so they don't show."

Naghan pushed the hammer down and then, as we approached the inn, looked up. "You'll never get me in there!"

"Not like that, no."

We went around the back and I told Naghan to wait quietly as I dug into my urvivel's saddlebag and produced the clothes I hoped would fit Naghan. He put them on, a decent dark brown tunic and a pair of almost brand-new sandals, and then he flexed his arms and hung his tool bag alongside the saddlebag, turned to me and said, "Now what?"

"I have hired a room in the inn. It is quiet. You can stay there without attracting attention. I'll leave enough silver." I spoke matter-of-factly, having worked all this obvious detail out already. "Now, tell me all you know of Oby. His whereabouts. You said he worked for the yellows?"

Naghan the Gnat put his hands on his hips. "No," he said.

I glared, shocked. "You—" I began.

"You may be the prince majister of Vallia. All very well. But Oby and Tilly are my comrades, as well. I shall not tell you what little I know of Oby's whereabouts unless—"

I managed to close my mouth. I said, "Unless?"

"Well, it's obvious, isn't it? I'm not letting you go running off to rescue them on your own."

Talk about an echo, bouncing between Naghan the Gnat and those fearsome fellows of my Guard in Vallia!

## CHAPTER SEVENTEEN

# Of the Eye of a Vollerman

There is little communication—for obvious reasons—between the four color corners. Each corner is a world to itself. And the area reserved for the queen's kaidurs is, in those terms, a double world to itself. We found Oby flat on his back under a half-dismantled voller. He worked—as a slave—for one of the managers of the yellows who fought for the diamond zhantil.

Naghan kicked his foot. He bent down.

"Oby! Come on out—and quietly."

"Go away, rast, whoever you are," said Oby's familiar voice. He had been a mere youngster, and now he was a man, nimble, strong, adept with a knife, obsessed with vollers.

I said, "I am Chaadur the Iarvin, and Naghan the Gnat kicked your foot, for he is no respecter of persons."

Oby came out so fast he hit his head a crack on the rim of the voller. He rolled out and looked up, swearing. "By Vox! It is—but—but—"

Oby's left eye was puffed and swollen and closed to a mere tear-oozing slit. It was a shiny purple color, with tasteful admissions of green and black.

"Damned overseer gave me that. . . . Naghan? And. . . ."

"Chaadur," I said. "Make no great fuss—"

"But the guards?" Then Oby saw the four Fristle guards slumbering at the foot of the trestles on which the voller was supported. The wooden shed allowed a mingled radiance of the suns to fall through cracks between the warped boards.

"Precisely. Now gather what you want. We will leave here now."

Oby's wits had always been like quicksilver. He was off the platform, scooping up a raggedy cloak of off-cuts of ancient gray blankets sewn together. He, too, picked up a leather tool bag.

"D'you know the way?" He was, at once, apprised of the situation.

"Yes. Talk later."

So, quietly, we went out from that area of the yellows. We did, this time, tend to leave a trail of unconscious guards. But I was in a hurry. A single quick question and a surly answer elicited that Oby had no chance, no chance in a Herrelldrin hell of stealing a voller.

"You'll have to ditch that cloak."

Oby looked annoyed. We walked not too close together along an alleyway between booths on one side and cages on the other. The wild-animal smell remained strong and evocative, but all the cages were empty. Tame slaves scurried with buckets and brooms and pungent ibroi. The disinfectant smell battled feebly with those primeval odors of the wilds.

"It took me a season and a half to collect all the scraps of blanket and sew them together. But if I must, I must."

The multi-gray cloak went in an arc into a trashbin where the slaves dumped what they cleared out of the cages. We walked on. When, at last feeling free, Oby and Naghan reached my urvivel and I could fish out clothes for Oby that only just fit, they began to jabber. They could have talked all day and all night.

"Yes, I know," I said, interrupting. "When you found yourselves sorcerously transported back here. But we aren't out of the woods yet. There is Tilly."

Oby looked up from the knife I had, as a matter of course, included in the kit I'd brought for him.

"I know where they took her. She is a serving wench in the household of a nulsh of a noble called Noran. Vad Noran."

"I know him." I felt the glow of successful accomplishment. "This is good news—if Tilly remains unharmed."

"She has sharp teeth—and her nails." Here Oby shook his head. "Fristle fifis can scratch a fellow's eyes out."

"If they've a mind to it," added Naghan, comfortably.

"That is all well and good. Now you two will stay—"

"I have given you my thoughts on that, prince," said Naghan, very stuffily.

Oby said, "I do not think I shall stay behind—prince."

When these two princed me—for they did not know I had become the emperor—they were pulling my leg, being sarcastic, in modern parlance, sending me up rotten. I sighed.

"I own I am glad to have you with me, but. . . ."

"That's settled, then," said Oby briskly.

You may be sure there was much to talk about, fathoms and fathoms of it, as we took ourselves off to the sumptuous villa belonging to Vad Noran. I wondered what I would do to him if he had harmed Tilly. I had no doubts at all what Oby and Naghan would do, no doubts whatsoever.

Our new clothes made us look respectable horters of the city, gentlemen with a purse of gold and a cutting way with slaves. Any searches for runaway slaves from the arena would take time to be mounted outside the jikhorkdun. As Naghan said, "They'll wonder, at first. They'll not believe we could have won free. There is a little time."

"We will make the time," said Oby. I glanced at him, seeing in his dark, scowling face with the strong lines that suffering had etched there but a pale ghost of the sprightly lad I had once known.

Then he laughed and said, stretching his arms wide, "By Vox! What it is to feel free!" As he spoke his whole face changed, the scowling lines vanished, his mobile lips curved and he looked like his old self. Then he winced and swore again, feelingly. "My damned eye!"

When I explained that as soon as Tilly was with us we would have to take a voller to fly to Vallia they treated it as the most natural thing in the world. Oby said he could fly anything that flew, and repair anything that was broken—always excepting the silver boxes.

Naghan said, "I suppose some fat notor of Huringa will miss his voller. I'd like to roast 'em all!"

When you looked at it like that, at the fact that the man from whom we would steal the voller sat in his plush seat in the amphitheater and howled with glee as some poor wretch was disemboweled or pierced through. . . . That did tend to reorientate my pious doubts. All the same, and I did not confide the decision to these two, I would reimburse the man for his flier.

Even if he was. . . . I said, "It might be possible to seize a voller from this Vad Noran."

"Capital!" said Naghan.

"Diashum," said Oby. And, indeed, the thought was rather

magnificent, rather capital. So we walked on in the strengthening rays of Far and Havil, and the hour of mid approached and I licked my lips and cocked an eye at them.

"There will be time," said Oby.

"I am dry," said Naghan. "And it is a long time, a very long time, since I have tasted anything respectable."

So we went into a moderate eating establishment and I watched these two stuff their faces. The place was decent and doing a brisk trade and we attracted no attention. The clepsydra on the shelf dripped away.

As a simple precaution I had provided us with red favors. This might not fool the searchers for long if Oby or Naghan were recognized, but it might give us a mur or two in which to jump.

When we went out I began to feel itchy. I know that feeling. It comes over me when I shilly-shally, and yet I was not delaying now, was I? So why should I feel this unease?

There was no denying that uncomfortable sensation. I was in the throes of one of those itchy sessions when I shilly-shally. The suns shone, there was a pleasant breeze, we were comfortably filled with good if plain food, we could jingle silver in our pouches, we were armed with thraxters taken from slumbering guards. And yet. . . . Yes, we walked the streets of a hostile city that would show no mercy if we were caught. Thc stink of the jikhorkdun pervaded the place. But that should not trouble me overmuch, surely? A whiff of peril? Never. . . .

Something was itching away at the back of my old vosk skull and I was too dim-witted to grasp it and drag it forward into the light.

Unmok!

I stopped.

Naghan and Oby stared at me.

"How would you two," I said, "like to be slave again?"

I gave them just enough time to start reacting nicely, and then I said through their gapes, "We need to find three juts at once." I did not specify the type of riding animal we would take, saying jut covered anything we picked up, from a totrix to a preysany. I started off walking rapidly toward the nearest tavern. They hurried to keep pace, and they did not expostulate or call out questions. We needed to remain inconspicuous, and they were probably more aware of that than I was.

We found three freymuls—the poor man's zorca—their

hides sleek and well cared for, tethered up at the side of the tavern. We slit the leather hitching thongs and mounted up. At a sedate walk we went out and along the avenue, mingling with the traffic. We looked so ordinary that no one was going to remember us, particularly as a Hyrklanan hat was hung over the saddle of my freymul. I put it on and pulled the brim down and slouched in the saddle, and we rode out to the camp where Unmok was busy working himself up into a frenzy.

"It seems to me," I said as we reined up and dismounted, "that you, Naghan, had best be Nath the Long (which is another example of the warped Kregan sense of humor) and you, Oby, had best be Nalgre the Eye." I started off for the tents and then swung back. "Oh, and I am Jak the Shot, here. Remember."

People on Kregen do remember names. They know if they forget too often the chances are they'll wind up with a length of steel in their guts investigating their backbones.

Unmok's middle left stump quivered. His little Och body quivered. His face quivered.

"And you've come back, Jak, to—"

"I come in friendship, as ever, Unmok." I made the pappattu, introducing Unmok and Nath the Long and Nalgre the Eye. The Llahals changed to Lahals. "There is no time for me to explain, Unmok. You know I have work to do."

"Aye." Unmok eyed my two companions, and Froshak eased nearer, his hand on his knife hilt.

"Your werstings. If you have not yet decided to sell them to Vad Noran, then I will buy them from you and sell them to him. I warn you—I will sell for more than I buy."

"Naturally."

He digested this. Then: "When?"

"Now."

"Well—"

"Now. Right this instant—as soon as I take them in."

"But, Jak, why?"

I breathed in, then out. "I have to see Noran and this is the surest and quickest way. You know how he hungers for the werstings."

Unmok clasped his upper right over his stump. "Then we are still partners? You will make the next voyage with me?"

Now, as you know, I am a rogue, a reprobate, a sinner among men. I have done things for which I am heartily repentant; but in the same circumstances I know I'd probably do the self-same things again. I try not to hurt people. Now I thought I understood what that itchy feeling had been about. Struggling to answer Unmok's unanswerable question, I saw. I said, "A moment, Unmok." Then, to Oby and Naghan: "You came here together? You know what I mean. Tilly was with you?"

They nodded. "Yes. We were taken up into slavery together." They had evidently decided not to risk names at all.

So that was it, that was the cause of my unease.

"There is no time to lose." When you say that and mean it, it sounds damned different, let me tell you!

Oby saw it, and then Naghan. "They'll know! They'll put two and two together . . . !"

"Yes." I turned back. "Unmok. We have been partners, we are still partners. I must see Noran—*at once!*—and the werstings will turn the trick. Please. We will talk about our future plans afterward."

He did not look convinced. "Have I your word?"

I shook my head. "No, Unmok. For any one of the many gods in their mutual wisdoms might strike me down. I must go. I will take the werstings."

My thraxter flicked out. Froshak halted at once.

"Froshak the Shine! I value your friendship. Do not seek to prevent this."

Froshak said nothing, as was his wont. But his knife, that knife so like my old sailor knife, slid up and down in its sheath.

Oby looked shattered. "By Vox," he said, and he spoke in a shaky whisper, staring up at me. "I've been saying we had plenty of time, speaking so grandly. We've plenty of time. Fool! Onker!" He began to curse himself then, and with a manic spring leaped for his freymul. He was up on the animal's back and driving in his heels as I got to him.

"Still, Oby! Wait! Think!"

"I've waited too long—if they've—Tilly—"

"Think! This rast Noran will not let us in—he thinks I spy on him for the queen—we will only enter by a subterfuge."

All the time I was holding onto him and dragging at the freymul. Naghan ran across and joined in. It took a little of the precious time we had been squandering; but we calmed Oby down.

"No time to fix you out as slaves." They had incontinently thrown their gray slave breechclouts away when they'd donned the clothes I'd brought. "Unmok!" I bellowed. "In this show me the value of your friendship! Let me have the werstings and the slaves to run them." I turned my face to Oby and Naghan. "You run the slaves running the werstings."

Unmok hovered, pitched to a frenzy between despair and hope. I felt for him. Also, I feared—oh, how I feared!—for what might happen to golden-furred Tilly while we delayed.

I picked up the thraxter, for that had been dropped any old how in my spring after Oby. Froshak had not moved.

Unmok unwrapped himself, letting his middle left stump jerk up, his right upper lifting. His right middle joined his left upper, and then spread wide. He bowed.

"Very well, Jak the Shot. For our friendship—new and yet of great value to me. Take the werstings. Froshak also. And, Jak—" Here his little Och face screwed up into a fearsome grimace. "I shall come with you to make sure we get a good price from Vad Noran."

There could be no further argument.

So, mounted up, urging our mounts on, we left that deserted camp. We followed the slaves who ran fleetly dragged along by the werstings. The killer dogs howled and barked and ululated, racing ahead, straining in passion against their collars and the long leather leashes.

## CHAPTER EIGHTEEN

# In the Recalcitrants House

"Obfaril!" said Naghan the Gnat. The sword smith spoke with a tone of sharp rebuke. We roared along after the slaves and the werstings, Huringa and a beautiful golden-furred Fristle fifi ahead. "Young Oby!" said Naghan. "The managers will not connect us that quickly. Yes, they will in time—"

"We have no time, Gnat!"

"Time. It will take them time to connect. Two mangy slaves run off—they'll expect to recapture them very quickly. Only when they do not will they think to look deeper. Then the records will be hard to find—there will be time." Naghan clenched his fists around the reins and lifted his head defiantly. "Dear Opaz! There has *got* to be time enough!"

The mention of Vad Noran's name and the business that brought us to the city did not perhaps carry as much weight with the guards as the bright fangs and lolling tongues of the werstings. Their howls echoed under the arch of the city gate.

"They'll have to be muzzled in the city." The Deldar of the guard swelled his chest against his armor. He wore a scale-metal kax, and was no doubt proud of that. "You know the laws are strict—"

I was about to knock him over, not having time to argue about the matter, when Unmok said quickly, "Of course, Deldar. The slaves are doing it now." I looked. They were. They did not have too much trouble fitting the bronze muzzles, and the dogs' tongues still lolled, evilly. Unmok knew his business. Had he not accompanied us with the tame slaves. . . .

We pressed on, striking directly toward Noran's villa.

Noran loved ostentation. His villa, a palace in miniature, was equipped with all the paraphernalia for gracious living. He boasted his own swimming pool, his own ball courts and his own small private arena. The cadade happened to be in the courtyard into which we were ushered, talking to four or five of his men, and I heartily wished him and his men a million dwaburs away from here. Oby glanced at me, and Naghan licked his lips.

"The master will come at once, almost at once, I feel sure," said the majordomo, dancing on pointed toes as he led us through. His retinue of slaves and fan-wavers and scroll-bearers, with a hefty Brokelsh to keep them in order, tagged on. Our slaves stayed with the werstings in the yard. My plan, if you wish to dignify the scheme by that name, was for us three to slip away and get into the slave quarters. We would pick up three slave breechclouts from the first three to walk by. It is easy enough to become a slave on Kregen, the trick—and it is often a damned difficult one—is to become free.

Oby nodded his head toward the cadade. The man was big and rugged, with a florid face. He was apim, like us, although some of his men were diffs, as was normal. He wore a splendid bronze kax, trimmed with silver, and his helmet bore a panache and plumes. He happened to be a Jiktar—well, a noble in Noran's position would have to employ a reasonable rank as the captain of his household guards—and he looked useful. No doubt it was sure that Noran paid him far more than the cadade could earn by hiring out as a mercenary in the wars.

As we padded along I reflected that I could not understand the attitude of many of the nobility on that score. Mercenaries fighting a war are one thing, but they are not as important as the mercenaries you hire to protect your skin. No, sir! Not in many parts of Kregen!

I didn't want Vallia to go down that road.

We walked past a clump of gregarian bushes and Unmok said in a throaty whisper, "Leave the talking to me."

"With the greatest pleasure," I said. "But, Unmok, we will not be with you. When we vanish you need not mention us. If asked, you say we must have returned to the werstings."

He cocked his face up at me. "But, Jak—"

"Around that column with the statue of Mahgoh of the Two smiling at the top. There we will leave you."

"What will—"

"You must, if necessary, deny me. Say the truth, that we have only recently become partners. Froshak will bear witness. Talk your way out of it, if necessary, man of the nets."

"But—*Jak*—!"

The statue of Mahgoh of the Two cast a large shadow. We entered the shadow from the left side and as the others walked on into the mingled rays of the suns shine we three skipped away around the corner and vanished from their sight.

The vanishing trick was, if I may say so, neatly done.

The urgency began to bite into us. Not one of us liked the idea that the cadade had been in the outer court. Perhaps news of the runaway slaves had already been received? Perhaps the guards from the jikhorkdun were even now closeted with Noran, telling him, hatching a plan?

No immediate signs of the household being aroused alarmed us. Slaves came and went with the usual hurried slave shuffle. The shadows rested on the walls and paths, tinged with green and red, and the muted surf roar of the villa continued. In ten murs or so we had three slave breechclouts, and three slaves slumbered under the hedge. Poor devils, that was probably their first decent rest in months.

We carried our weapons and gear bundled up, acting the part of slaves carrying a burden for the master. Then we plunged boldly into the slave warrens.

Our very first question had elicited the reply, gasped out with a fist around throat, that, yes, the golden-furred Fristle fifi was here, quartered in the Recalcitrants House.

Not a one of us liked the sound of that, by Vox!

Outside the Recalcitrants House a hefty Rapa, stripped to the waist, was flogging a Xaffer. I stopped.

The walls lofted here, with spiked tops, and the house itself was pierced only with small windows, high up, barred. The courtyard echoed with the Xaffer's shrieks.

With his nervous laugh, Naghan said, "It is no business of ours."

"No." I forced myself to walk on. "But what kind of insensitive offal orders a Xaffer flogged?"

Xaffers are diffs of a strange remote race, vague, used when slaves as stylors and in other like capacities. They never—or practically never—give trouble. We passed the wooden triangle and I saw the dark bloodstains fouling the wood. The Rapa went on lashing, and a stylor in a blue tunic at the side chalked down the strokes on his slate.

The door of the Recalcitrants House was narrow. A Rapa guard held his post there. I took Naghan by the ear and ran him up to the guard.

"Here's another one—and I'll get an extra portion of palines for bringing him in." Naghan was squirming most realistically. Oby chipped in and gripped his flailing arm.

The Rapa hawked and spat. His feathers quivered.

"You scum—sell your own mothers for a bowl of porridge."

"Yes," I said, approaching fast. I let go Naghan, who spun away in Oby's grip, kicked the guard betwixt wind and water, and caught him as he fell. We all bundled inside. Oby had the guard's spear out and pointing along the corridor. It was deserted and all the doors were shut.

"So far, so good." I picked the Rapa up by his wattled neck. His eyes were unfocused, and spittle ran out of his vulturine beak. "Tell me where the golden-furred Fristle fifi is chained up, and you may live."

He gabbled.

I shook him.

His eyes popped. He slobbered. Then: "Cell eleven."

"Cell eleven," I said to Oby.

Naghan rubbed his ear with his left hand and lifted the key ring from the guard's belt with the other. Then he and Oby padded off along the corridor.

"I see you wear a red favor, so do I," I said to the guard, trying to make refined conversation. "I hope our fortunes improve soon."

He boggled away, and then he spat out, "You are mad."

"Oh, aye. And my friends. Believe it."

The clitter-clatter of keys followed by the wheeze of a heavy door drew my attention. Oby and Naghan went into cell eleven. Presently they came out. Between them walked Tilly. I own to a throb of thankfulness—she could walk. She looked dazed. She was trying to rub her wrists, and wincing. Much of that glorious golden fur had been rubbed away, the skin raw. Oby and Naghan supported her.

"But—" she was saying, half laughing and half crying. "But—dear Oby—dear Naghan—"

This was all going splendidly.

With Tilly safe, why, what was there that would stop us now?

The Rapa guard gave a twitch and I shook him, just to remind him. Tilly saw the guard, and she saw me.

"Hush, Tilly," I said. "I am Chaadur the Iarvin."

"Yes," she said. "They told me. But it is all so, so—" Then she broke open those inner springs that men are not supposed to have and that they do have, witness the feelings they try to hide. "I have been chained, *master,* and not in silver chains, and not by you."

By the digusting diseased liver and lights of Makki Grodno! But that took us back, Tilly and me, and her flirty golden tail, and our talk of silver chains for impudent fifis!

I swallowed.

"You're going to be all right now. You're safe. All we have to do is find a voller—and we're free and flying."

"Yes, master."

She knows I detest her calling me that.

"Let us clear off, then," said Naghan. He looked about as though the shadows would leap on him.

Tilly held onto Oby and Naghan. "There is a Fristle—he has tried to be kind to me here. I am new here. He is called Fordan. He is locked in one of these cells."

"Open them all," I said. "But step lively. I do not think these slaves will break for their freedom, being cowed. But it will add a complication." The Rapa in my fist had swooned away so I dropped him. "Start at the far end and warn 'em all to silence. Not that they will."

The doors opened one by one. A motley collection staggered out when the chains were unfettered. Some refused to budge, aware they had no hope of extended liberty and fearful of the flogging at the end. We could not take them all. The corridor turned with a dog leg at the end, and there were more cells, some holding more than one inmate. We opened them all.

Fordan turned out to be a strong-bodied Fristle, his cat's face bewhiskered splendidly, his fur a lustrous ginger with gold and black patterns. I liked the cut of his jib, even though his face was swollen from beatings. My dealings with Fristle men had often been ambivalent at best, and downright hostile at worst. Probably, I considered as we went along opening doors, probably Tilly's quick and instinctive gesture of pleasure at seeing Fordan, and her little squeal of horror at the state of his face, predisposed me in his favor.

"I thank you, notor—" he began.

"Thank Tilly," I said. And then, with meaning, I added, "My friends and I will gladly kill anyone who hurts Tilly."

And Fordan, quickly, on a breath said, "And I, too!"

"Then stand just inside the doorway and keep watch."

"At once, notor." He went off, limping, making nothing of the pains he must be suffering from his swollen face.

I said to Tilly, "A likely lad."

Her little chin went up. "Well—I like him!"

A small crowd gathered in the corridor, bemused, wondering what to do for the best. I threw open a door and said to the golden-furred numim who attempted to strike me down, "Steady, steady, dom! We're letting you out—no noise."

The lion man let his clenched fist drop. He reached the end of his chain. Quickly I unlocked him. He looked savage, fierce, with such anger in him as boded ill for those who had chained him and abused him.

"Letting us out—where to?"

"That is for you to decide. I have no love for Noran, nor have you, as I judge it. If we can break free, then you are free. If not, then you are slave again."

"I shall not be slave again!"

His lion face expressed absolute determination. He must have put up a fight before they chained him. He flexed his muscles, no sign of the pain reflected on his features, and pushed past to the door.

"Perhaps you would like to stand at the outer door, and—"

"Aye."

He went along to stand with Fordan. Fristle and numim stood side by side, concealed, looking out. I fancied if a guard walked unwarily by he would face two formidable opponents in these two. They did not speak to each other, and I guessed they were strangers.

Only a few doors were left.

The crowd grew restless. And who can blame them? If they were going to break free, they wanted to start *now*.

For every one who stayed miserably in his cell, too frightened to venture forth to certain punishment, there were two who came out filled with vigorous determination to run for it and never be caught again.

There were only two doors left.

"Let them go," I called to Fordan. He nodded and stepped aside and the crowd ran out. Pretty soon their uproar would attract the guards. We would be well away by then, taking our own chances. Most of the slaves made up their own minds what they would do; it was every man for himself, *sauve qui peut,* and to the devil with the hindmost.

A girl tottered out of the last door. She looked in a distressed state. She wore the remnants of fine clothes, and there were weal marks on her naked back. Her hair tangled in an untidy mess about her face, and tear streaks cut through the grime. She saw me. Her eyes, wide brown eyes, closed. She tottered and Naghan went to catch her, thinking she was about to fall. But she was not falling; she was going into the full incline.

I said, "My name is Chaadur the Iarvin. Remember that, Fransha. Now we are taking you home."

She started to cry.

Tilly put a hand out, and the gesture of friendship from the Fristle girl spoke volumes. One distress called to another.

"You know her?" Tilly did not sound surprised.

"Aye. The Lady Fransha, who ran off with her lover and put all Vallia into a turmoil—"

"No!" Fransha looked up, shaking. "No, majis—no, Chaadur! Voinderam and I were kidnapped! By the Racters!"

I felt the ice clench around my heart. The damned Racters!

"Tell us as we run, Fransha. You are with friends, now."

We stepped over the Rapa guard. The suns shine smote down. The dwindling uproar from the slaves indicated they had split up, as we had anticipated, and were running every which way. Some of them would be running in circles, I had no doubt. But some, too, would win free.

The Rapa who had been flogging the Xaffer lay with his whip wrapped around his throat. There was no sign of the stylor and his chalk and slate. The Xaffer was gone, too.

We crossed the open space swiftly, and now we ran with naked steel in our fists. Fordan stayed close to Tilly.

"The Racters sent a note to each of us, saying the other must desperately meet. So I went to the meeting place, and Ortyg went too, and—"

"The Racters surprised you and kidnapped you, and sold you as slaves!"

"Yes and no." We slowed our run to a walk and Fordan assisted Tilly and Oby and I helped Fransha. "No, Strom Luthien wanted to kill us out of hand—"

"He would."

"But the Kov of Falkerdrin would not permit it. He said

we would go to his estates and be held prisoner until the Time of Troubles was over."

"Nath Famphreon, you mean? The son of Natyzha?"

"Yes."

"I know him. In this, he acted as I would expect, I think. He has notions of honor and loyalty. The pity of it is, in one cynical sense, that his loyalty is to his mother."

"He was kind to us. He apologized for what had been done. And I believed him."

We went down an alleyway between hedges, heading toward a squat, flat-roofed building supported on many thick pillars. That had the look of a landing platform.

"Nath Famphreon betrayed you?"

"No." Fransha was now gaining better control of herself. Her memories of what she had gone through were being pushed aside as she spoke of the very beginning of her ordeal. "No. Our airboat had to come down—well, you know how unreliable they are. We were captured by flutsmen. The kov was not with us, and his men fought, but they were overborne. He employs mighty paktuns to work for him. But some were slain and others were captured. We were sold. . . ." She stopped. She did not like to recall this part of her adventures; it brought back the hideous nightmare, and she shook.

Tilly said, "Leave her alone for now."

"That is the platform," said Fordan. He carried the Rapa guard's thraxter. I was pleased to see he gripped it in the fashion of one who knew how to use the sword.

"No, Tilly." I spoke as gently as I could. They all jumped anyway. "No, there is yet one more thing I must know."

Fransha laughed, too shrilly. "Ortyg? My love, Ortyg Voinderam?" She was shaking so much now her hair swung and matted before her face. "I do not know. I have not seen him since they brought me to this hideous place!"

The racter party had been very clever. They had spiked our guns in the matter of our plans to invade them. But, all the same, I was glad to have confirmation that Phu-Si-Yantong was not instigating this latest plot against us in Vallia.

We paused in the shadows of the landing platform. An ornate staircase built of stone, with iron balustrades and chemzite facings, led up to the roof. Hyrklana is rich in iron. On the roof the overhanging eaves of hangars for the fliers told us the private flierdrome was of some capacity.

"Listen," I said. "Other escaped slaves will probably come

this way, seeking vollers. You, Naghan, and you, Oby, will see to it that our party gets onto the roof and into a voller. Fordan will care for Tilly, I feel sure—"

The Fristle nodded. "With my life."

"So that leaves the Lady Fransha to you two."

"And you?"

"Listen! Take a suitable voller and lift off at once—"

"Now just a minute!" started Oby, furiously.

Naghan began expostulating.

I quieted them down.

"Listen, you two! I want you up and away and out of it, with the two ladies. There are still chores I must do here. For one thing, I can't just walk off and leave old Unmok the Nets, can I? He risked it coming here with us. And there is Ortyg Voinderam. If he is here I want to find him. That is for the good of Vallia." I did not add that, also, I had an appointment with Prince Tyfar and Jaezila and their retainers, Barkindrar the Bullet, Nath the Shaft and Kaldu.

"But *we* can't just fly off and leave *you*!"

"You can. And you will. I came to Hyrklana to get you three out of the jikhorkdun. Thank Opaz, that has been done—or nearly done as soon as we bag ourselves a voller. And we've found the Lady Fransha, which is a blessing, and unexpected, although all of a piece, given the habits of flutsmen and slavers. But I have other things to do."

Well, there in the shadows, with the shouts of guards beginning to rise from the grounds of the villa, these two wanted to start a fierce whispered argument. I wouldn't have that. I was somewhat fierce.

In the end we padded up the stairs and knocked over a few guards who wanted to stop us, and we found a palatial voller with a cabin amidships and a steeply lofting poop aft. She had fast lines. She was worth much gold in Hyrklana and a small fortune in Vallia. Oby said she would do.

"No more arguments! Up and away. All the way home to Vallia." I gave them a very rapid rundown on the altered state of the empire, and cautioned them to beware of everyone until they reached the imperial palace in Vondium. I did not think that would have fallen again. They wanted to know all about the Time of Troubles, but Fransha said she would explain. She called me majister as a matter of course. When, in his biting tones of argumentative sarcasm, Naghan addressed me as prince this and prince that, Fransha looked alarmed.

"But, Naghan—this is the emperor!"

Naghan looked at me. Oby shut his one good eye.

"Emperor?"

"It doesn't matter," I said impatiently. "For the sweet sake of Opaz! Take off. Guard yourselves. I'll be back home in Vondium in no time." I told them that Delia and a gang of cutthroats might be following me and added that they were to be told what I'd told Naghan and Oby. Privately, I hoped the two parties would not meet up. If they did I knew what would happen. The whole raving bunch would come roaring down to Huringa ready to take the place apart stone by stone.

Of course, that might be a Very Good Thing, as Deb-Lu might say; it did not happen to fit in with the plans we had for Vallia. First things first.

"Now," I said, and a brusqueness harshened my voice. "Get in the voller and take off!"

And then a party of slaves ran shrieking into the area below the landing platform. That did it. Fordan helped Tilly up into the voller, and I noticed how they both observed the fantamyrrh as they entered. Oby turned to Fransha. But she was looking over the parapet, her fists gripped on the stone.

"Ortyg!" she said, choking, shaking, trembling uncontrollably. "My love! Ortyg!"

Down there vicious guards were herding slaves into a huddle. Whips rose and fell. Shrieks rent the air. And, clearly in the mess of slaves, beaten to his knees, Ortyg Voinderam staggered and fell.

## CHAPTER NINETEEN

# Mazdo the Splandu

What a confounded mess!

I swung to glare at my friends.

"Stay here!" I spat it out. I know my face must have blazed that old devilish look, I know I sounded like the craziest of all mad emperors. "Stay here. Keep a watch from the voller. Slay any guard who tries to molest you. If I fail—lift off."

"But . . . !"

"We will. . . ."

"We won't let you. . . ."

"By the Black Chunkrah! Will you do as I ask?" Then, cunning with the frantic pressures of the moment, I bellowed, "For the sakes of Tilly and Fransha!"

They had not seen what I had glimpsed among the trees and shrubbery beyond the corner of the landing platform. A small stairway led down over there. Without giving them any further chance of argument, I leaped away, raced across the roof.

Their faces must have shown shock and horror in that fraught moment—for I ran away from the ornate stairs with their iron balustrades and chemzite facings. I ran away from the brutal guards and their whips below. I ran away from Ortyg Voinderam, so cruelly beaten into the ground.

I, Dray Prescot, Lord of Strombor, Krozair of Zy, must have seemed to them to be fleeing.

Just as my head whipped below the level of the platform I half turned and bellowed, "Do as I say as you value your lives—and my friendship!"

Then I was down, haring like a maniac for the secluded path leading to the space before the landing platform.

Along that path, hurrying, came the cadade.

With him half ran, half scurried, a gesticulating guard, a Fristle, who had evidently brought the bad news to the cadade. The florid face was more flushed still, the eyes mean, the jaw fiercely set. Sweat dripped from the brim of that splendid helmet with its panache and plumes. He hurried. But he would not sully his own dignity by running.

That pompous self-esteem of his gave me the chance to get down the little back stairs from the landing platform and into the corridor between the hedges.

There was little time for finesse. The Fristle saw me coming and started to yank out his sword. He was slow.

The cadade let rip with a blinding bellow of rage and ripped out his own over-elaborate sword.

Now, I had no wish to slay them, either of them. But this had to be done nip and tuck. I belted into the Fristle, slid the blow of the thraxter, slammed his head back with a simple and unsubtle right cross. Before he slumped to the ground I'd ducked, spun, kicked the cadade and then dug my thumb into his windpipe. After that it was a mercy to tap him alongside the head—having first picked up his sword and tipped off his helmet. He went to sleep.

A voice said, "By Opaz! As neat a piece of work as—"

The voice stopped. It stopped abruptly and on a choked grunt. The reason for that was my fist wrapped around the throat of the speaker. I recognized the golden-furred numim we had released from the Recalcitrants House. I let him go and stepped back and instantly bent to the unconscious cadade.

"You were nearly a dead man there, dom," I said, matter-of-factly, stripping off the ornate bronze and silver kax, ripping the silver-tissue vest away, getting at the blue tunic beneath. The kilt was mostly bronze and silver. That went on me first, wrapped and thonged with swift and sure knots. I was driving my arms into the tunic before the numim got his breath back.

"You—you are mighty quick, dom."

"When necessary." I still did not pause, dispensing with the silver tissue—it had ripped clean across, anyway—getting the kax on. Without being asked, the lion man stepped up and helped me buckle up the straps.

"My thanks, dom—"

"My fist wrapped around the throat of the speaker."

"I am Mazdo the Splandu." He spoke the name simply. But I grasped much by the cognomen—not that there was time for the pappattu. I had to get out into the open space among the slaves before my bunch of revolutionaries came boiling down those ornate stairs to rescue Voinderam themselves.

"There are vollers up there. You had best take one swiftly—I have other work to do."

"I shall take an airboat from these rasts. But, cannot I help—?"

"Again, my thanks, Mazdo the Splandu. But—no. Best for you to take your freedom while it is still on offer."

The cadade's sandals would have to be high-thonged, of course. I slapped the leather thongs about as fast as I could. My heart was beginning to let me know it could beat a right old tattoo. The sword belts, the last check to make sure everything was shipshape, and finally, grabbing the helmet and lifting it up and feeling the weight, and settling it on my head. The kax strained as I raised my arms. But the cadade was a big fellow, as I've said, and I could wear his armor albeit with some constricting discomfort.

"You—"

"If you must, call me Chaadur. Now I am off. Remberee, Mazdo the Splandu. We may meet again."

I bustled along, half-turning, and then banishing that superb specimen of the race of diffs we call numims—lionmen—from my mind. He called after me, soft-voiced, "If we do meet again, Chaadur the Sudden, I stand in your debt."

I lifted my arm, not looking back, and so rounded the last hedge.

Here I concentrated. I knew the lineaments of the cadade. I forced my face into an approximation, thinking of what Deb-Lu-Quienyin had said, pumping up the blood, getting a flush to spread. Mind you, that wasn't difficult, not after the rushing about I'd just been doing. I was not exactly panting, but I was breathing faster than usual when I rounded the end of the landing platform and paced rapidly out toward the knot of cowed slaves and the belligerent guards.

They sprang to instant attention as the glory of the bronze and silver kax, the waving plumes, the glittering helmet, bore down on them.

Now for it. . . .

I started bellowing in the hoarse commanding voice I had heard in the outer courtyard. Deb-Lu was right. Habit, acceptance, seeing the clothes and hearing the vicious words of command, all these things added up to the cadade to these guards. I was the cadade. Who else?

This was quite clearly a random collection of slaves. They'd been going about their unending labor when the guards had rounded them up. Quite probably there was not a single one of those who had escaped from the Recalcitrants House.

I stalked across, giving the guards the rough edge of the cadade's tongue—for a few moments of listening to him in the outer courtyard and experience of his kidney before had given me his measure.

"Take them away," I foamed. "They are not the ones—fools, dolts, onkers! Nulshes! Pick up this one." I pointed at Voinderam who lay, a dark trickle of blood staining his pale face. He looked in a bad way. "Bring him. I will question him. He will know the answers."

Peremptorily, I indicated that two Rapas should drag the slave I had picked out. "The rest of you—about your business, or I'll have the skin off your backs jikaider! Grak, you yetches, *grak!*"

The guards started to lead the rest of the slaves off. The two Rapas, blank-faced, petrified with fear, followed me. I headed for the ornate stairway. Halfway up I turned and bellowed down, "What are you skulking for! Hurry, you cramphs! Bring him up here!"

They hurried. The sounds of the others receding gave me little comfort. But, by Zair, a man can do only so much in this wicked world.

At the top I walked half a dozen paces across the roof. The two Rapa guards, shaking in their sandals, started after me, dragging Voinderam between them. His shoulders stuck up like windmill sails, his head hung down, draggling. I quelled any feelings of pity—for anyone.

"Thank you," I said, and turned back and with a simple one, two, put the Rapas to sleep. I managed to catch Voinderam before his face hit the paving of the roof. A scuffle at my back brought me around—it was Oby with Naghan. Half hysterically, Fransha threw herself forward. Between us, we levered her free, carried Voinderam across to the voller, pushed and pulled Fransha into the airboat.

"Now, take off, keep low, and then go fast. Go as fast as you can. And may Opaz go with you."

My face did not hurt, and I realized that somewhere up

those fancy stairs I'd been forced to let the cadade's features slip away. I looked at my friends, and I felt the glow of comradeship. Then they started up their protests again.

"I will not tarry long. But you would not—in honor—have me abandon Unmok? Surely?"

"But we should go with you—"

"I am not starting again. By Vox! I left Vallia to get away from that!"

Well, there was little time. A group of slaves ran up the back stairs down which I had gone, and I saw that one carried a bloodstained sword. I fancied he'd got that from the Fristle I'd knocked unconscious. So one did not need to be told whose blood sullied the blade.

The slaves simply raced for the nearest voller, clambered in, and in heartbeats she lifted.

Among that group of ex-slaves maddened by near despair and now gripped with the determination to be free, there was no sign of the splendid golden numim, Mazdo the Splandu. I fancied he'd make his own way out of Noran's villa, aye, and crack a few heads in the doing of it.

"That does it." I had to make my friends grasp the essentials. "That lot will arouse the dead. You must go now!"

Finally, reluctantly, but anxious for the welfare of Tilly and the Lady Fransha, they shouted down the remberees and the voller lifted off. I did not intend to lollygag around. The flags of the roof were hot underfoot, bathed in the mingled streaming radiance of the Suns of Scorpio. Shadows lay hard and tinged with the old emerald and ruby fires. I darted across into the shade of the hangars, caught the first lifting yells of approaching guards and raced flat out over the roof for the other small stairway, twin to the one down which I had descended on the cadade. As I reached the top and bolted down the first guards boiled up onto the roof.

Below me stretched a maze of little outbuildings. Vegetation smothered the alleyways. This was a relatively neglected quarter in Noran's villa that offered capital concealment. I stripped off the fancy armor and chucked it down under a bush. With my own clothes once more revealed I sprinted on, twisting and turning, heading back for the outer courtyard, and Froshak and the werstings.

Slowing to a walk and going along briskly but with caution, I angled around the main buildings and so came up to the courtyard from the flank. The uproar in the grounds of the villa really was rather satisfying. Slaves looked uniformly scared; which did not please me. I saw no guards until I reached the courtyard, and they were all staring the other way. I looked, right along with them.

"No," Froshak was saying. "Not me. Know nothing."

He stood in the grip of two Rhaclaw guards. By reason of their immense domed heads, Rhaclaws are often badly served in the way of helmets. These two wore helmets fashioned from strips of iron, filled in with boiled leather. They held Froshak firmly.

Callimark, nervously pacing, fiddling with his sword, looking agitated, swung back to glare at Froshak.

"I do not believe you! By Flem! If you're lying. . . ."

"Know nothing—notor."

The werstings, still handled by our tame slaves, were being herded into wheeled cages. The pampered dogs, killers or not, went in eagerly enough at the sight of the red meat within.

I walked slowly forward.

This might be a little tricky.

I was still unobserved.

The well where the old bent-over Fristle woman had drawn me a copper bowl of water partly concealed me. The stone coping was dry. No dried, perhaps, than my mouth.

"Take his weapons, nulshes!" Callimark had made up his mind. The Rhaclaw guards snicked out Froshak's knife. He made a single gesture; then he remained still.

Callimark pulled his thraxter around. "Guard him. I shall consult the vad in this." So saying, Callimark marched off. He took with him, I noticed with amusement tinged with concern, an audo of his guards, the section—not a rank—of eight men marching along closed up around him. With his going a visible relaxation took the guards left. As for the slaves, they chittered and chattered about their business, and the dust plumed and the suns shone and, for all I could see, no one here cared aught of a mass escape of slaves from the Recalcitrants House.

A bronze bell rang above the outer door.

The noise among the trees and pathways fluctuated as the guards searched and this outer courtyard must have been checked over at the very beginning. Certainly, as I observed, no one, slave or guard, gave sign of excitement or concern over that escape. The escape that concerned them had taken place here earlier. The bronze bell rang again and with its second summons the majordomo and his retinue who had admitted us appeared, hurrying toward the gate. He had to pass by the cage which lay on its side, its iron-barred door flapped open. At first this had seemed to me to be a wersting cage, but it was not, as I looked closer. Something had been brought into the courtyard in that cage and the cage door had been opened and the something—or somethings—had escaped.

So that was why Callimark questioned Froshak the Shine.

The outer gate was thrown open and a file of slaves entered. They carried sacks and pots and their backs were whipped every now and again to urge them on. They scurried beneath the trees away toward the vad's storerooms. Despite the noise the business of the villa had to go on.

One of the Rhaclaw guards gave Froshak a prod. Just why he did this I do not know; all men in these positions of petty power are not insensate beasts—of course not. But some are.

Froshak reacted. He twisted away, violently, avoiding that prodding sword.

The other Rhaclaw guard joined in, bellowing his anger.

The swords beat down. Froshak defended himself, pushing up his arms, taking the blows as best he could. He saw the open gate. If he broke free now—he and I were both aware that any resistance the Fristle might make would be punished, he could be killed, and no one would bother overmuch. The vad's writ ran here. The Rhaclaws used the flats of their swords. Froshak would have to take his punishment, take his beating, or make a break for it.

The slaves took no notice. The other guards guffawed.

Froshak tried to grab a sword arm, and missed, and the thraxter came back and belted him alongside the ear. He tumbled over. I saw his right hand. It snaked down to his belt and an expression of anger was followed swiftly by a look of bafflement so furious I felt for the Fristle. His knife was not sheathed at his belt. He crouched, glowering. The Rhaclaws taunted him, obscenely, savage in their enjoyment of his frustrated savagery.

I drew my own sailor knife.

"Froshak!" I called in a voice directed to the Fristle. He looked up. I threw.

The knife glittered once as it flicked across the intervening space. Handle first it flew. Froshak put his hand up and—thwunk!—the knife slammed into his fist as though grown there.

One Rhaclaw yelled in abrupt alarm, and then Froshak slid

the knife in, and out, slashed at the other Rhaclaw, and was on his feet and running. He was quick, by Krun! The Rhaclaws staggered away, dropping their swords, the blood bright upon their legs. There was little point in hanging around any more. Froshak ran out through the opened gateway, and I dodged back the other way around the well, keeping below the coping, faded back into the bushes.

Very little time had passed since I'd hurtled off the roof of the landing platform.

Finding the statue of Mahgoh of the Two was not difficult. The lady was a somewhat prominent landmark. Beyond there a curving arcade led on and I padded along. Froshak the Shine was a tough and resourceful customer and I had no doubt that he would win free. What he would do thereafter I could not guess. He'd recognize the knife, for sure. He'd know who had thrown it to him.

The shrubbery at the side of the path flanking the arcade rustled. Bright green leaves moved aside and a couple of men staggered out, locked together. One was a slave, a Gon with a bristle of white hair over his scalp, the other a Rapa guard. The Rapa could not cry out because the slave's fists gripped a length of the chain about the feathered neck. The Gon struggled silently with his work. They pitched onto the pathway, flailing about, and the Rapa's struggles weakened.

I stopped in the shadow of a column.

The Gon stood up. He touched blood on his left arm, and along his ribs. He was panting raggedly.

I said, "I'll give you a hand to stow him in the bushes, dom."

The Gon spun about, his hands flicking the lethal chain up.

"You'd best hurry—there will be other guards." And I jumped across, grabbed the Rapa and started to heave him into the bushes. The Gon drew a breath.

"By Havil! You are a—"

I was ripping the Rapa's sword belt free. His thraxter was a plain and simple weapon, much like the one I had been forced to abandon when dressing up as the cadade.

"No time for jabbering! Listen!"

The sound of heavy footfalls reached us around the curve of the arcade. The Gon looked wild. He would not touch his bristle of hair, as another man might have done, rubbing his hand across his hair in perplexity.

"I'm off—"

"May Havil the Green go with you, Gon."

"You will need the protection of Havil more than if you stay here." The Gon shoved into the bushes, panting, holding his left arm where the blood ran. "Run, apim, run!"

He vanished between the leaves. I straightened my clothes and walked on a few yards past the place where blood drops might prove tricky to explain. Mingled with the oncoming tramp of studded sandals, the ominous clash of weapons indicated guardsmen. I finished buckling the Rapa's sword belt about me, flicked my fingers and walked on.

Vad Noran in the lead, Unmok bobbing along at his side, the party rounded the bend and bore down. He had a score of guards. Noran looked murderous. At his other side, Callimark, looking agitated, was fluttering his hands and trying to explain.

I stood to one side, looking at them, and—I own!—I drew my stomach in and pulled myself up and got ready to lie like a trooper for our lives.

## CHAPTER TWENTY

# Combat, Blood and Death

The lies tripped off my tongue smoothly enough once I'd figured out what the hell was going on.

In addition, I was now pretty sharp set. The thought of a slap-up meal inside me to fortify the inner man against the hazards ahead tantalized with its unrealizability at the moment.

". . . malignancy, and he'll be flogged jikaider if I have any say in the matter," Callimark was saying. He looked like a man bluffing away, blustering to conceal his own lapse in duty.

"When the truth is established, Callimark, we'll flog to your heart's content." Noran's face bore a most unpleasant expression.

"The schrepims have not been found—"

"Your pardon, notor," said Unmok, his middle left twitching. "But there could be no reason for Froshak to let loose the schrepims! Believe me, notor, we are too conscious of your kind patronage—"

"As to that, Unmok, we shall see. I paid good red gold for those four schrepims and I intend to have my money's worth!"

Now it was plain. The overturned cage with its iron-barred door flapped open had contained four schrepims, and these diffs, rather like overgrown lizards with cunning and intelligence, had escaped. I, too, doubted that Froshak would have done that; there was no reason for it. Well—no reason beyond the ordinary person's aversion to schrepims. It was reputed that these scaled men had the powers of the Dark, that they could scry almost as well as a Wizard of Loh—that, I did not believe—and that their cold reptilian natures set them always in opposition to the ways of the gods of Kregen.

I stepped forward.

Unmok twitched. Callimark cast a worried look at me and then started to argue his case again with the vad. Noran did not stop. He went to bustle past without even looking at me.

I said, "Your pardon, notor." I went on very quickly. "I believe there has been an escape of slaves, and they overturned the cage and the schrepims escaped in the confusion."

Now Noron half stopped and regarded me as he continued on along the curving arcade.

"And you?"

"I do not know for sure, notor."

"If you are right this Froshak may keep his head—and Unmok here and you may escape a flogging."

That was as cold as the Ice Floes of Sicce.

Noran stopped. He eyed me up and down.

"The schrepims cost me money. They are renowned kaidurs—hyr kaidurs. They must be coddled. If they are damaged before I see them fight. . . . By Glem! Am I or am I not the vad!"

Everyone around him hastily assured Noran that, indeed, he was the vad.

Up to now on Kregen I had not much faith in receiving any help from the Star Lords or the Savanti. Oh, yes, there had been times during which I thought that, well, perhaps either the Everoinye or the Savanti might have arranged things to favor me. But these occasions were few and far between. As far as I knew, and as far as I was concerned, I was battling along alone.

Now, a large missal tree overhung the arcade a few paces along and its leaves brushed the tiled roof. The arcade curved around Vad Noran's private arena. A movement among the branches of the tree drew my attention, and then the quick looks of the others.

Up there, quickly glimpsed and vanishing, the green-scaled visage of a schrepim glared down on us.

As I say, it was probably mere chance. But, perhaps, just perhaps, the Star Lords did have a hand in it. . . .

"They have run into the arena!" shouted Callimark.

Noran swung to bellow at his guards.

"Go and round them up—and treat them gently until I get there." He guffawed then, suddenly back in good humor.

"After that you may fight in my arena as though in the jikhorkdun!"

There were a score of guards. They ran off obediently enough, but it was very clear they did not much fancy the task ahead of them. I felt a stab of pity. Schrepims are the very devil as antagonists. They are quick and sudden, skilled with weapons, able to take a great deal of punishment before they are killed. Their vigorous energy is cold and reptilian, and exceedingly vicious.

The memory of that time over in Higher Ripolavi where we'd been forced to fight a roaming band of schrepims came back to me. There are schrepims and schrepims, and that lot had been of the Soparan race. These four who would give the twenty guards a nasty time, as I judged, I gathered were of the Saradush race. Over in Ripolavi we'd lost Nath the Langon and Nalgre the Forge before we'd even got properly to handstrokes. We'd lost half a dozen more good men before we'd seen the scaled fighters off, and there had been only thirty of them in the band.

Noran was rubbing his hands together. Callimark was looking relieved.

"We will go up into my arena and witness the fight." said Noran. "It is what I paid for, and I will not be balked of my pleasure." He set off at a brisk trot around the arcade toward the flights of steps leading up to the stand seating. We followed.

Managing to fall in beside Unmok as we trailed along after the vad, I said, "Froshak got away."

"Thank his Fristle gods for that! We're like to have our heads off if—"

"No, Unmok! It will turn out all right. Remember the wer-stings."

"I do. Money will not stitch my head back on my shoulders."

Noran's private arena had been built as a miniature copy of the arena in the jikhorkdun. Strewn with silver sand, ringed by comfortable seatings, shaded by a velarium which could be pulled across on its yards if the suns burned too hotly, it waited in the true style of an arena—an area dedicated to combat, blood and death.

He even had the four quarters arranged with their various colors, each with a prianum to receive the trophies of victory and the four staffs with the colored symbols. At the moment the ruby drang lifted highest. Noran was of the reds. The sapphire graint, the diamond zhantil and the emerald neemu were all at the bottoms of their poles. I wondered if he altered this when he invited guests of different color persuasions.

His own box, although lavishly appointed, flanked by columns garlanded and wreathed and with sumptuous hangings of cloth of gold and ruby velvet, did not dare match the opulence of the royal box in the great arena of Huringa. Queen Fahia was conscious of her regal dignity and touchy on matters of etiquette. But the display of wealth was dazzling.

Noran took his seat. It was a throne in everything but name. We settled alongside on the lesser seats. Each one was softly upholstered, with padded arms and back, and with a small table alongside with wine racks beneath. As I sat down and looked out across the suns shimmer along those silver sands I caught my breath.

Here I was, looking out over the arena in Hyrklana instead of being down there, with a sword in my fist, facing death for the entertainment of gilded trash in the stands and the howling crowds!

Sitting in those plush surroundings with the waiting oval of silver sand spread out below me, I wondered what was going to happen next. My thoughts veered off to a vision of this kind of obscenity finding a place in Vallia. The bloody tradition of the arena flourished in many countries of Havilfar. Even the games of Jikaida City were in truth an offshoot of the jikhorkdun. No, in Vallia we drew spiritual sustenance and refreshment from other sports. There were precious few Vallians I knew who would wish it otherwise.

Three of the escaped schrepims moved into view below. They stepped cautiously backwards, feeling back with each foot in turn, moving with the reptilian grace of their kind. Following them in a curved line, the guards advanced cautiously. There was a sense of hunting animals closing in for the kill in the way that semicircle of guards shuffled steadily forward. But it was clear to us all that they were in no hurry to get to grips with the scaled men.

Noran picked a candied fruit from a box on his table. He bubbled now with good humor.

"This is more like the way life was meant to be led." He popped the fruit into his mouth. His cheek distended, glistening. "I paid my money, now I want my entertainment."

"The guards are not happy," commented Callimark. He, too, sat forward in his chair to watch, and a lick of spittle drooled from the corner of his mouth.

"Get on with it!" Noran abruptly shrieked down. He waved a fist at the guards. "A dozen gold pieces for the first to attack!"

My small knowledge of the fighting habits of the scaled men told me the guard who accepted the offer would not live to collect his dozen gold pieces.

I studied the schrepims.

Their greenish-grayish scales were dull. Different races have different shapes and colors of scale, of course, and the edges glister with different contrasting colors. These three had orange edges to their scales under their fighting harness. The straps were all of scales. Their armor was scale. But their swords were solid thraxters, efficient weapons in the hands of experts, although in nowise the finest swords of Kregen, as you know. The tails of the schrepims were thick at the root, and heavy, flat, flailing instruments. They were nothing like the supple whip-tails of Katakis, for instance, or the superb handed tails of Pachaks or Kildois.

"What are you waiting for?" bellowed Noran again.

The guards shuffled forward, swords pointed, shields up, the visors of their helmets pulled down.

"They're all jikarnas,"* said Callimark. He beat a fist on the marble coping before him. He looked contemptuous.

No one sought to contradict him. Also, no one suggested he might like to hop down there and set to himself.

The aura of the scaled men exuded a menace that comes as much from their reputation as from their mere presence. Ordinary mortals steer clear of them, and they have their own ways on Kregen.

"Jikarna!" Noran shouted the word down. It made no difference. Slowly and steadily the guards advanced and as steadily the three schrepims retreated. It was quite clear the guards had decided that no single one would rush forward—the notor's dozen golden deldys or not—but they would attack together, in a bunch, and overpower all three in a final massive onslaught.

* jikarna. Arna is a Kregish word having the meaning of "absence of." Hence Gilarna the Barren—the Absence of Pleasure. So that jikarna can be translated as the absence of warrior qualities, *i.e.*, coward. —A.B.A.

That made the sweetest of sweet sense to me, by Krun.

The three scaled heads, so much like those of lizards, turned this way and that, in purposeful summing up of the situation. When the action began the speed of the schrepims would be blinding. And, I own it with some diffidence, I began to calculate just how many guards might be left at the end, or even if any would be left alive, and whether or not the scaled men might win free.

"Fifty deldys," roared Noran.

One of the guards, a Khibil, reacted. Khibils with their overbearing ways and haughty fox-like faces always consider themselves to be a superior race of beings. Well, I own to a fondness for Khibils that although of a different nature from my affection for Pachaks shares much of that fellow feeling. This Khibil hoisted his shield, whirled his sword—and charged.

He shrieked as he went in, boring dead for the center scaled man. "Fifty golden deldys!" he screamed, and with all the cunning of the fighting man sought to overpower the center antagonist before the two flankers could strike at him. Taking his onslaught as the signal, with equal cunning the other guards rushed forward.

The Khibil had time for one stroke. It was a bold, slashing blow that would have taken the head off the schrepim had it landed. But the schrepim was not there as the blow whistled past. A superb sliding glance of the scaled man's body, a glint of greenish gray, and the wicked sword smote once, and was still.

The Khibil staggered away, his shield falling uselessly, his sword dropping. His foxy face was a mere mask of blood.

The remaining guards howled and flung themselves on. It was all a flurry of blows, and the quick scrape and ring of steel on steel, the screech of steel on bronze. How they fought, those schrepims! Superb in their reptilian strength and speed they danced on their massively muscled legs, balancing on those thick tails, striking and avoiding, chunking into the guards and slashing and hacking, and withdrawing with bewildering rapidity.

Yes, oh, yes, I remembered their style of fighting!

Four guards were down, then three more, their throats slashed, their unshielded sides cut through. Blood smoked on the silver sand. The uproar deafened. Three more guards staggered away, their legs unable to support them, sinking to the sand. Three more—and yet three more. The four remaining waited no longer. They cast down their shields and ran.

With long reptilian strides the schrepims chased them.

Swords lifted and blurred down in savage blows.

The last man, the single survivor, screamed and ran blindly.

One of the schrepims tossed his sword into the air. He caught it by the forte. His arm went back and he hurled, a vicious, cunning, superlatively destructive cast. The running man staggered on for four paces, lurching, before he fell with the sword burst through heart and lungs.

"By Havil!" Noran was on his feet, one hand to his chest. His face was flushed. "By Glem! They were superb, superb!"

"Money well spent!" declared Callimark.

I looked at these two with interest. None so blind. . . .

Unmok nudged me.

"Jak! They'll—!"

"Yes," I said.

Rich blood puddled the silver sand.

Vad Noran was suffused with pride. This villa was a palace and a fortress. Within its walls his will was law. My early impression had convinced me that it would take far too much time to break an entrance in my own old swashbuckling way. The trick with the werstings to gain us entry had been essential, and had worked. But, also, that very impregnability of his villa meant Noran, standing now flushed with the excitement of the combat, had no fear of the three schrepims. He looked down at them as they walked alertly back toward his box.

"Well done, Slacamen," he shouted, giving them a nickname common among diffs and apims, a name, incidentally, I had heard the Schrepims often chafed under. "There will be much gold for you, aye, and rich foods and fine clothes."

Still the three advanced, silently, across the sand. The blood glimmered most evilly upon their blades.

Unmok the Nets choked out some unintelligble comment. He started to scrabble over the back of his chair.

Noran did not turn.

"Sit quietly, Och! These Slacamen cannot climb up here."

Unmok collapsed onto his seat. He was quivering.

"You are sure? Notor—you are sure they cannot get at us?"

"Of course. Why should they?" Noran's contempt seemed

to me to reveal a sudden and unwelcome thought—the kind of thought he would not allow himself to think.

The scaled men couldn't climb up here, could they?

From my own experience I fancied they could—and would.

I said, "Van Noran! There are three down there. Were not there four in the cage?"

Callimark let out a squeal of pure terror.

"By Flem! He is right!"

"They will not harm me!" Noran bellowed it out. He put a beringed hand to the hilt of his sword. "I am Vad Noran! I bought them to fight for me! I pay them and feed them—they owe their lives to me."

"I do not think they see things that way." I looked along the seating, left and right. There was a fourth, and I did not think he would have run off and left his fellows.

The throaty sound of breathing, hoarse and rasping, came from Callimark trying to nerve himself. Unmok crouched in his seat. Noran yelled down, "I am Vad Noran! I pay you gold to fight for me, Slacamen!"

Left and right, along the seating, and up to the lip of the arena wall, along the trees, and down again, to the ornate entrance. My gaze flicked about. No sign. . . . No sign, *yet* . . . !

Very quick and sudden, schrepims, very fast and deadly.

But although Vad Noran's guards were not, in the judgment of a hard old fighting man, worthy of their hire, some, at least, of that score who had died in the arena had struck shrewd blows before they perished. Two of the schrepims bore wounds, from which a green ichor leached. Hard to kill, these reptilian humans, but die they could, given courage and strength and skill and the effort of willpower to pit against them.

Around the arena I looked, carefully, seeking a glimmer of greenish scales along the seatings or up among the overarching trees. Callimark continued to breathe noisily. Unmok sat up straight and hauled out his sword.

"I am not in the habit of doubting the word of a noble," he said, and there was an edge to his voice. "But it seems to me the schrepims will climb up here and we will die. I will strike a blow first, by the golden jeweled cup of the Och Kings!"

"Nulsh!" said Noran. But his voice faltered.

Around and around, searching, searching. . . .

The three walking toward us across the blood-puddled silver sand gave off that aura of menace that breathes from reptilian things. They walked easily and their thick tails were lifted high. You did not cut off the tail of a Slacaman as easily as that of a Kataki. Although the contest between Kataki and scaled man is instructive—in a gruesome way—and conducive to many serious lessons, it remains for all that a spectacle I would not cross the road to witness. All the time as these three advanced and Noran began to gnaw his lip and Callimark tried to get himself under control and Unmok quietly whistled his sword about to get his eye in, I twisted my neck and stared about, up and down, along and around, searching, searching. . . .

"Perhaps, vad, we had best depart," said Callimark, and his voice pitched up and down the scale alarmingly.

Give Vad Noran his due—he just could not understand why men he had bought to fight for him, men recommended to him as hyr-kaidurs, should want to slay him. That was too personal. He delighted in the atmosphere of the jikhorkdun, living its thrills and glorying in its valor and blood. But he hadn't considered that his own blood would be risked in any valorous combat. He would enter the ring to a challenge from an equal, he would fence with a professional kaidur, but that would not be for real, not for blood and guts real.

Just when he realized the schrepims would—damned well would!—climb that barrier and leap on him with lifted swords, with fang and claw, I do not know.

But, in the instant I spotted a staggering group of slaves boil out of the entranceway and totter, sprawling, shrieking, groveling, scrambling any-old-how along the seating, Noran's nerve broke.

Blindly, drawing his sword and thrashing about with it as though he slashed weeds, he bolted.

I said to Unmok, "Time we were leaving."

The little Och came up out of his chair like a gazelle.

"As Ochenshum is my witness you speak sense." He joined me as we moved back from the ornate seating. The uproar farther along grew. "But, Jak," said Unmok, and the avaricious old devil looked green. "This great noble, Vad Noran, has not yet paid me for the werstings!"

The slaves had scattered, shrieking, and Noran was rampaging along toward the exit with its curious carved nymphs upholding torches that were, at this time of day, as yet unlit.

"I think, Unmok, my friend, we will not get paid at all from that one." And I started to run.

Unmok let out a screech. Callimark took to his heels and ran the other way. Noran staggered back from the exit. He waved his sword about drunkenly. The schrepim who moved out of the opening between the torch-bearing nymphs looked no different from his three brethren in the arena. The same reptilian-snouted face, the heavily hooded eyes, the snaggle of sharp teeth, the same grayish-greenish scales with their bordering of orange. His clawed hand grasped a thraxter. His left arm was concealed by a shield. That, as I judged it, was the only difference.

Unmok screeched again. "Jak! They climb the barrier!"

Time for a single swift glance back. It was all there, the picture I remember and hate to recall. Callimark was flung across an ornate chair, his body slashed almost in two. The three schrepims leaped like lizards over the seating. Unmok was running toward me. Ahead Vad Noran, screaming in a paroxysm of fear, blundered back. The fourth scaled man followed him purposefully.

No doubt now remained that the schrepims would kill and go on killing until they were stopped.

I stopped running toward Noran. Unmok was my first concern. Noran would have to take his chances.

And then—and then, by Zair!

As I stared at the three scaled men in one direction, and was aware of the fourth in the other, I experienced for a fleeting moment of horror an image, scorched on my brain, of a splendid golden Kildoi, four-armed, tail-handed, brushing aside with superior swordsmanship all my efforts at swordplay.

Damn Prince Mefto the Kazzur!

But, with a little crippled Och to save, there was no time to blither-blather about the past and what was dead.

Not that Mefto the Kazzur was dead. . . .

Noran was screaming in a crackling voice for the cadade. I did not know if the cadade was dead or not, but he wouldn't be turning up here.

"Out of the way, Noran!" I said. My voice must have penetrated the scarlet fear cloaking his senses, for he jumped, shivering, and then fell over the backs of the row of seating, tumbling among the bright cushions.

The schrepim didn't mind whom he killed first. Just so long as he could get his sword into someone, just so long as he could vent the frustrations of being taken up and forced to fight as a kaidur in the arena, chained, caged, whipped, sent out to fight like a wild beast—and he a man!—and then caged again if he lived, and dragged off with a hook through his heel if he died.

He came at me with the flashing speed of a reptile.

Whatever happened with him must happen fast. His comrades were breathing down the back of my neck.

He used his shield with skill, for he was a hyr-kaidur, and I had to skip and leap and parry for longer than I liked before my thraxter managed to loop inside his. I shoved the shield up and the rim took him under that ferociously toothed snout. He grunted. His squamous body was like a wriggling eel. But the thraxter went in, punching through scale, sliding on, cutting. I withdrew at once, green ichor sliming the blade, kicked him as he went down and then jinked sideways without looking back. I leaped over the chair upward from the rank, landing and spinning about.

That dramatic exercise had been necessary.

The leading schrepim's blow chunked stuffing from the chair seat.

I leaned forward to strike down on that sleek scaly head, but with lizard-like swiftness he recoiled.

For an instant we glared, eye to eye.

The fourth tooth along each side of his lower jaw protruded up at an angle. Larger than the other teeth, it slotted into a groove outside the upper jaw. The jagged line his jaws made as they clicked together gave him a ferocious aspect, almost as though he grinned at sight of his prey. The scales hooding his eyes looked like monk's hoods. Just below and closer together than the eyes the two deep pits of his heat-sensing organs were no doubt picking up my sweaty radiations and helping him to locate me even more exactly. Although his eyes were dark, the pigment, rhodopsin, in them which gave him good night vision would appear to glow an eerie red-orange at night from any reflected light. To see the eyes of schrepims glowing at night, the Kregish saying runs, is to look on the watchfires of hell.

His thick tail thumped the ground between the seats. I did not wait but leaped to the side. Using his tail as a lever, he soared up, his sword flashing out at me. I landed first. With solid ground under my feet I was able to roar forward and slash him while he was still in the air. Green ichor gushed from his side. He fell awkwardly.

Now he uttered sounds, a spine-chilling hissing, a spluttering rush of words and a ferocious shrilling.

"He leaped up, his sword flashing out at me."

Schrepims mostly speak their own language, their forked tongues giving a sibilant quality to their words; but they are well able to speak the universal Kregish language. By reason of that genetic language pill given to me by the Savanti I am able to understand tongues. Even as he fell, he was shrieking, "You will be caught up in the coils of Ratishling the Sinuous and crushed until your bowels smoke, apim, for the indignities you heap on me."

Oh, yes, I could feel sorry for him. But his two fellows were leaping like lizards along the seating toward me, and I knew their rage was such they'd prefer to use their fangs and claws on me rather than the swords they wielded. The wound in this one's side leaked green; but that wouldn't kill him. I aimed a delicate cut along his neck, where the scales smoothed and were more tightly fitted and of a lighter hue, just above the black scales of his harness. The thraxter bit and drew, cutting cleanly.

I leaped away.

Noran was shrieking and blubbering, and that old devil Unmok the Nets, his sword gripped in his two right, upper and middle, hands was struggling up from the tier of chairs below to get in the way of the charging scaled fighters.

"Get out of it, Unmok, you fambly!"

"Jak—if we are to die—"

"We're not!"

And I fairly hurled myself forward. Just in time I got the sword before Unmok and swept away the first blow from the leading schrepim. They were so damned quick! He came back, screeching, and there was no time to play him, for the first and fourth were rampaging up, and now they, too, were shrilling. They filled the air with fearsome promises of what Ratishling the Sinuous would do to me and all non-schrepims.

Well—you couldn't really blame them, could you? But I do not like to stand still while someome tries to kill me, never have and, by Krun, never will, I daresay. So I fought.

That was a fight of which the details remain hazy to this day.

Instinct, pure primeval instinct, and skill and utter dedication to the Disciplines alone could aid me now.

The swords clanged and chirred, and one schrepim was down and his dark green blood flowed from a mangled neck.

The other two bore wounds, as did I, and I'd falter and grow weak long before they'd even realize their scaly hides had been punctured.

One of them swept in and tried to fasten that rat trap of a mouth on my left arm. I got away just in time, with a long shredding of skin hanging from between his ugly fangs.

I leaped sideways and his thick tail swept around like a barn door closing and slogged into me and I went end over end down among the seats. How I didn't crack my head open I don't know. He scuttled after me and with a long, low lunge I kept down and so, left hand pressed against the floor by the seats, stuck the thraxter up into him. He sailed on and over me, as though pole-vaulting in just about the most uncomfortable position for the pole you could imagine, and he did not drag the sword from my grip. It came out with a wet slurshing sound. No time to watch him writhing in agony, no time, no time!

The last one jumped the seating to get at me.

To dream he was the last would have been a mistake on my part, and one I did not make. He was the last one to come into action, but the others were not out of it. Oh, no! Slit throats, deeply punctured wounds, impalements, that kind of punishment does not stop your schrepim. Their dark, insensate energy, the vigorousness of their attack, the febrile swiftness of them—they have to be killed and then killed again before they are dead.

Our swords crossed, I used, as I recall, a middling clever passage and hit him clean across the snout.

My thraxter broke across.

Instantly, I raced away, drawing him with me away from Unmok.

The thraxter had been my only weapon. Never laugh at or decry the great old Kregan custom of carrying an arsenal into battle! If ever I'd needed a selection of weaponry, it was now. . . .

I ran.

The Sorzarts of the inner sea, the Eye of the World, do not compare with schrepims. The Phokaym do, of course; but they are of a world apart, there by that noxious cleft in the earth called the Klackadrin. Cousins in the realm of reptiles, Phokaym and schrepims. I ran and Unmok let out a screech and I half turned as I ran. The pursing scaled fighter was almost on me. Unmok's sword arched in the air, spinning, sailing up and over the schrepim's scaly head. It spun down toward me.

That was a tricky catch.

The sword hilt thumped into my fist and I failed to grasp it cleanly the first time and the schrepim slashed. I ducked, felt my sword that had been Unmok's slipping away, and grasped again. I put my foot into a scaled belly, thrusting, and then jerking instantly to left and then surging right.

His wicked tail lashed where I would have been.

The sword snugged into my fist. I thrust.

The blade squished in deeply. I drove it on, grinding it around, sawing on it, and I smashed my fist across his snout, driving back those wicked fangs.

He screamed and struggled to get at me past that steel tooth. I got a grip around his throat with my left hand and squeezed. I spat in his eye. If I'd had fangs I'd have ripped his throat out.

I kicked him, and we hopped about, locked together.

Somewhere out of the scarlet haze Unmok's yell: "Behind you!"

With a supreme effort I managed to spin us about. The blow hit the schrepim on the back of the head. If he noticed it, I do not know. It was a blow that would have split an apim's skull.

The fellow who had struck the blow drew back, setting himself for another try. His scaly body was slimed green with his own blood. He moved at a speed a normal eye could follow. He was dying. He didn't know that, or, knowing, pushed it aside in his insensate desire to kill me.

I shoved my man back, drawing out the sword with a loud sucking noise. The two schrepims staggered together. I was just about done for now. As the two collided I jumped. The sword went around in an arc of greened silver.

Two blows, two blows delivered with the failing dregs of my strength. Two reptilian heads popped off to roll thumping down the stairs. I turned wearily and saw the other two, who should be dead, advancing on me. I noticed the red blood on their swords, and gazed stupidly at the green ichor fouling my blade.

Unmok appeared at my side, carrying a sword. The thraxter was most ornate. I realized it was Noran's weapon.

"I would not believe, Jak the Shot—but. . . ."

"Do you stand aside, Unmok the Nets. They may pass me, but they will be dead doing it."

"And, my friend, so will you."

"If it is my time for Zair to whisk me up, my friend, then up I will go, and nothing on Kregen will prevent that."

A flash of gold just beyond the scaled men, a glitter of

steel. The first schrepim bore on for me, but the second swung back, not as quickly as he had once moved, to face the golden numim who leaped on him, sword held just so.

The two combats finished with a speed that astonished me.

My schrepim died, at last, poor devil, and I swiveled to see Mazdo the Splandu finish off his with a slicing cut that left the schrepim's head all a-dangling before he fell.

"Jikai!" called Mazdo. "Jai, Jikai!"

"Maybe," I said in a grunt of exhaustion. "I give you the jikai for your help—and, my thanks—"

"You did it all. I merely brushed up the crumbs."

And Mazdo the Splandu ran fleetly off along the seating to vanish past the curious carved nymphs. After that the guards turned up. I do not know if they had waited to see the outcome of the fight. But Vad Noran, shaking still, his face as green as the green ichor staining the seating of his private amphitheater, slowly came back to his senses. He started bellowing orders.

His guards, who may have waited and who may not have, were in for a very rough time of it. A very rough time indeed.

Presently, when the poor shredded schrepims had been carried away, and Noran had been petted and fussed over by his tame slaves, all aahing and oohing, and blandishing him with exclamations of admiration and praise for his valor—at which Unmok and I wisely held our tongues—we all went into the villa. Little to add to that. Unmok, brisking up, mentioned payment for his werstings, and Noran paid. He looked at me.

"I shall reward you, jikai—handsomely. You are, I think, a hyr-paktun. Will you fight for me in the arena? There will be much gold. You will be a hyr-kaidur very quickly, I know—"

"Much as you honor me, notor, I am not able. I am sworn."

He looked disappointed, but he had the sense not to press.

It was quite clear to everyone that Noran must have fought like a leem to have slain all the schrepims with my and Unmok's assistance. Unmok started to protest, but I hushed him.

"Give us our gold, notor," I said. "We have a cage-voller to buy and fresh animals to find."

"Yes, yes. You shall have gold—" He swallowed. "My life is precious—" And then he said, "I cannot understand the ingratitude of those vile Slacamen! I paid for them, I would have treated them well! Why did they choose the path of murder?"

His personal needleman had patched me up and stuck a few needles in to deaden the pain. I felt half alive. I said, "They are men despite all, despite what diff and apim may think of them. No man cares to be chained and caged and forced to fight in a battle that does not concern him."

"You speak foolishly, Jak. Men like that have only their swordarms to sell in the market. And I pay them well!"

You couldn't argue with him. At least, I couldn't at that moment. I nodded.

"Thank you, notor. Now we will take our leave."

The vad's palatial quarters reflected his tastes well enough. The fellow who so far had sat quietly in a deep armchair by the window, idly pulling leaves off a plant in a bowl at his side, looked across. He was a spare man—by Krun! he looked like a starving ferret!—and his tastes were most certainly not reflected in the sumptuousness around him.

"You sound as though you sympathize with these Slacamen."

I shook my head and waited for the Bells of Beng Kishi to subside. I had taken a few fair old knocks. "No, notor. Just that they made the mistake of not knowing when to stop killing."

"One that you will not make?" His voicc was like oiled steel.

I agreed, in the same deferential way I was talking, for I wanted out of here. He wore supple mesh mail from the Dawn Lands, and his dark hair was cut savagely short. His left eye was covered by a patch, a thing of crusted diamonds and emeralds. The stillness of him as he sat there, the deliberate movements as he stripped the plant, all conveyed the sense of suppressed energy. He was a man I would not seek to cross, and if, inadvertently I did so, would guard my back and put him down as quickly as possible.

He said, "You will not leave without the vad's permission."

"Assuredly, notor."

He turned his one good eye, sunken under a black brow, up to Noran. "I would have given much to have seen the contest in the arena, Noran. And more to have put my swordarm alongside yours in your battle with these yetches."

Noran laughed. His voice pitched a trifle high, his face was flushed, his eyes bright. I did not look at Unmok. I just wanted out. We had gold enough now to buy the cage-voller.

About to open my mouth again, I was brought to my senses by Unmok's grip on my arm. The two lords missed the byplay.

"Shut your black-fanged winespout, Jak!" Unmok's whisper was fierce and frightened.

Noran was speaking, trying to sound offhand, casual about his fight and yet driven by what the pretense demanded.

"I would have joyed to have had you at my side, Gochert. It was a High Jikai!"

I kept my craggy old face impassive. By Zim-Zair! The presumption! Not in claiming what Noran claimed—that could easily be understood, and excused, on the grounds of his natural vanity and the position he found himself in. No, not that. But to use those great words, the High Jikai, in this context. . . . No, I wanted out, by Zodjuin of the Silver Stux!

Then another portion of the puzzle that I sensed—and with a chilling unease, too!—was going to influence my life in the immediate future dropped into place. This jewel-eyed Gochert had finished with the plant. It was now a mere stiff skeleton of twigs. His deliberate fingers began to slide over the pommel of one of his swords as though it were a netsuke. This was his thraxter. He wore also a rapier and his left-hand dagger was larger than the usual main gauche. All the weapons looked to be plain and workmanlike.

Gochert's one good eye appraised Noran. He waited before he spoke, and that small pause was just not quite long enough to be insulting.

"A Jikai," he said. "A High Jikai. By Spikatur Hunting Sword, Noran, I think you are right!"

Even if Vad Noran's jaw drew in until his neck creased and his shoulders went back, he took the remark as a compliment. He had no desire, apparently, to cross this jewel-eyed, ferret-faced Gochert. He waved his hand to dismiss us.

I said, "With the vad's permission." Then I added, "It is now clear that Froshak the Shine did not release the schrepims."

"By Glem! Is not that what I have already said!"

He hadn't, but I did not wish to argue the point. We went out and I took a last good look at this Gochert fellow, who scared Vad Noran and who talked of Spikatur Hunting Sword. The gold weighed on us, and I, at least, was ready to fight for it. But Unmok knew what he was doing. He might be scared of the protocol surrounding nobles, but he assured me that Noran would honor his promise and payment. So we collected the tame slaves from the outer courtyard and left Vad Noran's villa and its secrets, and walked down into the busy bustle of Huringa.

In a weird way, somehow or other, I seemed to hear the echo of clanging iron bars back there in that villa.

As we walked along Unmok regained his usual perky self. "A cage-voller!" he said. There was awe in his voice.

"You told me you did not much care for this beast-caging life, Unmok."

"So I did, Jak, so I did."

"So why continue? We have enough gold. You could set up in business." I refrained from mocking him on what might be the current nature of that business.

He stopped and twisted to stare up at me. His middle left jerked in excitement. "It is your gold, Jak! You fought the Slacamen, not I!"

"Are we or are we not partners?"

"But—in this!"

"You'll find Froshak again all right?"

"Yes, yes. But tell me fair what is in your mind."

"I will, Unmok. I will—but. . . ."

The plans I had for Unmok and Froshak were dreams they would consider impossible. I did not want to force their destinies upon them, become an arbiter of their fates. If they wanted to go with me to Vallia, they would have to make the decision themselves. I was fully prepared for a refusal. Their lives were their own.

Amusement touched me at the thought of Noran and the pitiful figure he cut and his desperate desire to hold onto the reputation of a jikai he had acquired over the affair with the schrepims. The honor in his life was now caged up, locked with a lie.

As for my life, well, I had broken free of my iron-barred cage, if only for a time. Delia and my gang of ruffians were safe, for no warning of danger had reached me from Deb-Lu-Quienyin, but there was cause for concern over the safety of anyone foolish enough to stand in their way.

Tilly, Oby and Naghan the Gnat had been rescued. Voinderam and Fransha were on the way home to confound the plans of the Racters. Vondium and Vallia would stand. We would struggle through, that I passionately believed in, even against Phu-Si-Yantong. Life would open out for me again, the iron bars forgotten. Whatever Unmok and Froshak decided, I would find myself a handsome voller and fly home to Vallia through the streaming mingled radiance of the Suns of Scorpio.

There were Prince Tyfar and Jaezila to bid good-bye to first.

Saying the remberees to them would be painful, but, after that wrench—Vallia!

Vallia and Delia!